His ranch and his brother had been the most important things in Sam's life

Now he had only the ranch.

"Everyone says we need time. That eventually life will get back to normal," he said, parroting the words he'd heard all day.

"I seriously doubt that," his sister-in-law, Jenny, replied. Her voice was bleak. "You're forgetting one thing. Two, actually. The babies. Lara and Tucker."

Sam swallowed. He wasn't a coward. He simply wasn't up to talking about the twins tonight. "Can we hold off on that for a while, Jen? We just have to trust each other to do the right thing."

"Do you have any idea what that is?"

He stretched the aching muscles in his shoulders and back. "Nope. But we'll figure it out." He rose and put out his hand to help her stand. "You should get to bed."

She stood for a moment, then crossed her arms. "I wonder if my milk is coming in. Do you know where Andi put that box of nursing pads?"

He didn't have a clue, but he jogged to the bathroom. He needed to get away. Such frank talk struck him as too intimate for what they were to each other.

Sam stared at his reflection in the mirror.

He might be a *father*, but he wasn't a *husband*!

Dear Reader,

You're about to enter the world of Gold Creek, California. An imaginary town a bit like the gold-rush-era community up the road from me. In the twelve years that I've lived in this section of the Sierras, I've come to love the beauty of the landscape—lush green winters and burnt-gold summers. I've also come to respect and admire the unique individuals—true mountain characters—who populate these hills. A perfect setting for a book about three independent and strong-willed women—the Sullivan triplets—trying to find their place in the world.

This first book in the trilogy is Jenny's story. She married her high-school sweetheart, then after college returned to her hometown to teach school. Perfect. Until Josh's cancer returned. And she found herself giving birth as her husband lay dying. Jenny's story is about reaching deep inside for strength you didn't know you possessed.

I've witnessed this amazing courage firsthand. My niece, Amy, is the true inspiration behind this story. She faced a devastating crisis—the loss of a child—at a time when most of us rejoice: the birth of a new baby. The tragedy was inconceivable, the agony almost overwhelming, but Amy went forward with true grace and remarkable fortitude.

Life does go on. I have two beautiful grandnieces, Laura and Rachel, to prove it. And I hope you'll enjoy Jenny's sweet triumphs, as well. Her sisters—Andi and Kristin—will tell their stories in January and February in their books, *Without a Past* and *The Comeback Girl*. I hope you'll come to love all three of them as much as I do.

Debra

P.S. Please keep in touch. You can reach me at P.O. Box 322, Catheys Valley, CA 95306 or via the Internet at my Web site, www.debrasalonen.com, or at eHarlequin.com, where you can access the Let's Talk Superromance thread at the Authors' Corner Bulletin Board.

My Husband, My Babies

Debra Salonen

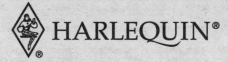

HARLEQUIN®

TORONTO • NEW YORK • LONDON
AMSTERDAM • PARIS • SYDNEY • HAMBURG
STOCKHOLM • ATHENS • TOKYO • MILAN • MADRID
PRAGUE • WARSAW • BUDAPEST • AUCKLAND

ISBN 0-373-71098-4

MY HUSBAND, MY BABIES

Copyright © 2002 by Debra K. Salonen.

This edition published by arrangement with Harlequin Books S.A.

® and TM are trademarks of the publisher. Trademarks indicated with ® are registered in the United States Patent and Trademark Office, the Canadian Trade Marks Office and in other countries.

Visit us at www.eHarlequin.com

Printed in U.S.A.

In memory of Kyle Woodrow Gray.
We miss you, sweet boy.

CHAPTER ONE

November 23, 2000
Thanksgiving

SAM O'NEAL GRABBED his younger brother by the collar of his sage-green brushed-cotton shirt and pressed him up against the weathered siding of the Old Bordello Antique Shop. "Jenny won't look me in the eye," he growled, after making sure no one was near. "Why does your wife run out of the room every time I walk in?"

Josh tried to shrug but was handicapped by the two foil-covered plates of turkey and trimmings that he carried like a circus juggler. Sam had one, too, in his left hand. In his right—the one at his brother's throat—was a grapefruit-size pink ball labeled Rosemarie. Ida Jane Montgomery—Josh's wife's eighty-something great-aunt who had raised Jenny and her two sisters—had insisted Sam and Josh use her so-named 1972 pink Cadillac to make their deliveries and pick up the other guests who were joining the family for Thanksgiving dinner.

"The old coots deserve some dignity," she'd told Sam as she pressed the hideous key bob into his hand. "Can you see those ladies trying to climb into your big fancy pickup?"

Josh rolled his chin away from Sam's fingers. "Jen's just getting used to the idea of being pregnant. It wasn't easy talking her into it, you know,'' he said, his voice slightly strangled.

Sam released his grip but didn't move away. He kept his voice low. ''What do you mean *talk her into it?* I thought it was her idea.''

Josh's color rose to clash with the key bob. ''The in vitro was her idea. I'm the one who pushed to use your sperm.'' He winked in a manner so typically Josh that Sam backed off. His brother knew all too well how to get around Sam's common sense.

When Josh had first broached the idea of Sam's donating sperm so Josh and Jenny could conceive, Sam had flat out refused, but Josh was...well, Josh. And when the three of them met in the office of the fertility counselor three weeks ago, Jenny, Josh's wife of ten years, had seemed guardedly enthusiastic. ''If Sam's okay with this, then I am, too,'' she'd said.

Sam had returned home to think about the idea. He couldn't come up with any real objection. The recurrent phrase in his mind was ''Why not?'' After all, the chance of his getting married and having kids of his own seemed remote.

''So why is she avoiding me?'' Sam asked again.

Josh eased sideways to put some distance between them. ''You're imagining things. She's just busy with all these preparations. You know how organized she is.

''And if you and I don't get these plates delivered and pick up the old girls—excuse me, the town matrons—we'll be dining on hot tongue and cold shoulder instead of turkey.'' He shuffled toward the wide steps leading to the parking lot.

Sam followed, mindlessly squeezing the pink ball to ease his trepidation. Something was wrong. He felt it. But Josh was right. This was Jenny's big day. The first

Thanksgiving in ten years that the Sullivan sisters were celebrating together. And at some point in the festivities, Josh would make the big announcement that Jenny was pregnant.

However, they'd unanimously decided that the role of Sam's sperm in the Petri dish would remain a secret. He'd made the commitment and signed the necessary papers. He was going to be an uncle not a father. And if that felt a little weird, he'd learn to live with it because—bottom line—he'd do anything for Josh. Always had. Always would.

THE ARTIST IN HER made Jenny Sullivan O'Neal yearn to capture every single nuance of the moment. The *Sullivan Sisters' Thanksgiving,* she named the imaginary piece.

She took a second to memorize the way Kristin's strawberry-blond hair glistened in the light, and the odd combination of Andi's Marine Corps camouflage pants and pumpkin-orange sweater that somehow worked.

Their first reunion in ten years.

Kristin—the youngest of the Sullivan triplets—stirred the gravy with one hand then dashed to the corner of the oak buffet where she was assembling a salad. A "will-o'-the-wisp," Ida Jane used to call her. Kristin had left home right after high school to stay with family in Ireland where she'd worked as a companion to their uncle's aged grandmother. Later, Kris and two of their Irish cousins, Moira and Kathleen, moved to Wisconsin where she became certified in massage therapy. Although she'd migrated back to the West Coast, she seldom made the seven-hour drive from southern Oregon to Gold Creek, their hometown in the historic gold rush corridor of the Central Sierras in California.

"Ida Jane is getting older," Kris was saying, shaking her head. "So she's a little forgetful and makes a few mistakes. Are you suggesting it's something more serious? Like Alzheimer's?" she added, lowering her voice.

"No. Not exactly. I don't know. But I think her business is in trouble," Jenny said, moving with care around the clutter of her great-aunt's kitchen. Ida Jane's idea of decorating was to fill every available nook and cranny with hodgepodge, from cobweb-laced pinecones in a battered copper urn to chipped vases stuffed with dusty peacock feathers and dried weeds. Jenny worried that the jumble might trip the eighty-one-year-old woman, but Ida loved her "junque," as she called it. Thankfully, so had the collectors who'd visited her antique shop, the Old Bordello, over the years.

The name of the shop reflected the original use of the turn-of-the-century Victorian building. The front half housed Ida's antiques; the second floor and rear section provided the home where Ida had raised Jenny and her sisters. Until recently, the store had been fairly successful. But something had changed. That was one reason Jenny had pushed for this reunion. There was a second reason, too.

Andrea, who'd shortened her name to Andi when she was seven, repeatedly plunged a potato masher into the crockery bowl resting in her lap. "Ida Jane Montgomery is the most astute businesswoman I've ever known. If her profits are down, then it has to be due to something else. Maybe she needs a new marketing angle."

On leave from the marines, Andi was seated cross-legged on the butcher-block countertop between the old-fashioned stove and the even more old-fashioned refrigerator.

"I was thinking about it on the plane," Andi continued. "You said foot traffic is sluggish and Ida refuses to have anything to do with the Internet." She took a breath. "What if we went with some kind of advertising ploy—like a ghost?"

"What ghost?" Kristin asked. "This place isn't haunted."

Andi shrugged. "Maybe not, but it's got history. It used to be a bordello. And I swear I remember Ida telling us a story about a young prostitute who was murdered in one of the upstairs bedrooms. That sounds spooky enough."

Jenny shook her head. "She just said that to keep us out of Grandma Suzy's stuff." The triplets' grandmother, Suzanne Montgomery Scott, a tragic soul who'd been in and out of mental institutions, had passed away decades earlier, leaving behind a daughter, Lorena. Lori and her Irish-born husband had returned to Gold Creek to give birth, when tragedy struck. A car accident claimed Mick Sullivan's life first, then—after an emergency cesarean section to deliver the triplets—took his wife's, as well.

Andi put a finger into the bowl and popped some potato into her mouth. Chewing, she said, "Doesn't matter. I think the story has just the right combination of tragedy and mystery to attract antique hunters and curious skeptics."

Jen agreed. "I like the idea, Andi. When can you come back to implement it?"

Her sister stiffened. "Move back here?"

The inflection she gave the last word left no doubt in Jenny's mind that Andi wanted nothing to do with Gold Creek. She thought she understood Kristin's antipathy toward the town—people had unfairly labeled her a screwup—but Andi had always kept her reasons for leaving home to herself.

"Yes," Jenny said bluntly, giving both her sisters a look they'd understand. "Ida Jane isn't getting any younger. She needs our help."

As she pried the cornmeal muffins from the speckled enamel tin, she told them, "Warren Jones stopped me on the street a couple of weeks ago and told me we'd better do something before our aunt loses the bordello. But when I asked to see her books, Ida told me to mind my own business."

Andi made a grumbling sound. "Warren Jones has always been a worrywart."

Jenny agreed, but if Warren, who'd filed Ida Jane's income tax returns ever since his father, Walter, retired three years earlier, was worried, then they owed it to their aunt to find out what was going on.

After Jenny transferred the muffins to the warming basket, she brushed back several strands of deep-auburn hair that had escaped from the lapis clip at the nape of her neck. "All I'm saying is that we need to stay on top of the situation. Remember Sandy Grossman...Grimaldo?"

Jenny noticed the way Kristin threw herself into opening a can of ripe olives. Her exaggerated disinterest in the conversation made Jenny wonder if her sister might still harbor feelings for her old boyfriend, Donnie Grimaldo. "Sandy's mother got hooked on bingo and lost everything. Sandy didn't discover how bad it was until Poopsie was facing eviction."

Andi pitched the potato masher into the sink then hopped down from the countertop. She scraped the fluffy white potato into a serving bowl, added a dollop of butter and covered the dish with a plate. "Ida Jane's no gambler. How many times has she repeated the cautionary tale of her father losing the Rocking M in a poker game?''

Kristin, who'd driven down from her home in Ashland that morning, nodded. "For years I was afraid to buy a lottery ticket for fear I might turn into a gambleholic.''

Andi opened the oven door and leaned down to pull out the golden–breasted turkey. "So we'll talk before Kris leaves. No problem. Is that the only reason you pushed for this reunion, Jen?'' She heaved the enamel roasting pan to the counter then whipped about to face her sisters.

A tremor fluttered in Jenny's belly. She knew it wasn't the baby. They'd only received confirmation of the success of the procedure on Tuesday. "Well, there is one other thing, but I thought I'd wait to make the announcement at dinner.''

Andi and Kristin glanced at each other. The two hadn't been on good terms since high school, but they still seemed to be able to communicate without words. "Tell us," Andi ordered.

"Josh and I are pregnant.''

"Told you so," Kristin said smugly.

"You knew?'' Jenny sputtered. "How?''

"Lucky guess," Andi said sourly. "It's not like you haven't wanted to be a mother forever. What I can't figure out is why you're not shouting out the news from the upstairs porch.''

Because we cheated.

"We've been seeing a fertility specialist," she admitted, her words tumbling over each other. "We used in vitro. There was a chance it wouldn't take.'' But it did take. *I'm going to be a mother. Of my brother-in-law's child.*

Andi left the turkey to rest and walked to Jenny's side. She looped a slim, muscular arm around her shoulders and squeezed. "I understand. You're Jenny Perfect. You shouldn't need technology and Petri dishes to make offspring. But, hey, sometimes even the best of us need help."

The teasing might have stung if Jenny hadn't heard it a million times. Her sisters had nicknamed her in kindergarten when she'd brought home her first report card: all S's and O's—Satisfactory and Outstanding. No N's—Needs Improvement. Unfortunately, the name had stuck.

Just last week, Gloria Harrison Hughes, author of "Glory's World," a local "news" column in the weekly *Gold Creek Ledger,* had reported:

Jenny O'Neal, the Sullivan triplet better known as Jenny Perfect, will host her sisters and select friends at a Thanksgiving dinner at her great-aunt Ida Jane Montgomery's home. This reporter can't help but wonder how long it's been since the Sullivan triplets have been together. Isn't it a shame when family is torn apart by poor judgment?

The dig had infuriated Jenny, but Josh had cajoled her into laughing at the vindictive woman who held Kristin responsible for her son's premature departure from high school. "Gloria Hughes is a small-town, small-minded harpy," he'd stated. "Everyone knows she got the job because her brother owns the paper. Nobody pays any attention to her column."

Jenny knew that wasn't true, but there wasn't anything she could do to change Gloria's mind. She'd tried.

She stuck out her tongue at her sisters, knowing it was the expected response, then walked to the pantry to retrieve the folding stool. Kristin and Andi laughed, and peripherally Jenny saw them exchange a look that she remembered well from their teen years.

Triplets shared a dynamic wholly different from twins. Much of the time they were a threesome—''Our Sullivan Girls,'' the people of Gold Creek called them, partly because many of the townsfolk felt they'd lent a hand in raising the orphaned triplets. But factions arose, too. Sometimes one combination, sometimes another.

Kristin finished preparing the garnishes then slithered a second can of jellied cranberries onto a ruffled crystal dish that had belonged to their mother. Earlier they'd culled some turkey and fixings for Ida's housebound friends. Josh and Sam were due back any minute from their taxi duties.

Chewing on a stalk of celery, Kris tilted her head and asked, ''Why in vitro? You're young, healthy. Why didn't you and Josh just try harder? Isn't that half the fun?''

''We've been trying to get pregnant ever since we got married, Kris. The fertility clinic finally determined that Josh has some problems left over from his bout of testicular cancer when he was twelve.''

Kristin's expressive face showed concern. ''I'd forgotten about that. Is there a problem?''

Jenny shook her head. ''No. He's fine. He's been cancer free for nearly fifteen years. But unfortunately, the treatment affected his ability to make viable sperm.'' *Like he doesn't. Period.* ''So, it came down to in vitro or adoption.''

Jenny plopped open the wobbly oak, A-frame stool beside the sink and gingerly climbed up to reach the overhead cupboard. ''Frankly,'' she continued, poking through the clutter to hide her nervousness, ''I favored adoption. There are a lot of kids out there who need a family, but Josh felt strongly about carrying on the O'Neal family genes.''

The O'Neal family genes. Saying the words made her feel like a fraud. The genes in question were Sam's not Josh's. But Jenny was determined to honor her husband's wish that this be kept between the three of them. ''If it ever becomes an issue, for health reasons or whatever, you can tell your sisters, but you know as well as I do that the only way to keep a secret in a small town is to seal your lips,'' he'd argued.

''And I'd appreciate it if you keep this—the in vitro part—to yourselves,'' Jenny added. ''Josh says it doesn't bother him, but you know how guys are.''

Andi, who'd been in charge of carving the turkey since age eight—the year she'd taken up fencing—sharpened the carving knife on a whetstone. ''Having lived in testosterone-ville for the past four years, I can attest to that. Men can be very strange when it comes to things having to do with the penis.''

Jenny thought she detected a certain edge of bitterness in her sister's tone, but she didn't have a chance to question it because the dining-room door suddenly opened and Sam O'Neal walked in.

''Deliveries made, dowager queens present and accounted for,'' he said with a lazy, John Wayne–style salute.

Jenny turned back to hunting down the gravy boat she knew was lurking somewhere in the cluttered cupboard. She told herself she wasn't deliberately trying not to look at her brother-in-law.

''We're just about ready,'' she mumbled, stretching to the far corner where she spotted the vessel. Unfortunately, the stool—an antique like everything else in her aunt's home—chose that instant to wobble. Jenny reached for the cupboard door again, but it swung out of reach. She would have fallen if not for Sam's quick action. He wrapped his arms around her thighs to steady her. His chin was level with her womb.

The intimacy, given their situation, made Jenny react poorly. She yelped and tried to squirm out of his hold, which resulted in her losing her footing.

"Hold on a sec," Sam murmured, trying to keep her from toppling backward.

Before she could blink, she was safely on the ground, gravy boat clasped to her breast. Sam gave her a puzzled look. "Are you okay?"

Jenny felt her cheeks fill with color; she knew her sisters were watching. "Fine, thanks," she said, quickly turning toward the sink. "I have to wash this."

Sam closed the overhead door then moved a foot or so to rest his backside against the counter. Casually dressed in what looked like a new camel-colored shirt and black jeans and low-heeled boots, he seemed remarkably at ease. As he chatted casually with her sisters, it occurred to Jenny that she really didn't know Sam very well at all, even though he'd been a part of her life for ten years.

Jenny watched him surreptitiously. He was a big man—six inches taller and forty pounds heavier than his brother. In his youth, he'd been a movie stuntman and even put in a few years on the rodeo circuit. At thirty-nine, he still possessed a restless, untamed quality that made the town matchmakers eager to find him a wife. To Jenny, he'd gone from enigmatic brother-in-law to raw bone of contention in less than a month.

Jenny knew Sam was not to blame. It wasn't his fault that his virility was an affront to her, considering what her poor, beloved husband had been going through. It just wasn't fair.

"I asked, 'How is the book coming?'" Sam turned slightly to face her.

Darned if his casual attitude didn't irritate Jenny, too. It was as if he thought they could all go back to life as usual now that the deed was done. Jenny knew otherwise. She knew nothing would ever be the same again. Everything had changed the moment the decision was made to use Sam's sperm to impregnate her egg.

"It's not," she muttered, attacking the fragile gravy boat with a woven plastic scrubber.

"What book?" Kristin asked. "The last I heard you were a fourth-grade teacher."

"Jenny's a gifted artist and writer, too," Sam said. "I saw some of the watercolors she did for a children's book last summer."

"Cool," Andi said. "Maybe you could do a book on our ghost, too."

Jenny ignored their banter. Her book project was a dream, and Josh had promised her the summer off to work on it, but knowing Josh, something would come up.

"I plan to work on the text this summer," Jenny said, not liking the testy edge to her tone, "but we all know June through August is Ida Jane's busiest season. But, if Andi moves back after her enlistment is up…hint, hint."

When Sam asked Andi about her plans, Jenny tuned out the conversation. Her sister would do what her sister would do—that was Andi. "Willful and stubborn as the day is long," Ida always said.

Instead, Jenny pictured how she'd begged Josh to consider choosing a donor from the impressive list their fertility counselor had provided. But Josh had pleaded, sweet-talked and pressured her into believing this arrangement would be better than using an anonymous donor.

"This is a win-win scenario, Jenny," he'd argued. "Even though we had different fathers, Sam is my closest blood relative. My *only* relative besides Mom."

Jenny knew Josh was sensitive about the fact his mother hadn't married his father. Diane claimed that the reason she gave her second son Sam's surname was to make things easier for Josh, but Jenny wasn't sure she believed that.

"This way we get a child that's at least *part* me, and Sam can feel good knowing the O'Neal line isn't going to die. That's more important to him than you think," he'd quickly added, anticipating Jenny's reply.

She and her sisters had long speculated about why such a virile, handsome man as Sam O'Neal didn't have a wife and children. Josh attributed his brother's decision to remain single to Sam's teenage marriage and subsequent annulment. Although Jenny didn't know the details, Josh maintained that Sam was "once burned, twice shy."

Sam's love life is not my problem, Jenny reminded herself. *What I need to figure out is how to treat him in light of his magnanimous donation.*

When she reached for the cotton towel her aunt kept hanging under the cupboard, Sam beat her to it. "Here," he said. His deep voice sounded strained.

Jenny accepted the cloth with a forced smile. "Thanks." Their fingers touched briefly, just enough to make her insides flutter in a way she didn't recognize. She quickly stepped back and nearly tripped over the dilapidated stool.

Suddenly angry, and very close to tears, she kicked its slightly askew leg. "Would somebody please throw that damn thing away before we end up with a lawsuit on our hands?"

The kitchen door swung open and a blond head popped in, a video camera to one eye. "What's that? Did I hear my wife use profanity? Lord have mercy. Jenny Perfect cussed."

Jenny saw Sam slip out of the range of fire, as if he could read her temper brewing. This irked her, too. As did her husband's use of the ridiculous nickname she couldn't shake. She grabbed a corn muffin out of the basket and pitched it at the video cam. Josh ducked.

The soft biscuit bounced off the door and rolled to a crumbly stop a foot from Josh's loafers. He picked it up and took a bite. "Mmm, good, but it'll be better with honey. Won't it, honey?"

Grinning, he sauntered across the room. He set the camera on the counter then pulled Jenny into an embrace. He nuzzled the sensitive spot on her neck until her knees grew weak and she had to laugh. "Stop it, you goofball. Everything's ready."

"I'm ready," he said, making his fair eyebrows dance up and down. "Oh, yeah, baby. Any time. Any place."

Amid the laughter and kisses, it struck her. Finally, after all the tests, thermometers and frustration, they were going to have a baby. Did it matter in the long run where the sperm came from? Not if they loved their baby as much as they loved each other. The child now growing in her womb would be *their* child—hers and Josh's.

"You are completely nuts," she said, cupping his cheek with her free hand. "But I love you."

Josh tossed his half-eaten muffin in the sink then pulled her tight against him. He lowered his head and kissed her. Jenny felt herself blush, even though her family had seen them kiss before—many times. But for some reason, she felt weird this time. She tried to focus on the pleasure of Josh's touch but couldn't relax.

Apparently sensing something was wrong, Josh lifted his head and said, "Okay, everyone, dinner's up to you. Me and my woman are heading upstairs for a little quality time in one of the bedrooms."

"Maybe Andi's ghost will show up," Kristin joked.

"Ghost?" Josh righted them so quickly Jenny's vision blurred. "What ghost?"

Andi repeated her suggestion with obvious reluctance, probably because she knew the only way the marketing scheme would become a reality was if she returned to Gold Creek to implement it.

"Have you ever seen this ghost?" Josh asked seriously.

Jenny punched him. "No, but you've got to admit, a *haunted* bordello carries a certain appeal. Remember that restaurant we ate at on Jackson Square in New Orleans? Muriel's? It's supposed to be haunted. Just because we didn't see a ghost didn't detract from its charm."

Andi walked to the cupboard for a serving platter. "We'd just be embroidering on a story Auntie used to tell us about a young prostitute who lived here. She died when two men fought over her and a gun went off. Right, Jen?"

Before Jenny had a chance to answer, a diminutive elderly woman entered the room. "What's the holdup here?" she asked. "My dinner guests are waiting. Joshua, are you making trouble again?"

Ida Jane Montgomery, dressed in a purple and green silk jogging suit that would have put a peacock to shame, looked around, a mock frown on her deeply lined face.

"M-me?" Josh sputtered. "It's the girls' fault. They were holding a séance to get the bordello's ghost to join us for dinner."

"A ghost? What ghost?" Ida Jane exclaimed. "If there's a ghost, I want to know about it."

Sam approached Jenny's great-aunt and bowed with dignity. "Miss Ida, these wayward youngsters are holding up dinner with their tomfoolery, but I'd be delighted to escort you to the table. Maybe if we set a good example they'll take the hint."

Ida Jane, her cap of stiff blue curls sticking out at odd angles, lifted her chin regally. "Lord knows I've tried to raise them right, but those girls were a handful from the day they came home from the hospital." Her sigh fooled no one. Everyone knew Ida Jane loved her grand-nieces more than anything, even the dilapidated old bordello that served as both antique store and home.

"Did I tell you about the time one of 'em filled the wringer washer with baby ducks?" she asked, taking Sam's arm. "I believe it was Andrea."

Together they made such a charming picture that Jenny's heart constricted, and her eyes filled with tears. Another memory to paint.

"Me?" Andi howled. "Why is it always me? I hated ducks. Still do. It was Kristin." She picked up the platter of turkey in one hand and the muffin basket in the other then followed after her aunt.

Kris gave Jenny a mischievous wink before wrapping an arm around the salad bowl. She also managed to carry the crock of mashed potatoes as she hurried after the others, loudly proclaiming her innocence. "It wasn't me, Auntie. I don't remember any ducks. Are you sure it wasn't Jenny? Just because she never got in any trouble doesn't mean…"

Before Jenny could follow, Josh pulled her into his arms. His Paul Newman–blue eyes were unusually serious. "Have I told you today how wonderful you are?" He kissed her lightly. "I love you more than giblet gravy."

Jenny relaxed into his safe, loving embrace. She'd been far too uptight lately. She had to try to be more like her husband, who could dash away the slightest worry with a wave of his hand. That same devil-may-care attitude was what had attracted her to him when she was sixteen.

"I love you, too," she returned. She didn't know what she'd do without his beaming smile, his spontaneous laugh. If even a fraction of his personality somehow found its way to their child, Jenny knew the agonizing choice would have been worth it. Setting her worries aside, she kissed him back.

A muffled chant, "Gra…vy, Gra…vy," filtered through the wall.

Josh grinned. "Duty calls, my sweet, but we're going to sneak away later. I promise. Is there really a ghost?"

Jenny shook her head. "Of course not. It's a marketing gimmick that might attract customers to the antique store. Ida Jane's been very closemouthed about it, but I think her business is in trouble. I'm trying to talk Andi into moving home when her enlistment is up. She has a lot of good ideas and she knows computers. Maybe we can gently nudge Ida Jane into the twenty-first century."

Using two oven mitts, Josh pulled a bake dish of marshmallow yams and another of pecan stuffing out of the oven while Jenny filled the gravy boat with the golden, aromatic sauce. She grabbed a serving dish of green beans on her way through, and together they joined the others in the dining room.

"Make room for the good stuff," Josh said, leaning forward to deposit the dishes on waiting trivets.

The yellowish glow from the candles in the center-piece cast an odd shadow across Josh's face. A shiver raced up Jenny's spine.

She hastily deposited her two bowls on the table and sat down. *Get a grip,* she silently chastised herself. *Must be all those extra hormones I've been taking.*

"This is wonderful," Ida Jane said, clapping her hands with glee. "The Sullivan girls are back together. Plus Sam and Josh and my dearest friends are here, too. What a joyous day!"

Four elderly women, as familiar to Jenny and her sisters as blood relatives, cheered with approval. The dignified Lillian Carswell, a retired librarian, sat beside Kristin. Directly across from her was Beulah Jensen, who lived around the corner and had left three May baskets on the porch of the old bordello every May Day until the triplets moved away from home. To Ida Jane's left was Mary Needham, whose poor hearing was probably a result of thirty years of driving a school bus. To Sam's right sat recently widowed Linda McCloskey, one of the nurses who had been at the hospital the night the triplets were born. Linda's only son, Bart, was celebrating the holiday with his wife's family in Santa Rosa.

Josh took his place at the head of the table opposite Ida Jane then reached out to take Jenny's hand. With his left, he made a "gimme" motion until Andi complied. She in turn connected with Kristin, who linked with Lillian and so on. Jenny and Sam completed the circle.

When everyone was holding hands, Josh spoke, his voice uncharacteristically serious. "Thank you, Father, for the gifts we are about to share. Thank you, too, for giving us each other, and never let us forget that we're connected through time and space, spirit and heart. We are family."

He squeezed Jenny's hand; she did likewise to Sam, who held her hand in his big rough paw. Glancing sideways, she saw his lips compress slightly. Instinctively, she knew what he was thinking. They were connected all right. In a way, hopefully, no one else would ever know.

Josh lifted his head and slowly looked around the table. "And speaking of family," he said, pausing dramatically, "Jenny's pregnant."

After a round of cheers and congratulations, Andi said, "As long as you don't have triplets, right, Auntie?"

Ida Jane's gaze settled on Jenny. She lifted her wineglass in a toast. "To new life. The number's not important, it's the love that counts." Her gray eyes clouded a moment then she went on. "You girls never had a chance to know your parents, but I can tell you, they loved you from the instant you were conceived."

Jenny felt a flush creep up her neck. Her grip on her glass of cranberry juice tightened.

"To families," Sam said quietly, his deep voice making a big impact. "Thank you, Miss Ida, for always making me feel a part of yours."

A chorus of "Hear! Hear!" echoed around the table.

After each glass touched, the feast began, every bit as festive and noisy as any Jenny could remember. She went through all the motions. She smiled and chewed and answered questions when asked, but a part of her was out of sync.

"A little faith, please," Sam said softly, their shoulders almost touching.

Jenny startled. "I beg your pardon?"

"A little turkey," he repeated. One thin, sable eyebrow quirked in question. "Are you feeling okay? You look pale."

Jenny swallowed the lump in her throat. She reached for the platter and in the process dragged the sleeve of her blouse across the mound of untouched mashed potatoes on her plate.

Sam made a harsh sound between his teeth, and rose. He pulled out her chair and said to the others, "Gravy stain. This calls for quick action."

Jenny rose without thinking and followed him into the kitchen. He led her to the sink and carefully rinsed the brown smear from the ivory material. "Jenny," he said softly, "what's wrong?"

Distracted by his roughened fingers working the delicate material with exquisite care, Jenny didn't answer. Her emotions were too jumbled, too close to the surface. She couldn't put her anguish into words.

Wrapping a towel around her wrist, Sam squeezed firmly. "What is it? Tell me."

"This is so *not* my style, Sam. You know me. I'm a born-again flower child. If nature had intended for Josh and me to have a baby, it would have happened. I can't help thinking something bad is going to happen because we were greedy. We wanted more than we were supposed to have."

The last came out as a blubbering cry. Sam cursed softly then reacted as any compassionate person would. He pulled her into his strong safe arms and soothed her with quiet, calming words of encouragement.

"Jenny, you took advantage of a medical miracle. What's wrong with that? Nature's changed the game, sweetheart."

The endearment wasn't anything she hadn't heard him

say a hundred times, but it made her throat close. "You've seen my breeding operation at the ranch," he went on. "Not to be crude, but *I'm* Mother Nature in my part of the world, and nothing terrible has happened. The Rocking M has the healthiest, strongest stock around."

Jenny made herself take a deep breath. His scent was different from Josh's but comforting, fortifying. She pulled back enough to look up at him.

"You haven't done anything wrong, Jenny. If it weren't for Josh's cancer, he'd have enough sperm to get you both in a lot of trouble. It's not his fault, and he shouldn't have to pay. Neither of you should."

"Your mother blames herself for Josh's cancer," Jenny said. "She said she didn't get his vaccinations on schedule and somehow that made him prone to testicular cancer."

Sam's expression turned sour. His less-than-congenial feelings for his mother were well known, but even after all these years she'd never discovered the reason behind them.

"That's just Diane being Diane, but none of that matters. What's important is that you and my brother have a chance to start a family. I'm just hoping this doesn't ruin our friendship."

Jenny knew she had to try to get past her qualms. Josh loved his brother almost as much as he loved Jenny. It would tear him apart if the two people he loved most couldn't be comfortable around each other.

"You're right, Sam. It'll all work out."

He touched his knuckle to her chin—a gesture he'd employed since Josh introduced them when she was sixteen. "Can I finish my dinner now?"

Smiling, Jenny tossed the towel on the counter and

looped her arm through his. "Just save room for pie. I bought them from the new bakery in town."

Sam's low chuckle reassured her even more. "That is not going to be a problem, believe me."

SAM WATCHED JOSH WALK the last of the dinner guests—Lillian Carswell—to the door of her neat-as-a-pin mobile home. The old gal was a veritable font of knowledge about Gold Creek's history.

The subject on the drive to her mobile home in Restful Trails Senior Park had been the triplets. She had stories galore. "Ida Jane was forever trying to dress them alike," she'd said with a chortle. "I'll never forget the Easter when the girls turned six. Marge Grover—she passed away a few years ago—sewed these darling little pinafore-type dresses, and Betsey Simms, at McAffey's department store, donated white anklets trimmed with tiny daisies and the cutest little bonnets you've ever seen. But the triplets had other plans."

She'd leaned forward to pat Josh's shoulder. "Not Jenny, of course. She was a perfect angel, like usual. But Andrea claimed the shoes hurt her feet. She preferred to wear sneakers without socks. She wouldn't even consider wearing the hat. Kristin wore the hat but insisted on sticking a bunch of flowers from Ida's garden in it. By the time she got to church, the lilacs were drooping like clusters of grapes."

Sam found the tale reassuring. The triplets were unique individuals, even at age six.

Once Josh was seated, Sam put the car in gear. He drove slowly to negotiate the park's many speed bumps. "Your wife has some concerns about this arrangement, Josh," he said. "We probably should have waited, maybe talked it through a little more."

"There wasn't time, Sam," Josh said. "You had the China trip scheduled."

"So? We could have put it off a few months."

Josh, who'd been diagnosed as borderline hyperactive as a child, went atypically still. "We've waited long enough, Sam. It was now or never."

An icy chill down his spine made Sam lean forward to click up the heat.

Josh turned in the seat to face him. "Jenny's happy about it. I know she is. She's just had a lot on her mind."

Sam could believe that. Getting her sisters to the same table after all these years was quite a feat. And talking Andi into returning to Gold Creek next spring seemed very unlikely. "Well, I hope you're right. Jenny's a good lady, and I don't want this to come back to haunt us."

"*Haunt,*" Josh repeated. "Ida Jane really liked Andi's idea of a resident ghost, didn't she?" Josh was a master at changing subjects, but his laugh—chipper, familiar and reassuring—eased Sam's odd feeling of trepidation.

"Don't worry, bro," he said, lightly punching Sam's shoulder. "Everything is working out just the way it's supposed to."

Sam hoped so. For all their sakes.

CHAPTER TWO

March 2001
St. Patrick's Day

SINCE THE DECK off the master bedroom afforded the best view of the courtyard, Sam headed there to take stock. He threw open the balcony doors off his bedroom and stepped to the railing to scan the crowd below.

Thanks to Josh's insistent nagging and organizational skills, the Rocking M sponsored a benefit barbecue each year on St. Patrick's Day weekend when the surrounding hills were their greenest and the California buckeyes were swathed in shiny new leaves. Members of the Gold Creek Garden Club—Ida Jane's pet group—handled the kitchen; the volunteer fire department cooked the chicken. Sam made sure he stayed in the background, while Josh played host.

Sam spotted Andi Sullivan sitting on the top rung of the corral chatting with Lars Gunderson, a cantankerous old miner who made Sam's solitary habits look downright social. Andi had only been back in town a week, but according to Josh, the changes she had in mind for the Old Bordello Antique Shop weren't sitting well with the store's owner.

His gaze circled the crowd of familiar faces until he spotted what he was looking for—a kelly-green Stetson. He had no idea where his brother had managed to find such a thing, but there it was atop Josh's head, pushed back at a jaunty angle to accommodate the video camera that never seemed to leave his eye.

Sam let out a long sigh. At least Josh was sitting still for the moment. Sam was almost out of patience where his brother was concerned. The past three months had been stressful. Jenny's full trimester of morning sickness and fatigue had coincided with Josh's seemingly unconnected series of colds and flulike symptoms, which had finally been diagnosed as something far more serious.

Josh's cancer had returned, popping up as a difficult-to-spot mass behind his liver. The oncologist Josh saw last week in Stanford had recommended an aggressive protocol of radiation and chemotherapy.

It couldn't be aggressive enough as far as Sam was concerned. His main problem was Josh's attitude.

"I beat it before, I can do it again," Josh said repeatedly. "Will you two lighten up?"

He was referring to Jenny and Sam. Sam hadn't spent a lot of time in his sister-in-law's company the past few months—he knew she still felt awkward around him. In hindsight, especially given Josh's condition, the timing of the pregnancy was all wrong, but there was little anyone could do about it at this point.

"He's going to wear himself out, isn't he?" a voice said from the doorway behind him.

Sam glanced over his shoulder, but he recognized the voice without looking. Jenny. Beautiful, glowing, very pregnant Jenny. "Not if I have anything to say about it," Sam replied, his voice gruff.

She sighed as she joined him at the railing. "You're not your brother's keeper, you know. But I do appreciate everything you've done to help."

Sam inched over to put more space between them.

Lately she seemed to possess an ethereal glow that made him yearn to touch her. Which, he reminded himself, was not a good thing. He knew this confounding attraction had to be based on the fact she was carrying his babies—her first sonogram had alerted them that she was carrying twins. His connection to her was purely biological, he told himself.

"Josh is lucky they finally diagnosed this," Sam said, staring at a group of people standing beside a patrol car. His buddy, Donnie Grimaldo, a local deputy, leaned against the front fender while his boss, Sheriff Magnus Brown, held court. The older man was a blowhard who'd never been one of Sam's favorite people.

"What do you mean?" Jenny asked.

Sam didn't turn his head but sensed she was studying his face. He regretted his candor but said, "I hate to admit it, but I was beginning to think Josh was turning into a hypochondriac, like our mother."

Jenny chuckled under her breath. "That summer in college when your mother stayed with us she practically lived at the clinic. She was on a first-name basis with all the pharmacists at Long's."

Sam turned slightly and said, "Good thing her new husband is a retired doctor. He's got just what she needs—money and a prescription pad. Maybe she'll keep this one."

Jenny frowned. "You really don't like her, do you?"

"I just don't like talking about her." His feelings were a mixture of anger and disgust, far too convoluted for casual conversation and best kept locked in the darkest recesses of his mind. He shrugged and looked away from Jenny's all-too-sympathetic eyes.

"Josh doesn't seem to hold as much bitterness toward

her as you do, but I guess you two have more history together, right?''

History. *I guess you could call a stab in the back that cost me my wife and unborn child "history."* ''Is that a polite way of saying I'm old?'' he teased.

She smiled wryly. ''Eleven years seemed like a big deal when I was seventeen and you were pushing thirty, but now that I'm almost thirty…''

Sam let his skepticism show. ''Twenty-eight is still wet behind the ears.''

''Oh, no. Not the old-age talk,'' a cheerful voice said, taking them by surprise.

Both Sam and Jenny spun around. For some reason Sam felt guilty, but fortunately, his brother didn't seem to notice. Josh strolled forward and looped his arm across his wife's shoulders. ''I was filming the festivities and happened to scan upward and what do I see but Romeo and Juliet on the balcony.''

His teasing brought a shot of heat to Sam's face, making him grateful for the setting sun. ''Yep, that's why I built this place. So I could spout poetry to my sister-in-law,'' Sam said, hoping his joke didn't sound as lame to Jenny and Josh as it did to him.

Jenny's lovely cheeks seemed to hold some extra color, too, but Sam attributed that to the afternoon's activities. She'd been in charge of the egg race.

''I guess it's about time to sound the gong for dinner,'' Sam said, starting to leave.

''It can wait. I, um, wanted to talk to you a minute,'' Josh said, his tone uncharacteristically serious.

Sam pulled over the folding chair he kept on the deck. ''Have a seat. I'll get you a chair, Jenny.''

She shook her head. In the mellow sunset, her wind-tossed locks looked bloodred. ''I'm fine.''

Josh squeezed her shoulders then whisked his silly green hat from his head and placed it on Jenny's. "She's a trooper, isn't she, Sam? Do you know anyone better than Jenny Perfect?" he asked, sitting down.

Jenny's lip curled up in a snarl, and Sam looked away to hide his smile. He knew she hated the nickname—even if it did fit.

"What do you want to talk about, Josh?"

"The big C. The ugly little growth in here." He pulled up his T-shirt, exposing his belly. The bluish-white scar that dissected his pale skin from sternum to navel was a product of the last go-around. When he was twelve, doctors removed a large mass near his liver along with the diseased testicle where the cancer had begun.

Sam shrugged, faking nonchalance. "What's to talk about? You fight it and beat it—just like last time."

Jenny nodded. Sam thought she looked close to tears.

Josh lowered his shirt. He closed his eyes and let out a long sigh. "I know that. But, I want to be up front about what's happening. I'm not going to give up living while I get these treatments.

"Jenny wants me to quit work. Being a park ranger has been my dream ever since I watched my first Yogi and Boo-Boo cartoon," he said, with a chuckle.

"Sam, you want to do your big-brother thing, which I appreciate all to hell, but the bottom line is—it's my life, my cancer, and I have to deal with it my way."

Something about Josh's tone, something too fatalistic for Sam's taste, made him blow up. "You mean laid-back? Take it as it comes? I don't think so, little brother. This isn't a game. It's war. We're fighting for your life, and I'm damn well going to be in the trenches with you."

Jenny put her hand on Josh's shoulder. "Listen to Sam, Josh. He remembers what it was like the first time. He—"

"You think I don't?" Josh exclaimed, jumping to his feet. "I was the one puking my guts out, not Sam. I'm the one who got razzed about my bald head. Been there, done that, Jen. And I'm not wild about doing it again."

Sam felt as breathless as he had when a horse had fallen on him, breaking three ribs.

Jenny threw herself against Josh and cried, "You don't have a choice, Josh. We have to think about the babies."

Josh's arms came up slowly, but finally he wrapped them around his wife and soothed her sobs. But over her shoulder, his gaze found Sam. There was something sad and very tired in his brother's eyes. Something that made Sam want to sit down and weep.

Three months later

"I'LL BE BACK in a minute. I'm going to put away some of this stuff," Jenny called, closing the door to the spare bedroom behind her.

Once the latch clicked, she leaned against it and slowly sank to the floor. Her belly made her feel graceless and top-heavy; her swollen ankles looked like gross stumps connected to her Birkenstock-clad feet. Her sleeveless denim maternity jumper was wrinkled and stained with Kool-Aid handprints from the end-of-school party. Happy tears, sweaty hugs and another year was over.

Then, before she had time to catch her breath, her colleagues had converged on her room to give her a baby shower. She'd survived both ordeals without breaking down, but her emotions were very close to the surface. When Sam's big white pickup pulled up to her classroom door and her husband gingerly lowered himself to the ground, she'd had to fight not racing to help him. But Josh, despite the weight loss and bald head, was still proud and independent. He tried to carry on as if the horrible disease wasn't getting the better of him. But everyone knew otherwise. Everyone except Sam, who refused to see the obvious.

She took a deep breath, readjusting her position to give a child's foot or elbow more room beneath her rib cage. As she eyed the booty piled on the daybed—a complete layette, bath provisions, stuffed animals and a vast assortment of tiny clothes—her gaze was drawn to the brilliantly painted rocking horse sitting on the floor in front of her easel. A gift from Sam.

"Your husband picked it out," he'd said, amid the oohs and aahs of her fellow teachers. "The last time we were in Stanford."

A month earlier. When there'd still been hope. When a miracle seemed possible, and Josh seemed to be responding to the high doses of chemotherapy pumped into his body.

Sam had taken charge of Josh's treatment schedule. It had made sense since Jenny couldn't take the time from work, nor was her body up to the long drives, but there was a tiny part of her that resented him. Sam had those hours on the drive to and from the clinic. He had the opportunity to talk to the oncologist and the nurses. He was the one Josh turned to with questions or concerns.

But her logical mind knew that way of thinking was petty. Sam was doing everything in his power to help Josh beat this disease. More, she feared, than Josh himself, who each day seemed less involved in his body's war.

A light knock on the hollow door echoed through her chest. "Jen?"

Andi. Lifesaver. Frustrated entrepreneur.

After several months of arm-twisting—combined with the kind of guilt trips sisters can lay on each other—Andi had agreed to come home. She'd moved in with Ida Jane in March and had immediately begun to implement her haunted bordello campaign. Unfortunately, Ida Jane had lost interest in the idea, and the two seemed to lock horns daily.

Jenny still worried about her great-aunt's health, but Ida's doctor blamed the memory slips and emotional swings on age. Jenny wasn't convinced, but she simply didn't have the energy to investigate further.

Struggling to her knees, she slowly rose and opened the door. "Sorry, I got sidetracked."

Andi, who was dressed in shorts and a tank top, shrugged. "No problem. I just wanted to tell you I'm taking Ida home. That punch went right to her head. You wouldn't believe the things I overheard her say. We really need to keep her off the booze."

"There was no alcohol in the punch."

"Really?" She looked puzzled. "I just assumed...well, I'm taking her home anyway. Sam just left, and I think Josh is ready to crash. He looked good today, though."

True. Josh had been his laughing, charming self, but Jenny knew he'd pay for the effort with a long, restless night of pain.

Andi seemed to understand. Her smile was tinged with sadness as she glanced at the gifts. "Nice haul. Do you need any help?"

Jenny shook her head. "It can wait until tomorrow."

"First day of vacation. Maybe you can find some time to work on your book, huh?"

Jenny looked at her easel and frowned. She finally had her wish—a summer off. But how could she paint the carefree, whimsical illustrations of a children's book, when terrifying questions assaulted her—questions like "How am I going to live without Josh?"

Two and a half months later

"JOSH, SNAP OUT OF IT," Sam barked.

He hated using that tone on his brother. Lately, though, it was the only thing that penetrated the foggy blur of morphine-induced haze. Josh's eyes opened. Glazed with pain and painkillers, the blue eyes that usually danced with humor were dull and out of focus.

Sam put his face two inches from his brother's. "Josh, concentrate. Your wife is on the phone. Do you hear me, Josh? Jenny wants to tell you about the birth."

The babies. Andi had already given Sam the news. A boy and a girl. But he wasn't about to deprive Jenny of the right to share the news with her husband, even if there was only a slim chance that he'd understand what she said. In the past three days, even Sam had lost contact with Josh, who was slowly distancing himself from his body in preparation for death.

At least that was the hogwash the hospice nurses tried to sell. All Sam knew for sure was he was losing the baby brother he'd practically raised on his own, and Sam wanted to throttle someone—preferably the person in charge of fate. Never had he felt this helpless. Well…once, when he was nineteen.

A voice came on the line. "Josh? Can you hear me?"

Sam recognized his sister-in-law's tear-ravaged voice. He held the phone to Josh's ear. Being careful not to disturb the tubes leading from Josh's body to the bags dangling from the portable hospital bed's metal sides, Sam rested his elbows on the railing and looked beyond the bed to the scene outside the picture window. The view wasn't as spectacular as what you'd get at the Rocking M, but this little house on one of Gold Creek's quiet side streets is where his brother had wanted to be.

"Promise me you'll let me die at home, Sam," Josh had asked shortly after they learned that the months of chemotherapy had been unable to stop the disease. "No more hospitals. I'm done with doctors."

While Sam hadn't been ready to concede defeat at the time—after all, Josh had beaten this enemy before—he'd agreed to honor Josh's request. "This is the place I've been the happiest. Other than the ranch, this was my first true home. I don't want to die in a hospital, Sam. You have to promise me."

Sam had given his word, but at the same time had extracted a promise from his brother that Josh would continue to fight the cancer with all his strength and will. "Miracles happen if you want them badly enough. You're going to beat this thing, Josh. You have to."

But none of the alternative treatments had contained a cure. Sam had even flown to Mexico to check out a facility that claimed to have a seventy percent cure rate. But Josh had deteriorated dramatically by the time Sam returned and had been too weak to travel.

Jenny spoke loudly, and Sam tried not to listen to what might well be the young couple's last exchange, but her words were unmistakable, as was her furor.

"You *cannot* die, dammit. Do you hear me, Joshua

Peter O'Neal? Not today. Not on the day your babies were born.''

Josh's eyes widened a tiny bit, and Sam's heart contracted. She was getting through in a way he hadn't been able to. Silently, he urged his brother to speak, to answer this woman who'd just spent twelve hours in labor, refusing drugs so she'd be alert enough to call her husband.

"I mean it, Josh," she said, her tone stern. Sam knew *he'd* pay attention if Jenny talked to him that way.

Josh's mouth opened slightly but no words came out.

Jenny let out a low cry of frustration. "Oh, honey, I know you're trying, but you have to try harder. You have to hold on. For the babies' sakes."

Josh's eyes closed.

Sam jostled his brother's bone-thin shoulder. "Josh, stay with us, buddy. Hang in there."

Apparently hearing Sam's low murmur of encouragement, Jenny made a high keening sound. "No, Josh, no. You can't die. I don't care if the twins are Sam's biologically—you're their dad. Your name is on that birth certificate, and you can't die on the day they were born. Believe me, that's something a child never gets over. I won't let you do that to them."

Josh's eyes opened again. For an instant, the briefest of seconds, his gaze met Sam's. Against all reason, Sam knew his brother would hold on.

He took back the phone. "Come as soon as you can, Jen. He's hanging in. For you. And the babies."

He hung up the receiver then reached out and took his brother's hand. Tears clouded his vision. He hadn't let himself cry. Not once in the past five months had Sam allowed himself to feel the loss that was coming.

He was losing the best thing in his life. His brother. The boy who had—in a way—saved Sam's life.

At twelve, Sam had been floundering. He'd just lost the only stepfather who ever meant a thing to him, and his mother was pregnant. "Never mind who the father is," she'd told him. "He's made it clear he won't be in the picture."

Sam wasn't surprised. Men passed through Diane O'Neal's fingers faster than money.

His mother had been hired as a makeup artist at Paramount a few months earlier. Sam was street smart; he knew about adult liaisons and the sexual dynamics involved in the entertainment industry. Rumor had it Josh's father was a popular television actor who wasn't divorced from his older, very rich wife.

Diane lost her job because the "star" didn't want a public relations risk, but miraculously came into some money. "An inheritance," she called it. She bought a small, cozy house in Culver City. After Josh was born, she went to work for a travel agency, and Sam became a makeshift daddy. Fortunately, the facility for troubled kids where he went to school offered enough flexibility for him to manage.

When Diane married Frank, the owner of the travel agency—and a man Sam detested—Sam left home. He dropped out of school to become a stunt double. The following spring, he got a break and landed a speaking role in a movie.

Eight months after that, everything went to hell. He lost his job, his bride, his unborn child and his dream of being a movie star. Worse than all of that was his mother's betrayal. Dangerously angry, Sam followed a friend's advice and joined the rodeo circuit. His career as a cowboy lasted until his mother tracked him down.

She'd divorced Frank and needed help taking care of Josh. Sam went home.

He stayed with Diane and Josh on and off throughout Josh's childhood, moving out whenever he couldn't get along with the current man in his mother's life.

It was never difficult to be with Josh—a child as cute and loving as a puppy. Josh was Sam's touchstone. The only time Sam didn't feel alone was when he was caring for Josh.

Walking to the kitchen for a glass of water, Sam looked around the living room. Josh had spent much of the past few months on the couch, until the night he'd fallen and been unable to get up. Jenny had called Sam in a panic. Sam had rushed into town—he made the half-hour trip in fifteen minutes—desperately afraid that Josh would be gone before he reached him.

Together, Sam and Jenny decided it was time to contact Hospice, the health-care professionals dedicated to helping terminally ill patients die with dignity. A hospital bed was set up in the living room to make it easier for the visiting nurses to tend to Josh's bathing, bedsores and bodily needs.

Soon after that, Sam moved his camper into town and parked it in his sister-in-law's driveway. "I need to be here," he'd explained to Jenny. "Josh needs me, and I think you could use a hand, too. You've been doing a great job, but it's going to get rough. I know. I went through this with Clancy."

Clancy Royson was the only one of Diane's husbands Sam had ever called Dad. A grizzly bear of a man, Clancy had given Sam the guidance and love he'd needed. Sam had been at his side when Clancy died of lung cancer. After his death, Sam's mother had sold Clancy's beautiful Pasadena ranch, and the proceeds were put in a trust for Sam until he turned twenty-five. Sam had used the money to buy the Rocking M, and not a day went by that Sam didn't wish Clancy were alive to see it.

Jenny hadn't put up a fuss about the travel trailer. Exhausted from worry and her pregnancy, she barely seemed to notice him. Since the St. Patrick's Day party in mid-March, Sam had watched his sister-in-law put every spare bit of energy into saving her husband. Fortunately, Andi and Ida Jane were nearby to help, and the women of the Gold Creek Garden Club stocked the kitchen with casseroles and baked goods. Even Gloria Hughes at the *Ledger* had written a tribute to Josh, suggesting the creation of a Josh O'Neal scholarship fund.

Josh made a soft groaning sound, and Sam checked his watch. He'd administered a shot of morphine just an hour and a half earlier. Hurrying to his brother's side, Sam took Josh's hand and squeezed it gently. "Hang tight, kiddo, Jenny's coming. I'll give you another shot after she gets here, but you don't want to be sleeping when she comes, right?"

Josh's eyelids fluttered and his lips moved but no sound came from his throat. Using a special sponge, Sam swabbed Josh's dry lips and tongue with water. Sam's chest felt tight and his hand shook. "Hang on, Josh. You can do it. You're Josh the Magnificent. Remember?"

Sam pictured his brother shortly after Diane divorced husband number four—a real loser who'd taken his frustrations out on Josh. Josh had been in his daredevil phase and he'd rigged up a body kite that he hoped would allow him to fly. Although he'd planned to test it on a bluff by the ocean, he'd opted for a practice flight from the top of the garage.

The words Josh the Magnificent were scrawled in blue

Magic Marker across the wings. Josh had suffered a broken arm in the fall, but his spirit had remained undaunted.

The sound of a car pulled Sam back to the present. He recognized the headlights. "Your wife's here, Josh. Jenny's here."

JOSH WAS GONE. That's the word they used. Not "dead." *Gone.* "When did he *slip away?*" one of the nurses had asked upon arriving at the door, minutes after Josh had taken his final, tortured breath.

Jenny had almost yelled at the woman, "He didn't *slip away.* He left. Josh left me."

But she didn't say anything. As the first light of dawn changed to pinkish-gold, she sat beside the cold stiff body of the man she loved more than life and blocked out everything, even the panic roiling beneath her skin.

"Sam, would you take Jenny outside? The nurses need a little space to finish up." Andi talked past Jenny as though she were mentally challenged.

Perhaps she was. Perhaps her brain had stopped functioning the minute Josh had stopped breathing.

"Jenny," Sam said softly. He put his hands on her shoulders and guided her to her feet. "Let go."

He broke the lock she had on Josh's hand—his oddly artificial-looking hand that felt too heavy, too cold to be real. Maybe they were right. Maybe he had slipped away when she wasn't looking, but when was that? She hadn't closed her eyes all night, even though she was so tired she felt as though she could sleep for a week.

"Would you like to lie down?" Sam asked, steering her toward the hallway. Toward her bedroom. The room she'd shared with Josh.

"No," she cried, turning so suddenly Sam's hands fell

from her arms. She rushed past him, not able to look at the scene by the window. At the hospital bed where two nurses were unplugging things that had been plugged into Josh's body.

She hurried through the kitchen and stumbled out the rear door, almost slipping on the dew-slick steps. She ran to the middle of the yard and bent over, trying to force air into her lungs when the pain made it almost impossible to breathe.

Her emotions were too jumbled to know what to do—scream, cry, rant and rave, shake her fist at a God who would rob her of the best part of herself? She squeezed her eyes shut tight to keep her tears locked inside. To cry would be to admit it was over. And it couldn't be over. Josh couldn't leave her. He wouldn't.

"Can I do anything to help?"

She recognized Sam's voice. "What can anybody do?" she said, her words passing through clenched teeth. "It's over. Everything good is gone. Just like that."

Sam didn't try to contradict her. Maybe he agreed with her. He simply stood beside her, waiting and saying nothing.

She looked back at the house. The sun had barely cleared the treetops. A beautiful summer morning. Josh had died at six twenty-two. He'd given her the time she'd begged for last night, but not the time he'd promised when he married her.

"We'll grow old together and die within a month of each other," he'd predicted. "You first, of course. And I'll be right behind you because I know your ghost would haunt me if I hung around here without you."

Anger bubbled up in her throat. "I'm never going to forgive him for this. Never."

Sam moved to a spot across from her, his bare toes

almost touching hers. Jenny straightened; her entire body ached from sitting in one position for too long. Her gaze met Sam's. His forehead was lined with deep grooves. The white around his hazel eyes was noticeably bloodshot. *When's the last time he slept?*

"Jenny," he said, his tone humming with feeling, "I know you're hurting. You have every right, but we have to be clear about something."

A lump formed in her throat. She pressed her hand to the saggy flesh at her middle—flesh that just hours earlier had been stretched to the breaking point to house the two children within her womb. Her babies...Sam's babies.

"I loved my brother more than anything in the world," Sam said, his voice raw with emotion. "I'd have traded places with him in a heartbeat if I could have met the devil to make the deal."

Jenny believed him too, so great was the suffering in his eyes.

"The Hospice people laid out all that stuff about the steps of grief, and I know that anger is part of the process, but don't take your suffering out on Josh. He suffered enough at the end. His pain—" Sam's voice cracked. He looked down, as if ashamed to let her see his weakness.

Somehow, without seeming to move, she was swallowed up by his arms. His low, rasping cry opened a floodgate of tears—tears that broke through her anger, her fear, to the grief below. They held each other like strangers who'd survived some mind-numbing catastrophe.

A single thought penetrated Jenny's fog of pain and grief. She recalled something Josh had told her right after his cancer had been confirmed. She hadn't been pay-ing too much attention because she'd known without a doubt Josh would be okay.

"I'll beat this, Jen, I always do, but if anything happens to me, at least you'll have Sam. He's always adored you and he'll never let anything bad happen to you and the babies."

Was that what Josh had said? She strained to remember. Or had he said *his* babies?

CHAPTER THREE

SAM SLOUCHED BACK on the couch and kicked his feet onto the now-empty coffee table. Someone had cleared it of the nursing clutter—the pink plastic spit bowl, the stack of towels, the box of tiny glass vials of morphine and the syringe that had pushed the stuff directly into the "butterfly," as the nurses called the portal on Josh's belly.

Gone, too, were the packages of swabs, the bottle of alcohol and the baby monitor device, which had allowed Sam to hear Josh from the travel trailer. The bed was still in front of the window but it had been stripped. Someone from the rental place would be by tomorrow to pick it up. Just as someone from the mortuary had been by this afternoon to pick up Josh's body.

Sam glanced at his watch. Had it only been sixteen hours since Josh stopped breathing?

Ridiculous details had filled the void he'd left behind. Questions to answer. Plans to finalize. Friends and family members to call. Thankfully, Ida Jane and Andi had taken charge of those tasks.

To Sam's surprise, Jenny hadn't fallen apart. Maybe she couldn't believe it was finally over. Josh had labored so hard all night to breathe, but he'd made it past the deadline she'd given him. "You can't die on the day your babies were born," she'd screamed on the phone, and somehow Josh had found the strength to comply with her request. Each breath had been such a struggle that from midnight on, Sam had started telling Josh it was okay to let go.

"You've done all you can, buddy. This one got the best of you, but you gave it a good fight," Sam had whispered. "Let go, Josh. Go find your peace."

At some point—Sam didn't know when—Jenny had added her consent. "I love you more than life, Josh O'Neal, but your body just can't fight this anymore. Take my love with you, sweetheart. It'll help you find your way to heaven."

Tears had streaked her face, but she'd remained strong right up to the end. Sam's respect for his sister-in-law had increased a hundredfold. She'd come from an entire night in labor and delivery directly to a deathwatch.

Sam leaned forward and looked down the hallway at the closed door of the master bedroom. Andi and Kristin had finally managed to get Jenny to bed after they returned from a quick trip to the hospital where she'd nursed the babies. The twins were strong and healthy, but they would have to stay in the hospital until they reached five pounds.

That was just as well, Sam thought. The next few days were going to be hell for everyone. A funeral was no way to welcome home two new babies.

Rocking back, he picked up the remote control and turned on the television set. He pushed the play button on the VCR, then quickly lowered the volume.

The scene on the screen was the white-white background of a hospital delivery room. The camera moved in the jerky rhythm of someone walking. The lens panned down, and Jenny's face came into focus.

"So tell us, Jenny Perfect, when was it you decided

this wasn't a mutant watermelon-seed debacle after all?'' Andi's voice asked.

Intently focused on blowing out a long breath of air, Jenny growled something indistinguishable and turned her chin toward the wall. The camera lifted, zooming in on Kristin, who stood beside the gurney. Her serious expression looked uncompromising and protective.

"Sam's right about filming this. It's what Josh would have done if he were here, but if you get in Jenny's face with any sort of nonsense, I'll boot your ass right out of the delivery room."

"You and how many nurses?" Andi returned.

"Girls," Jenny groaned. "This is a happy time, remember?" The last came out as a hiss, as if she was expelling pure pain. Sam's gut clenched.

The pandemonium that followed was somehow brilliantly orchestrated—nature blending with modern medicine in a way that left Sam gape-mouthed in awe. Jenny was the star of the show, focused and intent, concentrating on each breath. He saw her forehead tense and her jaw stiffen with each command to push.

For someone who'd helped deliver hundreds of calves and foals, Sam could honestly say he'd never seen a more magical birth. When a shout of glee went up as Lara slipped into the doctor's hands, Jenny leaned back for three short breaths then lifted her head and said, "Don't forget. There's another one in there."

Sam sat forward, his fingers linked. He brought his knuckles to his lips. Andi had told him Tucker's birth was the more difficult of the two. "Jenny was tired from the first. It was like finishing a marathon then being told you had to run another ten miles," she'd said on the phone.

His gaze followed the camera, which panned back and

forth between Jenny and the baby, who was being attended by two nurses in masks. Lara Suzanne and Tucker William. Jenny and Josh had decided on the names after a sonogram revealed the sex of the twins.

Very red and most unhappy, Lara kicked her skinny legs like a bug on its back. The chatter in the room seemed elated and full of hope.

Sam couldn't help but marvel at that since he knew everyone involved had to have been aware of what was happening back here. Two lives entered the world as another prepared to leave it.

The camera returned to Jenny, who was obviously exhausted. She seemed to be breathing almost as hard as Josh had at the end. But she somehow remained upbeat, even joking with Andi about running out of tape if the second delivery took too long.

Sam was so completely engrossed in the drama before him he didn't sense another presence until a movement in the doorway caught his eye. Jenny. Like a little boy caught watching a dirty movie, he fumbled for the remote and hit the pause button.

"No. Leave it on," she said, walking toward him. "I'd forgotten she'd filmed it."

She was wearing a shapeless, faded pink robe that Josh had given her one Christmas. Sam knew that because she'd made a point of reminding Josh of its origins right before his downward spiral. "I was looking for something sexy and you bought me this grandma robe," she'd complained, her voice thick with love and humor.

"Warm," Josh had whispered. Speech seemed to drain his energy. "Pra…"

"Practical," Sam had supplied, immediately wishing he'd kept his mouth shut. When Jenny had looked his way, Sam had gathered up an armload of bedding and headed for the laundry room to give the couple some privacy.

Jenny moved stiffly and sat down gingerly. The robe gaped, exposing a nightshirt of fine white muslin with a lace insert that buttoned to the waist. Feminine, pretty— a gift from Ida's friends. Part of the bonanza she'd acquired at a recent baby shower—her only afternoon away from her husband's side until she'd gone into labor.

Sam fluffed up an olive-green couch pillow and put it behind her back. "Did you sleep?" he asked, noting something different in her smell. *Green apples?* Then he remembered the basket of toiletries and candles Beulah Jensen and her daughter had delivered that afternoon.

Aromatherapy, he'd thought with despair. Like anything's going to help.

But to Sam's surprise, the displaced reminder of spring eased his tension. He took a deep breath. Josh had loved spring.

"Kris gave me a pill," she said. "Something herbal. She said it wouldn't interfere with my nursing. She seems to know a lot about babies. I guess from living with our cousin, Moira, when she was pregnant."

"Whatever works. You're going to need your strength to get through the next few days."

She didn't acknowledge his words. Sam could have kicked himself. *Who am I to lecture her on strength? I've never seen this kind of courage in my life.*

"Is this the second one?" she asked, her tone the most expressionless he'd ever heard.

He nodded. "Andi told me it was more difficult."

One corner of her mouth twitched. "You could say that. Tucker was sideways. The doctor wanted to do an emergency C-section, but—'' She waved to the television. "Turn it on. You'll see."

Sam watched, both mesmerized and appalled. Kristin took her place at Jenny's side and intently massaged her sister's still-rounded stomach. Jenny's face contorted in pain as waves of contractions passed over her, but the doctor, who was working with his hand inside her kept telling her to pant. Finally, after what seemed like hours—but in truth was only ten minutes—she was given the command to push. Tucker put in an appearance just five hard pushes later. He immediately urinated all over the doctor.

Jenny snickered softly. "His father's son, right from the start."

The innocent words fell between them like a live snake.

Sam jumped to his feet and walked to the VCR and hit rewind. If Josh were alive, there'd be no question of the twins' parentage. But Josh wasn't here. The twins no longer had a father. Or did they?

"What's going to happen, Sam?" Jenny asked softly.

Squatting on his haunches, he faced her. "There's going to be a funeral, Jen. Saturday morning in the park—outdoors, just the way Josh wanted it. Let's concentrate on one thing at a time—just like you did when you were in that delivery room."

She closed her eyes. "I wanted it to be a joyous moment. Josh would have had balloons or kazoos or something crazy up his sleeve. I couldn't do that, but I could make the experience positive. Happy. Did you feel that? When you were watching it?"

The earnest tone in her question touched him. "Absolutely. I don't know how you managed to laugh through some of that, but you did. And your sisters were great.''

She nodded. ''I know. You were great, too.''

''Me? I wasn't there.''

She swallowed. ''You were where I needed you to be. You kept Josh focused. I know you did. You probably gave him a play-by-play as if you were watching. Right?''

Sam turned slightly to remove the tape. He spotted a pen on the coffee table and used it to print Tucker and Lara's Birth and the date on the label. ''I blathered on.'' He gave a dry chuckle. ''It probably sounded more like a mare giving birth, but I don't know how much he heard.'' He added softly, ''The drugs really kicked in at the end.''

''Thank God,'' she whispered.

Sam silently seconded that. Josh had been in excruciating pain for the past week. The doctor said the tumor had wrapped itself around his spinal column; every nerve ending was probably on fire.

''What else has to be done before the funeral?'' she asked. ''I haven't been much help today.''

Sam rose and walked the short distance to the kitchen to make her some tea. He put the kettle on to boil. Ida Jane had left a box of tea bags for lactating mothers. He took a bottle of beer from the refrigerator and twisted off the cap. After a long guzzle, he sighed.

''I've taken care of most of the arrangements,'' he said, knowing she could hear him. For some reason, he didn't want to face her. They'd shared an intimacy—the death of a loved one—and Sam was feeling strangely vulnerable.

''Tell me,'' she said.

"Just a second," he said, stalling. He took another pull on the beer.

When the teapot whistled, he poured the water into a cup and added a tea bag and a dollop of honey then carried it to her. "The wake is Friday at the Slowpoke Saloon. My foreman, Hank Willits, is handling it. Lars is coming down from the mine to help.

"The funeral will be in the park Saturday morning at ten. Ida Jane has asked her minister to say a few words, and Donnie will read the stuff Josh wrote out."

In early May—a time when the results of Josh's chemo and radiation still looked promising, Josh had checked out a bunch of books from the library dealing with the rituals of death. Although neither Sam nor Jenny had wanted to talk about it—the idea smacked of giving up the fight—Josh had composed a list of things he wanted at his funeral.

"I want it festive, Sam," he'd said one day on the trip to the treatment center. "No black armbands or dirges. This is a part of life whether we like it or not."

Jenny held the mug between her hands and blew on the steam. "What did you decide about the doves?" she asked.

Sam couldn't help but smile. Both he and Jenny had argued about the impracticality of releasing doves in the Merced River canyon where Josh had requested his ashes be strewn.

"I'm working on that." He started to sit down but walked to the hall table and picked up a sheaf of papers, instead.

Sam was still embarrassed about the scene he'd caused that morning. He'd ranted like a madman when the poor undertaker told him it might take a week to get Josh's ashes back. "A week?" he'd shouted. "Are you telling me we have to go through this a second time? That my poor grieving sister-in-law is going to have to do this after her two little babies come home from the hospital?''

In the end, the man had agreed to rush delivery. But Sam felt like a jerk.

"I filled out most of the info on the obituary, but I'd like you to look it over if you're up to it.''

She took a sip of tea. ''Tomorrow?''

"Whenever.'' He dropped the papers back in place then walked to the door and looked out the narrow side window. Dusk had fallen and long shadows filled the yard.

"You're not leaving, are you?'' she asked suddenly. ''I mean, you probably want to get back to the ranch. To your life. To—''

Sam pivoted. He was barefoot, and his heel made a squeaking sound on the parquet flooring. The muscles in his lower back felt as if he'd just ridden cross-country on a mule. He set his beer bottle on the counter and walked to the couch. Instead of sitting beside her, he chose the coffee table in front of her.

"Jenny, I promised Josh I'd be here for you, and I meant it. I won't leave until you kick me out. Understood?''

She kept her gaze on the liquid in her cup. For all her strength, she seemed very fragile at the moment. Vulnerable. Helping females in need was Josh's forte, not Sam's. Josh was the sensitive one, the proverbial shoulder-to-cry-on. Sam never knew what to do. Touching her shoulder seemed wrong. Holding her hand wouldn't work when she was using both hands to hold her cup.

He reached for the phone. ''Andi told me to call if you need her tonight. I overheard her tell Ida Jane that a number of ladies had volunteered to stay with you once the babies come home from the hospital—like they did with Ida Jane after you and your sisters were born. Should I call her?''

Jenny shook her head. "No. I'm too tired to talk to anybody, but I would like to thank Kristin. Is she here?''

Sam took that as a hint and stood. "Sorry. She already left, but she said she'd be back in time to help with the funeral.''

Jenny took another sip then said, "Poor Kris. Gold Creek is the last place she wants to be, but I couldn't have made it through that delivery without her. She has a healing touch. Too bad I can't talk her into moving home.''

"What's keeping her away?''

Jenny shrugged. "Bad memories. Disappointments. I don't know exactly. I get the impression something is holding her in Oregon—a guy, probably.''

Sam liked Kris, but her living arrangements weren't his problem. He had enough problems of his own—like what to do with his mother when she finally showed up.

"Tomorrow morning, I have to run out to the ranch to take care of a little business, but I'll be back by noon,'' he told Jenny. "Maybe Andi could drive you to the hospital to feed the babies.''

"Have you seen them yet?'' she asked.

Sam felt his cheeks color. He couldn't explain the crazy emotions that had hit him the instant he'd set eyes on the two tiny bundles in the covered isolettes. He'd been forced to duck into the men's room to give himself time to recover.

"Yup, I sure did,'' he said, his tone sounding artificially chipper. "I ran over while you were sleeping. They're beautiful, Jenny. Absolutely perfect.''

She looked past him. Sam knew she was seeing the hospital bed, not the view beyond. "The whole time I was giving birth, I kept thinking that this is what life is all about," she said, her voice barely louder than the tick of the mantel clock. "Birth and death.

"Yes, it seems more dramatic when the two happen right on top of each other, but reality doesn't use a calendar. No matter our personal drama, life goes on."

She lifted her chin, her eyes not really seeing him, as if she was talking more to herself. "When we stopped at the store, I saw a flyer about the music festival in Strawberry. We went every year. Josh loved bluegrass. And all the people." She sighed. "It's this weekend, Sam. Labor Day weekend. Don't you feel like you've been living in a vacuum?"

Sam knew exactly what she meant. When he'd called the Rocking M to discuss the wake, Hank mentioned they'd lost two calves to a mountain lion the night before. Normally, a loss of that nature would have disturbed Sam, who took his role as caretaker of his animals very seriously, but Sam had merely grunted, "You'll have to handle it," and hung up. He didn't have it in him to care.

The Rocking M was his life, his escape from the unreality of Hollywood and all the bad memories it held. The only thing he'd brought with him from L.A. was Josh—a rebellious teenager with long hair and plenty of attitude.

The ranch and Josh were the two positives in Sam's life. Now he was down to one.

"Everyone says we need time. That eventually things will get back to normal," he said, parroting words he'd heard repeated all day.

"I seriously doubt that," Jenny said, her tone bleak.

"You're forgetting one thing. Two, actually. Tucker and Lara."

Sam swallowed. He wasn't a coward, but he knew he wasn't up to talking about that subject tonight.

"Can we hold off on that awhile, Jen? We just have to trust each other to do the right thing."

"Do you have any idea what that is?"

He sat back and stretched the aching muscles in his shoulders and back. "Nope. But we'll figure it out." He rose and put out his hand to help her stand. "You should get back to bed. It's still early but I plan to take the phone off the hook and crash."

She stood a moment then crossed her arms. "I wonder if my milk is coming in. Maybe I should try pumping my breasts. Do you know where Andi put that box of nursing pads?"

Sam didn't have a clue, but he jogged to the bathroom, ostensibly to look around. Mostly, he needed to get away. For some reason, such frank talk struck Sam as too intimate for what they were to each other. Brother-in-law. Sister-in-law. *Parents*.

"I found them, Sam," she called out.

Sam looked at his reflection in the mirror. He might be a father, but he wasn't a husband. Jenny's husband was dead, and nobody was ever going to take Josh's place—not in her heart, anyway.

MOST OF THE MOURNERS began to disappear within minutes after the close of the service, Jenny noted with relief. She didn't blame them—the heat in the river canyon was hellish.

She felt a little light-headed and giddy, but she wasn't sure that could be blamed on the heat. More than likely it was her mind coming to grips with the surreal nature of watching her husband's ashes drift in the air.

As an old friend from high school played taps on the trumpet, Jenny—with Sam at her side—had stood at the midway point of the Briceburg Bridge and somehow managed to empty the polished metal box of its gray ash. For the space of a heartbeat the ash had floated—a visible reminder of all that would never be—then melted into the water and disappeared.

Despite the glare of the sun, Jenny continued to stare at the river from her vantage point near the edge of the parking lot. At Sam's gentle prodding, she'd handed him the empty box before returning to the gathering place for handshakes and hugs that she was too numb to feel.

Why the river, Josh? she longed to ask. *Why couldn't you at least have left me a burial plot that I could visit with the children on your birthday or holidays?*

But there was no answer. Only Josh's four-page script. A final itinerary that had included a memorial service in Gold Creek's park then a motorcade following Donnie Grimaldo's patrol car to the Bureau of Land Management recreation area on the Merced River.

Behind her, Jenny sensed the exodus of cars. People were heading back to Ida Jane's for food and refreshments. *Maybe no one will notice if I don't show up.*

Fat chance, she heard a voice in her head answer. Josh's voice—Josh, who would have loved this send-off. Hundreds of friends, business associates and townspeople had put their Labor Day plans on hold to say goodbye.

She recalled their argument over the band. "People love music," Josh had insisted. "If you put up a tent in the parking lot, you could get the Lone Strangers to play," he'd suggested, naming a popular local band.

When Jenny had protested that the idea was "too up-beat," Josh had appealed to Sam. And so far, Sam had carried out Josh's wishes to the letter, even managing to find twenty-seven white doves to be released as Jenny started sprinkling the ashes.

"Jen?"

Jenny heard her sister but didn't answer. She had a feeling if she opened her mouth a terrible cry would spew out. As long as she nodded and smiled, like one of those toy dogs in the back window of a car, she'd be fine.

"I've got to get Ida Jane out of this heat, sis," Kristin said. "Andi went back with the Garden Club ladies to set out the food. You'll come with Sam, okay?"

Jenny nodded. *Maybe.*

She glanced over her shoulder to watch her sister walk away. Jenny would have been lost without her sisters, Ida Jane and the citizens of Gold Creek, but that didn't keep her from wishing they'd all just disappear.

"Jenny," a low voice said beside her, "you need to get out of the sun before you melt."

Sam.

He gently took her elbow and started leading her toward his pickup truck. In his other hand, he carried the empty mortuary box.

"No," she said, yanking free. "Just...no."

The word came out like the long, eerie screech of an owl hunting in the night. He stepped back, dropping the box in surprise.

"Okay," he said levelly. "I'll wait for you in the truck. Come whenever you're ready."

"Ready?" she cried, tearing off the woven straw hat Kristin had insisted she wear. A gust of hot dry wind snatched it from her numb fingers and sent it end-over-brim into the prickly branches of a nearby buckbrush. The same breeze pressed the gauzy material of her pale yellow sundress against her sweaty body. Instead of offering any kind of relief, the blast felt like the breath of a dragon trying to sear her skin.

"Ready for what?" she repeated hoarsely. "What's the plan, Sam? Did Josh mention what I'm supposed to do? Say, for the next twenty years or so? He didn't dictate that to you, did he?"

Sam ducked his head as if wounded by her anger.

"This isn't the way we had it planned, Sam," she said, her voice squeaky from the tightness of unshed tears. "We were going to die in our eighties, with our children and grandchildren nearby. We wanted to be buried side by side in the old cemetery, near the war veterans." She hauled in a ragged breath of scorching air.

"Why'd he change the plan, Sam? Why?"

Despite the kilnlike temperature, Sam wore black. Black jeans, black boots, black shirt. And a green cowboy hat—Josh's hat.

See me sweet hat, Jenny luv? Josh had teased in his deplorable Irish brogue last St. Patrick's Day. *'Tis the luck of the Irish that belongs to the man wearin' this hat.* That had been in March—right before all hell had broken loose.

"The only plan I care about at the moment is getting you out of the sun and back to Ida's. Your family's there. Your friends. By the looks of all the food I spotted before we left, the whole town's there for you."

The town. Her town. Josh's adopted hometown. *Leave Gold Creek, Jenny? Are you crazy?* he'd once admonished her when she suggested moving. *This is a dream come true. The place where everybody knows your name. I finally feel at peace here. Why would I want to leave?*

For *me?* she'd been tempted to cry, but, of course, she hadn't. While no one would have believed it of affable, easygoing Josh, the fact was, he turned pure mule once his mind was made up.

"Can we go now?" Sam asked.

She looked down. Her feet and ankles were swollen—probably a by-product of labor. Her breasts were three times their normal size, her stomach flabby and the incision the doctor had made to keep her from tearing itched.

And she was burning up. The sun was melting her hair into her scalp. If she could just cool off, even for a minute, maybe she'd be able to think straight.

She spun on one heel and took off. Zingers of pain shot up her legs as she scrabbled clumsily across the stony embankment to the water's edge.

The Merced's high-water days of spring and summer were long gone, leaving behind a wide ledge of polished gravel and throw-pillow-size boulders, but the river's main channel still churned with the last remnants of melted snow from the Sierras.

Jenny's slick-bottomed sandals made the trek treacherous, and she was forced to keep her gaze on her feet instead of picking out a safe wading spot. Even this time of year, the river held danger—less of drowning than of being pummeled against exposed rocks.

She had her left foot in the water, sandal and all, when a firm hand grabbed her shoulder. "No," Sam growled. "No. I won't let you go, dammit."

The anguish in her brother-in-law's voice pierced Jenny's red haze. She understood instantly what he thought she'd intended to do, but before she could explain otherwise, her foot slipped on a moss-covered rock and she fell to one knee. Her ankle twisted awkwardly, and she lurched forward, scraping her palms on the abrasive rocks. Frigid water soaked the hem of her dress.

"Jenny," Sam cried.

One minute she was on her knees in the river, the next she wasn't. Jenny had never known the sensation of being lifted off her feet. Her vision swam, and she thought she might pass out, whether from the heat, the pain in her extremities or Sam's death grip, she wasn't sure.

"Sam, I didn't...I'm not...put me down."

He ignored her. Or maybe he couldn't hear her, since her voice seemed to come from the end of a long, hollow tube. Jenny closed her eyes and took a deep breath. Perspiration and fabric softener filled her senses. Not my brand of fabric softener, she thought for no reason at all. Where has he been doing his laundry?

Sam's broad chest was heaving from exertion by the time they reached the sparse shade of the dusty oak trees that ringed the parking lot. He set her down on a large boulder. Her soggy sandals made a squishing sound when they hit the ground. She looked down, but Sam grabbed her chin and made her look at him. "What the hell are you thinking? You can't...you just couldn't. You're a mother, Jenny. Doesn't that mean anything to you?"

Although his tone was harsh, bitter even, his hazel eyes expressed pure anguish. Jenny covered her face, ignoring the grit that was still attached to her bloody palms. "I didn't mean to scare you, Sam. I wasn't jumping in. I was just so hot..." Her excuse sounded lame. Maybe it wasn't even true. Didn't a part of her wish she'd died, too?

"What's going on in your head, Jenny? This isn't like

you. Maybe you need to join that grief group Linda Mc-Closkey mentioned. She said it had helped her.''

Am I grieving? Yes, she thought, but not for the reasons everyone thinks. Mine are selfish reasons. I'm a coward. I'm afraid to be alone. I don't know how to be a mother. I can't do this without Josh, she silently cried.

That isn't the kind of truth you confessed to a group of people—especially in a small town.

"I'm okay," she said, starting to scoot forward to hop off the rock. "I'll be fine."

Sam removed his hat and tossed it onto a nearby table. He let out a deep sigh and said, "I suppose we might as well get this out in the open and deal with it, but first we've got to cool down."

Jenny knew what he was going to say and she didn't want to discuss it. Not now. Not yet. Her heart started hammering the instant he grabbed her hand and pulled her to her feet.

"Come on."

To her surprise, he led her in the opposite direction of the truck. His grip tightened as they rounded a dense cluster of scrub oaks. The water had undercut the embankment, creating a tiny cove shaded by the pines and oaks on the steep mountainside.

He let go of her hand to bend over and take off his boots. His thin white cotton socks were next, and then he rolled up his jeans. "Coming?" he asked before gingerly wading into the calm water.

Jenny kicked off her sandals. The pebbles in this area had been worn smooth but she moved with care, since her ankle still throbbed. The chilly water brought instant relief. Just an arm's length away from Sam, she bent over and splashed scoop after scoop of water across her face and over her neck. The chilly water dribbled down her dress's neckline, soaking into the heavy-duty nursing bra she was wearing. For a girl who almost never wore a bra, this lactating physique took some getting used to.

Josh would have loved this, she thought, glancing down at her bustline.

Sighing, she cupped some water in her hands and studied it. Sunlight made the suspended particles of grit glitter like flecks of gold.

"Are you thinking you'll see Josh there?" Sam asked.

The question unnerved her. Given their relationship, she wasn't sure she liked the idea of Sam being able to read her thoughts. "Maybe," Jenny answered.

Sam didn't say anything, which, for some reason, irked her. "What do you think happens when you die, Sam? Heaven or hell?"

He looked at her a moment, as if hearing something she hadn't intended to share. "I don't know, Jenny. But I do know Josh didn't do this on purpose."

"I didn't say he did," she said, facing him.

"No, but you're angry. I can tell. And I'm assuming you're mad at him for going off and leaving you with two babies and...me. I'm a complication that doesn't help."

His empathy unnerved her, and it suddenly struck her that she wasn't the only one Josh had deserted. Sam was here, too. In limbo. As were Lara and Tucker.

"What are we going to do, Sam?"

"Do we have to decide today? Can't we just carry on like we have been?" He looked toward the bridge. Beads of water glistened in his dark-brown hair. Jenny could see the imprint left by Josh's hat. His squint made the lines around his eyes seem more pronounced. *This has aged him,* she thought.

He turned and caught her staring. "Can we at least wait until after Diane leaves?"

Jenny had received a call this morning. Diane and Gordon, Sam's mother and stepfather, had been held up by engine trouble with their RV but would arrive later today. Sam had disappeared into his trailer shortly after hearing the news, not reemerging until it was time to leave for the park.

To Jenny, Diane's visit was just one more weight pressing down on her. She'd always gotten along with her mother-in-law as long as Josh was present, but who knew what would happen without him?

"Are you going to stick around while she's here or hightail it back to the ranch?" She hadn't meant to sound quite so much like a nagging wife.

"I'm not going anywhere."

Despite the flat, resigned tone in his voice, Sam's answer made her feel better.

He turned and walked back to shore. He sat down on a low rock, legs sprawled, while he used his socks to dry his feet. There was something very youthful in his pose. Sam never looked like a little boy, Jenny thought. That was Josh's department. For some reason, the thought irked her. Josh was gone—it was just her and Sam, now. Parents.

A shiver passed through her. "What are you going to tell your mother if she asks? Do you think she knew about Josh's condition?"

He looked up sharply. "Why would she? Josh and Diane weren't that close. Besides, she's not into babies. She'll show up, cry a little then leave. That's how she operates."

His bitterness made her shiver. It reminded her once again how different Sam was from Josh. Josh had often joked about his mother's unorthodox methods of parenting. "Mom believed in the free-range school of child rearing," he'd once told a group of friends. "If you survived childhood, you had it made."

"You can tell your sisters and Ida Jane, if you want. They might wonder why I'm hanging around so much, but it's up to you," Sam said. "Are you ready? We should be going."

Hanging around. What exactly did that mean? she wondered. She started to ask, but stopped. Did it matter? Did anything matter?

She limped to the water's edge.

"We'll stop at the hospital," Sam said. "You can get your ankle checked and feed the babies."

"I can try," Jenny said, picturing the trouble she'd had that morning. "Lara isn't taking to the breast well. I thought I was doing something wrong, but Tucker's not having any problems. He's positively voracious."

Sam's smile was sad and slightly wistful. Before she could ask why, he broke away to fetch first his hat then hers. Finally, he stooped to pick up the metal box that had held Josh's ashes.

Neither spoke as he helped her climb into the truck. He flicked the air-conditioning to high, and Jenny sank back into the upholstery and closed her eyes, trying hard to forget about the urn lying on the bed of the truck. But the image haunted her. It was, she decided, a perfect metaphor for her life—a pretty façade but empty inside.

"SAM, RUN ALONG to the party. You're the host, after all. I'll bring Jenny after she feeds the twins."

Like so much of what his mother had said to him over the years, Diane's words held a barely veiled put-down. *You're the host, after all.* As if he'd made some gaffe by not greeting the mourners at his brother's funeral personally.

He and Jenny had been sitting in the lobby of the hospital, waiting to see an emergency-room doctor when Diane found them. In her wake trailed Gordon, a likable fellow who'd retired from active practice last year. Gordon had examined Jenny's ankle and pronounced it, "Tweaked, not sprained."

"I'll wait," Sam said, relishing the small delight he drew from doing the exact opposite of whatever his mother wanted. He knew it was childish, but Diane had that effect on him.

Diane gave him a look he'd seen a hundred times—one of pure exasperation. "I would think this is the least you could do for your brother, since you weren't able to do anything about the cancer."

Jenny leaped to her feet—sore ankle and all. "Diane," she said sharply. "Sam did everything in his power to save Josh. We all did. If you want to blame someone for Josh's death, blame Josh. He's the one who kept insisting he had a cold or allergies or the flu. He put off going to the doctor until it was too late."

His mother's carefully made-up face crumbled and she walked away. Gordon rushed to her side, providing the necessary comfort. Jenny looked stricken.

Sam wasn't sure what exactly just happened, but he blamed his mother. "Why don't you head upstairs to the nursery?" he said to Jenny.

"I'm sorry," she whispered.

"What you said was true. Now, go. The babies need you."

Sam walked her to the elevator, then returned to where his mother was standing, repairing her makeup with the help of a small compact and a tissue. Sam didn't know if women used compacts like that any longer, but it was a sight and smell he'd forever associate with his mother.

"Diane, let's get something straight. Jenny is very fragile at the moment. I know Josh was the light in your life and you're hurting, too, but you will watch what you say around Jenny or you won't be staying."

Diane lifted her chin regally. "Who died and made you king?"

"Josh."

Her bottom lip trembled. "That's a rotten thing to say—even for you."

"I know, but it's true. Josh didn't plan to die. The cancer had metastasized by the time we started treatment. He was battling it on too many fronts—kidney, liver, stomach, lungs. There were things he wanted to do to help prepare his family and make sure they were taken care of, but he was just too sick, too fast. He asked me to look after Jenny and the kids, and that's what I plan to do."

"You're the executor of the will?" Gordon asked.

Sam nodded.

"Are you the twins' godfather, too?"

Godfather?

"Jenny can decide that. I don't need a title to know where my duty lies."

Gordon gave Sam an encouraging nod. Diane, however, looked unconvinced. "How much help can you be when you live on the ranch and Jenny and the babies live in town? You'd be better off putting your money where your mouth is and hiring a nanny."

"I'll hire a nanny if that's what Jenny wants. First, we have to get the twins home, then we can worry about fine-tuning."

She made an indignant sound and stuffed her compact

into her shoulder bag. "At least you didn't suggest taking Jenny and the babies to the ranch. You may be content to play hermit, but no woman would want that lifestyle. Obviously."

Usually Diane's jabs bounced off Sam like hot grease on Teflon. For some reason, this one penetrated. *Jenny and the babies at the ranch?* It might be the perfect solution, if he could get her to agree.

Not for long, of course, he told himself. Just long enough to bond with his children.

"Are you coming or not?" his mother asked contentiously. "I want to see my grandbabies."

Sam shook his head. Not yet. He wasn't ready for his mother to see the depth of his feelings. Or Jenny, either. He didn't want to frighten her. He would never do anything to jeopardize Jenny's bond with her children—he just wanted to be a part of it, too.

JENNY WAITED until the last of the kind souls who'd stayed to help clean up the old bordello left. She was exhausted. Numb in a way that kept tears at bay. A part of her brain knew this was unhealthy, but she had one more thing to do.

Josh had lied to her. He'd promised a life with love, children and happiness. She was done with lies.

"Sit down, you two," she said to her sisters. "I need to tell you something."

Andi and Kristin trudged toward the table. "Can't it wait?" Andi asked. "I'm dead."

A second later she realized what she'd said and bent over, groaning. "Oh, crap, Jen, I'm sorry."

To Jenny's surprise, Kristin walked over and gently rubbed Andi's back. "We know what you meant."

Jenny motioned them to join her at the table. "I'm

going to drop in a minute. But this is important, and there won't be time in the morning before Kris leaves.''

Andi and Ida had both implored Kris to stay for the weekend, but she'd insisted she had "commitments.'' Jenny didn't blame her; there wasn't much she could accomplish here while the twins were still in the hospital.

Andi hopped up to the counter across from them. Kristin sat opposite Jenny. "So?''

"I do appreciate everything both of you have done. You know that, right?''

Kris pushed a covered bowl of potato chips aside to squeeze Jenny's hand. "We know.''

Jenny tried to take a breath but her chest felt constricted. *How do I say this? How do I tell them about Sam?* "I have something I need to tell you. It's probably going to sound like something out of daytime TV, but when we discovered that Josh couldn't…''

A deep cough made all three jump. "Sorry,'' Sam said from the doorway of the screened porch. "Didn't mean to startle you, but I just got back from the ranch. You weren't at your house, Jen. I was worried.''

Jenny had planned to do this alone. It seemed befitting, but now that the moment had arrived, she was profoundly glad to see Sam. She motioned him forward. "Come in. I was just going to tell them about the babies.''

He crossed the room, stopping a few feet away. Outwardly, he displayed none of the fatigue that showed on her and her sisters' faces, but Jenny knew that was a ruse.

"Like I told you,'' he said. "It's your call.''

Andi, who'd never been easy to live with when she was tired, said crossly, "Tell us what?''

Jenny opened her mouth, but nothing came out.

"Josh was sterile," Sam said. "An unfortunate side effect of prepubescent testicular cancer. He asked me to donate sperm so Jenny could conceive. I did."

Kristin gasped. It took Andi a second longer to get it. "And Jenny went along with this?" she croaked.

Jenny felt her face flood with color. "Josh wanted it so badly," she said lamely.

Kris jumped to her feet. "Thank God he did. Where would we be right now without those two perfect babies to look forward to?" Tears filled her eyes. "And this way, they'll have a father, too." She surged toward Sam and gave him a hug. "Oh, Sam, you'll be a wonderful daddy."

Jenny read the bewildered look on his face. It wasn't what he was expecting.

Andi leaned back, thrusting her tanned, toned legs into the room. "That's well and good, but what about the logistics that comes with that kind of arrangement? Do you share the kids? You each take one? What?"

Sam lurched back as if struck. Jenny saw the look of horror in his eyes.

"No," they cried in unison.

"Jenny is their mother. Babies need their mother," he said, as if that was the last word on the issue. He turned and walked to the door. "I'll be at the house if you need me, Jenny. I assume you're spending the night here."

Jenny nodded; she wasn't ready to face her empty bed.

A minute later the low roar of the diesel filled the air. She wondered how she'd missed his arrival.

No one said anything. "I know this looks bad, but at the time Josh was healthy. Who knew this would happen?"

Andi made a gruff sound. "I'm sorry, Jen. That was a stupid thing to say. I'm used to dealing with jerks who think with their dicks, pardon my French. Sam's a good man. You can trust him."

Jenny felt a tiny glimmer of hope. Maybe there was a chance she could pull this off. "I love you guys. Thanks."

They started to leave the room, but Andi stopped suddenly. "Are you going to tell Ida Jane?"

Jenny sighed. "Not now. Maybe someday, but Josh's death has been hard on her. I don't think she can handle much more."

Andi stepped back to squeeze Jenny's shoulder. "I think that goes for all of us."

CHAPTER FOUR

"DON'T USE POWDER. Powder is bad for babies' lungs."

"Oh, phooey. We always used powder on your behind. Your lungs are fine, aren't they?"

"Andrea's right, Ida. My granddaughter told me that, too. She was picky about everything—even the kind of water she mixed with little Tory's formula. Water was water in my day."

Jenny tuned out the voices coming from the nursery. Her house was small, and the busy hum of people—her sister, her aunt, Beulah Jensen and the other volunteers—added to her exhaustion. She couldn't seem to find the strength to get up and care for her month-old babies.

Tears filled her eyes; sorrow twisted in her gut like a living, breathing monster. How was she supposed to be a mother to two tiny babies when her soul had been ripped from her body—right through the hole in her heart?

She curled into a fetal position. Her breasts were swollen—primed for feeding time; her cotton nightshirt felt damp against her knees.

She continued to nurse her babies, but each feed was a struggle. Lara fought the breast as if she were suffocating every time Jenny tried to put the nipple in her mouth. Tucker, on the other hand, latched on and suckled like a vampire then cried for more. And there just wasn't any more to give, which added to Jenny's sense of failure.

Staring at the glimmer of light filtering through the cracks in the miniblinds, she tried to make her mind go blank.

The door to her room—the room she used to share with Josh—opened a sliver. "Oh good, you're awake," Ida Jane said, peeking inside. "Sam didn't want to disturb you, but Tucker just will *not* take the bottle. He wants his mama."

Jenny longed to treasure each minute with her beautiful babies, but grief was robbing her of the ability. She didn't know what she'd have done without Ida Jane, her sisters and Sam.

"Go ahead and bring him in," she said. "I'm awake."

Ida disappeared. Jenny carefully scooted backward. She plumped a pillow against the plated-brass headboard. The bed—a wedding gift from Ida—was an antique that had been in the bordello when Ida's father bought the place. It took a double mattress, small by today's standards. When Jenny once suggested trading it in for a queen-size bed, Josh had argued against the idea.

"This our marriage bed, Jen," he'd said. "I can't walk by it without picturing your hands gripping those dowels...the look of passion on your face."

At the time, his words had embarrassed her. Now she'd give anything to hear his voice.

Blinking back tears, she tenderly ran her fingers over the metal.

"He's a bit cranky," a deep whisper said.

Startled, Jenny turned toward the door. Sam walked

to her, a tiny bundle in his arms. He carried the baby as if born to the role.

"Lara's happy as a little pig with the bottle," he said. "Beulah's feeding her now, but Tucker here won't have a thing to do with it. He says it's Mommy or nothing."

Jenny moved over to make room for Sam to sit down beside her. It made the transfer of the baby easier, she'd found. Plus, she liked Sam's unflappable calm. She'd always known he was rock-solid and dependable, but she'd never seen his leadership abilities put to the test. This little exercise in small-town helpfulness would have tested the patience of a saint.

During the eleven days that the twins were in the hospital, Sam had regulated visitations and food donations, shielding Jenny from the well-meaning but at times overwhelming support she'd received from the citizens of Gold Creek. When the pediatrician finally gave them permission to bring Tucker and Lara home, Sam had politely but firmly set restrictions on the number of volunteers who could help.

Although Diane regularly hinted that Sam should move back to the ranch so she and Gordon could park their RV in his spot, Sam seemed to ignore her. Jenny was glad. She liked her mother-in-law, but the woman was almost cruel in her criticism of her son.

For the most part, Jenny tuned everything out. One small part of her felt guilty about leaving Sam alone to deal with his mother—he was grieving, too. But ultimately, she just couldn't muster the energy.

His weight made the mattress sag. "Let me get you a pillow for your arm," he said, passing Tucker to her. Wrapped in a lightweight blue cotton receiving blanket and a yellow skullcap, Tucker was all face—a red, angry face. Sam disappeared before she could tell him not to bother.

Jenny took a deep breath and looked down. "Hello, son," she said softly. Jenny was ashamed of the fact that she'd spent as little time as possible with her children since they came home from the hospital. But her friends and family—including Sam—assured her that she would be her old self after she had time to mourn.

"Time," she murmured, unbuttoning her top with her right hand. "When will I even care about time?"

She was just reaching for the flap of her nursing bra, when Sam returned.

"Oops, sorry. Here. I'll be quick." He lifted her left arm—the one cradling the baby—and slid the pillow underneath.

"Let me fill your water glass, then I'll get out of your way. Somebody's hungry."

Tucker, as if sensing that mother's milk was near, let out a series of short, sharp cries. "Hang on, Buddy, Mom's coming. Just let Uncle Sam get this for her."

He paused midstep. A ghost of a smile flickered across his lips. "You know, Josh started calling me that when you first found out you were pregnant," he mused. "But he stopped a good month before he saw the oncologist. I wonder if he knew something was wrong even then."

"He knew," Jenny said flatly. *But did he know* before *I got pregnant?* The question plagued her.

"Call me when he's done, and I'll come get him."

With that, Sam walked away.

Jenny opened her bra and helped guide her son's lips to her engorged breast. She studied the baby's smooth pink cheek in the light from the lamp beside the bed. He'd changed so much in a month. Red wrinkles were gone, replaced by full cheeks and new hair—dark brown. Lara's was reddish blond—more Sullivan than O'Neal—but everyone insisted Lara favored her father. "I think Lara has Josh's nose," someone said just yesterday.

Jenny heard that kind of thing almost daily from the concerned friends and volunteers who stopped by. Everyone was eager to point out a resemblance as if that link might keep Josh's memory alive. Unfortunately, all it did was make Jenny feel guilty. She could have handled the duplicity with aplomb if Josh were at her side. But what was she supposed to do now?

Why aren't you here, Josh?

As her milk started to flow so did her tears. Tucker hung on while her diaphragm heaved. She used the sheet to staunch the deluge.

"Jenny? Are you okay?" Sam asked from the doorway.

She let a low cry of anguish. The door flew open. "To hell with modesty," he muttered, clearing the distance in three strides. "What's wrong, Jen? What can I do?"

"Nothing. Go away," she sobbed. She didn't understand how she could have a single tear left inside her body.

"I can't do that," he said, sitting beside her. "I'll do anything you ask—except that. You need me here. The babies need me."

He ran a hand through his uncombed hair. For the umpteenth time, Jenny noticed the pallor around his lips, the deep lines bracketing his eyes.

"Please don't ask me to leave, Jen," he said finally. "If I were alone at the ranch, I'd go crazy with worry." He looked at her, and in his eyes Jenny read the same anguish she saw in the mirror every morning. "Diane spends half her time at the golf course with Gordon. Ida can't handle a set of twins by herself, even with the Garden Club ladies helping out. And thanks to that advertising campaign, Andi's swamped at the store.''

Jenny knew he was right, but she wanted the world to disappear and leave her to her memories, her very private pain. Tucker's lips stopped their fishlike motion. Without thinking, she switched him to the other breast.

Looking up, she caught the expression on Sam's face—wonder and awe were the only words to describe it. Is that how Josh would have reacted? she wondered. *No, he'd have curled up beside me and tickled me until I laughed.*

She tilted her head back and closed her eyes. ''When, Sam? When will it stop hurting? I can barely breathe without feeling as though someone has scooped out my insides.''

He touched her knee. Even through her baggy sweatpants Jenny felt the warmth of his hand, his support. Sam was kind. He was wonderful…he just wasn't Josh.

''It wasn't supposed to be this way, Sam. I can't do this without him. It's just not fair.''

''I agree,'' he said, surprising her. ''It's not fair to any of us—Josh included. But it's not like he could help it. The cancer spread too fast.''

She'd heard others say the same thing, but she didn't buy it. ''I think he knew it even before we did the in vitro,'' she said, her bitterness obvious. ''He sensed it and that's why he pushed for you to be the one. He manipulated us, Sam. And I hate him.''

Sam didn't say anything for a minute. His profile could have been carved from granite, but then he blinked rapidly, as if suppressing his emotions. Suddenly, his handsome face contorted in anguish, and Jenny was filled with remorse.

"I'm sorry. I shouldn't have said that."

"You don't mean it," he said, his voice gruff.

Maybe I do, maybe I don't, but Sam isn't the person to burden with my anger.

"How are things at the ranch? Don't they need you?"

He heaved a sigh. "Does it matter? This is where I am."

She felt Tucker's lips disengage from her breast. Sitting forward, she quickly closed the gap in her gown. The baby lay on her lap, eyes closed, satiated. A smile tried to find its way to her lips.

"That should help," she said, feeling a tiny glimmer of satisfaction. She pushed back a lank lock of hair. "Would you take him for me? I need a shower."

Sam leaned forward to pick up Tucker. The movement brought him within an inch of Jenny. The intimacy of the moment struck her hard. This should have been Josh, she thought, swamped by bitterness again.

"Well, there you go, little man," Sam said, rising. He placed Tucker against his shoulder and efficiently burped him. "Good job. Just like your daddy. I used to burp him, too, you know."

Sam nestled Tucker in the crook of his arm and walked to the window. He turned the little plastic wand and sunlight flooded the room. Jenny could tell by the angle of light coming through the long silvery needles of the bull pine that it was still early.

"Diane's in the kitchen, by the way," he said flatly. "She wanted to fix us all a big breakfast to thank Ida for letting them park the travel trailer in the lot behind the bordello."

"Your mother can cook?" Jenny had been surrepti-

tiously fastening her bra and just happened to catch
Sam's smile. The oddity of the question suddenly struck
her, too.

"I've never thought of Diane as the domestic type,"
she added. To her surprise, talking with Sam seemed to
help perk her up a little. "Josh used to tell the most
bizarre stories about her."

"Did he mention the time she left him in the car at
the 7-Eleven because the beer-delivery guy offered to
take her out to dinner?"

Jenny immediately regretted bringing up the topic.
Sam's expression went sour, and he paced to the far side
of the room and back. His broad shoulders seemed
bunched with tension, but he continued to cradle Tucker
with utmost care.

"Usually, when something like that happened, Josh
would dig around for change and call me if he got scared
or too bored. I used to lie awake at night worrying about
what might happen if I missed his call."

"You never did, did you?"

"Not that I know of. He used to say he lived a
charmed life." The irony in Sam's tone was tinged with
anguish.

Again, Jenny felt guilty for dumping so much on his
shoulders. She slowly rose and walked toward him.

"He lived a good life, Sam. Too damn short, but Josh
packed a heck of a lot of living into his twenty-seven
years."

Sam leaned one shoulder against the wall. He stared
out the window, but his gaze seemed fixed on something
well beyond her small backyard. "I think he knew his
time was limited, Jen. I don't mean specifically last fall.
I mean years ago. Josh once told me he felt as though

he'd cheated death, and every minute from that point was borrowed."

Jenny returned to the bed and sat down. She looked at her bare toes. "Did you know he used to paint my toenails? He'd buy the wildest shades of magenta or green or lavender nail polish then make me sit still so he could apply it."

She wiggled her toes. The nails were dull and needed clipping.

"You have nice feet," Sam said.

Jenny smiled, remembering the first time she and Josh met. "You must be that Jenny Perfect girl I've been hearing about," he'd said, catching her outside the Frosty Freeze, where she was sweeping up cigarette butts.

"What makes you think so?" she'd returned.

"Because you have perfect feet."

She'd been wearing sandals because a tub of ice cream had fallen off a shelf and broken her baby toe the day before.

That was the summer Josh and Sam moved to the Rocking M. Josh had been in town registering for school.

"I've decided not to go back to work after my maternity leave is up," she said suddenly.

Sam pushed off from the wall and walked to her. He stood a foot away. "Good. You have a full-time job with the twins. The school will hire you back when the kids are older," he said equitably.

His tone irked her. She didn't want equitable. She wanted to lash out at someone. She wanted things to be different. "That's easy for you to say. You have an income."

He tilted his head as if hearing something she hadn't meant to say. "Hold on," he said. "I'll be right back."

When he was gone, Jenny walked into the adjoining bathroom. She glanced in the mirror, but quickly averted her gaze. Her hair was a rat's nest; there were bags under her eyes and her skin looked like freckled construction paper. She splashed water on her face and brushed her teeth then returned to where Sam was waiting with a tall glass of orange juice.

"Gordon says nursing mothers often forget that their body is feeding two—in your case three," he said.

Jenny accepted the glass and took a long drink.

"I'm worried about you, Jen. You don't eat enough."

She shrugged. "I'm not hungry."

"I know, but you need to make yourself eat—or at the very least, you need someone around to nag you to eat."

Jenny smiled then. Josh would have sat on her until she ate every bite.

"That's one of the reasons why I want you and the babies to move home with me."

Sam's tone was so nonchalant it took Jenny a minute to comprehend the meaning of his statement. "To the ranch?"

Sam nodded. "Think about it. I have plenty of space plus a housekeeper who could help with the twins. If you rent this place, you'll have a steady income. And you might even find time to work on your books."

Jenny swallowed. "And what do you get out of this?"

When he looked at her, his eyes—for once—were surprisingly easy to read. "I get to be a father."

MOVE TO THE RANCH? Was he crazy?

Jenny pushed her sunglasses back up on her nose and

returned her gaze to the road. Sam had been called to an emergency at the ranch before she could ask her questions. She'd waited as long as she could for him to return. Finally, she'd loaded up the twins for a drive to the Rocking M. The babies hadn't made a peep since the car pulled out of the driveway, but it bothered her that she couldn't see them. As per the directions, their infant seats were in the back seat of her Honda Accord, facing away from her.

"They're fine," Diane said, reaching over to pat Jenny's arm.

Ida had volunteered to accompany Jenny to the ranch, but Diane wouldn't hear of it. "I'll go," she'd insisted. "It's been ages since I've been there. I wouldn't mind seeing what Sam's done with the place. I'm sure it could use a woman's touch, but what woman would be content to live in the middle of nowhere?"

Jenny could name one. She'd always loved the Rocking M. Whenever Sam was away on business, or on those rare occasions he joined a few old friends on a fishing trip, Jenny and Josh would volunteer to ranch-sit. They'd take long trail rides, relax in the Jacuzzi tub, grill thick steaks on the patio and dine under the redwood gazebo. It was an idyllic retreat they both enjoyed, but Jenny had never imagined living there. Her mind churned. *Was this a ploy to gain custody of the twins? Does he think I'm unfit to raise them alone? What if he's right?*

"I used to despair that Sam would never marry, now I'm more afraid he might," Diane said as they passed under the Rocking M arch. "I can just see some woman imagining a life of peace and quiet on a beautiful ranch then hitting the reality of being stuck in the boondocks with a man who spends every spare minute reading cattle magazines and studying the pedigrees of longhorns.''

Diane's negative attitude baffled Jenny. It always had. But Josh had been philosophical about his mother's relationship with his brother. "Sam and Mom don't get along, Jen. It's their problem, not ours. Maybe someday they'll mend their fences, but I have a feeling I'll be long dead before it happens.''

The memory made her shiver.

Diane glanced at her. "Are you cold? Must be from not eating. No one could be cold in this heat. How do you stand it? Maybe you should consider moving to Santa Barbara. Gordon and I could help you find a place close to us. It's so beautiful there.''

The offhand suggestion was so *Diane*. "Mom loves to make plans. You just can't count on them," Josh used to say. Like the oft-promised trip to Alaska, Jenny thought. Josh's dream trip. Finally, Sam had taken Josh camping in Denali National Park and fishing in the Gulf of Alaska for Josh's twenty-fifth birthday; Jenny had stayed home to let the two brothers spend time together.

"I'm sure Santa Barbara is lovely, but I couldn't move that far away from Ida Jane," Jenny said. *Or Sam.* Somehow she knew Sam wouldn't like the idea of Jenny and the babies moving out of the area.

"Maybe you and your sisters should look into getting Ida situated in one of those assisted-care facilities. She isn't getting any younger," Diane said, her tone slightly bored. "She's amazing for her age. But it's obvious this ordeal has taken a toll on her. And that nonsense about the ghost isn't helping, either, if you ask me.''

Jenny kept her mouth closed and tried to absorb the peaceful setting. She never made the thirty-mile drive to the ranch without being filled with a sense of wonder.

At this time of year, the hills were a burnished gold, the sprawling oak trees scattered incrementally like pieces on a chessboard. As the road climbed, she began to see more live oaks, bull pines and manzanita bushes.

"I should have known Sam would buy another ranch. He always loved Clancy's place," Diane said.

Diane's perfume—something terribly expensive, no doubt—was making Jenny slightly nauseous. She rolled down her window a bit farther. "Clancy was Sam's stepfather?"

When Sam and Josh first moved to Gold Creek, there'd been a lot of talk about the rich southern Californian who'd dropped a bundle to buy the Rocking M, but Josh had been quick to tell people that his brother's wealth was a one-shot thing courtesy of his stepfather's estate.

"Yep, one of the best mistakes of my life," Diane said, her tone surprisingly wistful. "I was a single mother with a six-year-old kid. I'd moved West with a guy who turned out to be a real jerk. I was tending bar in a little dive and along came Clancy Royson. My cowboy. Too old for me, but damn, he was a good man. He made living on a ranch sound like a dream come true, so I married him."

Jenny had to slow down to turn onto the winding gravel road that led to the ranch house. "Was this in Pasadena?"

Diane nodded. "He raised prime cattle, thoroughbred horses, oranges and avocados. I gained twelve pounds the first year I lived there." Her tone was surprisingly light. "Sam fell in love with the place. And with Clancy. They bonded." She looked out the side window. "I knew right away the country life wasn't my cup of tea, but I stuck it out three years for Sam's sake."

Three whole years, huh? Jenny thought dryly.

"Actually, Clancy and I never divorced, but I moved back to town and went to beauty school. I had a dream of working in the movie industry as a makeup artist."

"Sam stayed with Clancy?" Jenny asked. She knew the answer. Josh had often talked about Clancy wistfully—not because Clancy left Sam an inheritance, but because Sam had had a true father figure in his life while Josh hadn't.

"Yes. Right up to the day he died." Her lips, shiny from a fresh application of berry-pink lipstick, pursed petulantly. "I'll never forgive Sam for not calling me sooner. He said Clancy wanted to die in peace and asked Sam not to call me, but I don't believe him. I should have been here when Josh died, too, but Sam didn't call me until it was over. So I missed my own son's funeral."

Jenny bit down on her tongue to keep from saying, "Sam was carrying out Josh's wishes." With a sigh of relief, she turned into the circular driveway leading to the two-story cedar-log home. The barn and corrals were some distance away.

"Over there," Diane said, pointing toward a cluster of men standing beside an empty corral.

She parked in the shade of a sprawling oak tree and got out. Her mother-in-law did the same, and both women simultaneously opened the rear doors to retrieve a baby. Three dappled cow dogs raced toward the car, barking a greeting.

Jenny picked up the tiny bundle wrapped in a blue-and-white-checkered cotton blanket. Her insides contracted painfully with a jolt of love. Lifting Tucker, she inhaled that wonderfully heady scent of baby lotion and spit-up.

"Well, this is a surprise," a familiar voice hailed.

Sam didn't sound overly pleased to see them. Jenny hoped that was because of his mother's presence.

"What have we here?" Sam's foreman of many years asked. "A couple of new cowhands? We sure can use 'em."

Jenny noticed a cowboy tossing gear haphazardly into the back of a battered pickup truck. Several other men stood together talking.

"You took off so fast, I was afraid something bad had happened," Jenny said. Diane joined her, Lara in her arms.

Sam looked uncharacteristically edgy. Jenny wasn't sure why. Was he regretting his impulsive offer? Perhaps he sensed that she planned to turn him down. There was no way she could move in with him, even if their relationship was entirely platonic. Gloria Hughes would have a field day with the gossip. It wouldn't be fair to Tucker and Lara, and, it might have an adverse effect on her career. Jenny knew she would return to teaching eventually—she'd need to make a living to support herself and her children.

They're Sam's children, too, a little voice said.

Jenny was going to have to do something about that voice.

SAM HAD THOUGHT he was imagining things when the little brown Accord turned into his driveway. Normally, he would have been delighted to see Jenny up and about—everyone was concerned about her depression, but Sam had a feeling she was here to talk about his proposal. The one he hadn't intended to blurt out the way he had. He'd planned to wait until his mother was gone, before sitting down and discussing the matter rationally.

"We had a little ruckus," he said, kicking a rock with the toe of his boot.

"Yep, two bullheaded horny toads who tried to kill each other," Hank muttered.

"Just hormones and old grievances," Sam said, trying to downplay the disturbance. He didn't want Jenny to think his staying in town was affecting his business—even if that were true.

By the time he'd arrived, the two men had been separated and disarmed. He'd talked to each man individually and had learned that a woman was at the core of the dispute. He'd fired them both for brandishing weapons on his property, but at the same time, he understood what fueled their tempers. Love could make a man act in ways he normally wouldn't.

"Bad blood and thick heads," Hank added, ignoring the look Sam gave him. "And now we're shorthanded."

Suddenly, the trio of Queenslands resting in the shade erupted into a frenzy and took off toward the gate.

A thin trail of dust on the road explained why. "Looks like Donnie," Hank said as Sam caught sight of the sheriff logo on the door of the car. "Greta musta called him."

Sam couldn't stifle his groan. "I wish she hadn't."

Hank stiffened at the hint of criticism of his wife. "Greta don't abide guns."

Sam saw his mother scowl. He knew Diane's opinion of the ranch and the roughnecks who worked for him. The last thing Sam needed was Diane influencing Jenny's decision—assuming she'd even consider his offer.

"Guns?" Jenny asked, her eyes going wide.

"Typical cowboy mentality. Settle things with a draw," Diane said snidely.

"Nobody shot anyone," Sam said firmly.

Before he could explain further, Donnie Grimaldo joined them. A big man, nearly Sam's equal in height, Donnie had the look of a guy who'd played football in high school and college. Sam had come to know—and like—the deputy through Josh's association with the man.

"Hi, Donnie," Sam said, shaking his hand. "What brings you out here?"

"Heard you had a little disturbance. Just wanted to make sure everyone was okay."

"Just two hotheads blowing off steam. They both got their walking papers," Sam said, nodding toward the man who'd just finished loading his truck. "Hank, will you take care of cutting Tim a check? Rory asked me to send his to his mom."

After Hank left, Sam invited his guests to the house. "I think Greta made fresh lemonade."

Donnie walked between Jenny and Diane, cooing over the twins. Sam followed a few paces back. It was a pleasure to see Jenny outside; the breeze played with her hair and she moved with natural, lissome grace. He could picture her at the Rocking M permanently. Too bad he had a feeling she was here to turn down his offer.

A few minutes later, they were seated at Sam's massive pine table in his country kitchen.

"What's new, Donnie?" Sam asked after he'd poured everyone a drink. "I haven't seen you since the funeral."

The man glanced briefly at Jenny and Diane but seemed to shrug off any need for secrecy. "You may not have heard, but there's been a rash of wildfires in the area. Nothing big. A couple of hundred acres in

Hunter Valley was the worst, but the state guys think they've been set on purpose.''

Sam didn't like the sound of that. The dry spring had left the area more vulnerable than usual.

''I just wanted you to be on the lookout for anything suspicious,'' Donnie said.

Diane sniffed loudly. ''How can Sam do that when he's living in town?''

Before Sam could reply, Jenny pushed back her chair. The wooden legs made a screeching sound against the Mexican tile. The blue bundle in her arms let out a thin wail. Jiggling Tucker, she said, ''Feeding time. Can I use your office, Sam?''

Sam shook his head. ''It's a mess. Better to take one of the bedrooms upstairs. Do you need my help?''

''That's my job,'' his mother said firmly. She rose and followed Jenny from the room.

Sam and Donnie spent the next ten minutes discussing the possibility of initiating a public-awareness campaign to alert people to the danger. ''Wildfires hurt everybody,'' Sam said. ''Not just ranchers and people who live in the country.''

''That's for damn sure, but most people are oblivious unless it happens in their backyard. Just stay on your toes, Sam. I know you've been trying to help Jenny and the babies, but if this was my place, I'd move home ASAP. You don't want to make the Rocking M an easy target.''

Both men stood, and Sam led his guest to the front door. ''You know how I felt about your brother. He was a good man.''

Sam nodded. ''He was quite a guy.''

After shaking hands, Donnie left, and Sam closed the

door. He leaned back and closed his eyes, feeling more exhausted than he could ever remember.

"If it's such a burden, you could always sell the place and move back to L.A.," a voice said from the top of the stairs.

Sam reluctantly opened his eyes. He'd never understood his mother's antipathy for the ranch—unless it reminded her of Clancy. Guilt, he supposed, from the knowledge she'd left her husband to die with a twelve-year-old boy at his side.

He didn't reply to his mother's suggestion but watched her descend. Even through jaded eyes, Sam had to admit Diane was an attractive woman. Now nearly sixty, she looked ten years younger. Her artfully frosted hair was styled in loose waves around her face. She wore lilac slacks with a print top; the color complemented her fair skin.

"Where's Lara?"

Diane turned at the foot of the stairs and glanced upward. "Sleeping on the bed while Tucker is having a snack. I'd like to use the phone to call Gordon, if you don't mind. I forgot to tell him I was leaving. He's probably worried."

Sam doubted that. Gordon didn't seem capable of worry so long as you put a golf club in his hand and pointed him in the direction of a course. "There's a phone in the kitchen. And Greta left some cake, too. I'm going to check on Jenny."

He strode past her, but she stopped him with a firm hand on his forearm. "She's still Josh's wife, you know."

The pointed remark stung like a poisoned barb—which was probably his mother's intent. "Thank God you reminded me, Mother. Who knows what lecherous thing I might have done if you hadn't told me?''

Her lips compressed in a way Sam remembered all too well from growing up. ''Don't be snide. I simply meant—''

''I know what you meant, Mother, and you can save it. Jenny and I have business to discuss. I want to help her. You're the one who suggested a nanny. Are you saying I shouldn't offer to hire one?'' He'd already decided his suggestion this morning was a bad idea. A selfish idea.

She gave a sigh of frustration and turned on one heel to walk away. ''Oh, do what you want. You always have.''

Not always, Mother. Not where Carley was concerned. Stifling the old, familiar ache that came from thinking of that time in his life, Sam took the stairs two at a time. He paused at the top of the landing trying to decide which way to turn—his suite was on the left, the two guest rooms and connected bath to the right. Knowing Jenny, he turned right.

Sure enough, he found her in a padded rocking chair in the alcove that overlooked the rear of the ranch. This was one of Sam's favorite spots. He often would sit in that chair and read on a Sunday afternoon when the last of his paperwork was done.

He approached slowly, not wanting to disturb Jenny's peace. As if drawn by a magnet, he detoured to the antique sleigh bed he'd bought from Ida Jane shortly after he and Josh had moved in. This had been Josh's room. Sam knelt beside the bed and lowered his chin to the down-filled comforter. Tilting his cheek to one side he had a perfect view of Lara's face.

Her soft cheeks had filled out nicely on a combination

of mother's milk and formula. Tiny heart-shaped lips puckered ever so slightly. Her lilac-hued eyelids were fringed with reddish-toned lashes. The fine down covering her head was a few shades lighter than her mother's auburn color. "You are going to be a beauty someday, princess," he whispered.

Jenny made a small sound, as if just becoming aware of his presence. Sam pushed back and turned around, letting his butt sink into the plush carpet; his back rested against the bed rail. "I didn't mean to disturb you," he said softly.

She stroked her son's cheek with the pad of her thumb and said, "You didn't disturb us. Tucker's just about done." Glancing up, she said, "Is everything okay? You look wiped out."

Sam felt wiped out. He couldn't remember the last time he'd gotten a full night's sleep. There was so much to take care of; two houses, a fleet of vehicles, the animals, the people, the funeral and Josh's affairs, and now the threat to his ranch. He knew where he needed to be, but the thought of leaving Gold Creek without Jenny and the babies made him feel ill.

But knowing the kind of gossip her moving in with him might generate was equally as unpalatable.

"Are you here to talk about what I asked you?"

Her rocking sped up a notch. "Yes."

"Before you say no, can I suggest something?"

She nodded. "Of course."

"Talk to Ida Jane before you make up your mind. Maybe she could move here, too." Jenny's mouth dropped open, but she didn't say anything, so he went on. "As I was driving out to the ranch, it occurred to me that Ida might benefit from a change of scenery. Josh's death has been hard on her. I think it brought back the memory of your parents' accident and her sister's death.'' Sam didn't know Ida Jane well, but he'd always regarded her as one sharp old gal. Something had changed these past few weeks.

"I saw something on TV the other night about depression in the elderly,'' he added. "The death of a loved one can trigger it. So could the changes Andi's been making.''

Jenny didn't say anything for a moment, but her expression was pensive. He held his breath.

"I'd planned to tell you flat out no way, but maybe I should discuss the idea with Ida and my sisters first.''

Sam nodded. "I want to help you and I want to spend time with the twins, but I can't be two places at one time.''

He slowly rose and walked to the rocking chair. He averted his eyes while Jenny moved Tucker, but peripherally he was struck anew by the beauty of seeing his child suckle from his mother's breast. It touched something deep inside Sam's chest, loosening a dam of emotion that had been held in check for almost twenty years. *My kid would have turned twenty-one this year. If he— or she—had been allowed to live.*

Pushing the thought from his head, he took Tucker from Jenny when she offered and walked away. Some things hurt too much to think about. Some gifts were too wonderful to resist. This ready-made family was the latter.

"WHAT'S GOING ON HERE?'' Diane asked as Jenny made the turn into the paved lot beside the old bordello.

"I don't know. Is that a flashing light?'' Jenny craned her neck to see past the truck in front of her.

"Looks like an ambulance," Diane said, her voice rising in pitch.

Jenny took the first empty parking place and jumped out. She reached in to grab Tucker. "Hurry," she urged Diane as she picked her way through the bystanders to the rear stairs that led to the veranda that wrapped around the front of the building.

"Your aunt fell," Lillian Carswell told her as she reached the door. "We'd just brought her home from Garden Club a few minutes earlier. Beulah and Mary and I were standing here talking when Andi called for help."

"Looks like her hip," Mary Needham said, shaking her head morosely. "Hips are bad."

"As long as it wasn't a stroke," Beulah said ominously.

Jenny's mind was reeling by the time she made it to the parlor where Andi stood beside a gurney containing a very vocal Ida Jane Montgomery.

"Auntie, what happened? How bad is it?"

Ida's right arm was strapped down with a drip line attached to it, but she managed to reach out with her left and clasp Jenny's hand. "Hello, dear, I banged up my hip. Don't know how. One minute I was fine, then boom." She closed her eyes and added under her breath, "Maybe Andrea's ghost pushed me." Her white eyebrows drew together.

Something about the way she said it made Jenny's heart turn inside out. *No. Not Ida, too. I can't lose Ida, too.*

One of the paramedics shouldered past Jenny, breaking her contact with her aunt. Apologizing, he told her they needed to transport the patient to Merced, where an orthopedic surgeon was waiting.

"We'll be right behind you, Auntie," Andi said, opening the door for the emergency crew.

Gordon materialized and offered to take Tucker from Jenny. After checking to see that Diane had the diaper bag and two bottles of frozen breast milk, Jenny followed Andi to Rosemarie, their aunt's big pink Caddie.

"Tell me what happened," Jenny asked a few miles later.

Andi's shoulders tensed. "I don't really know. One minute she was fine, the next she was on the floor."

"Maybe it's her blood pressure medicine. Or something she ate. She wasn't drinking, was she?"

"Who knows what they do at Garden Club?"

Jenny wasn't sure which idea bothered her more—Ida hitting the bottle or Ida thinking an imaginary ghost had pushed her. Neither sounded like the Ida Jane she knew and loved. Maybe what Sam had said was right. Ida Jane was emotionally fragile.

Aren't we all? All except for Sam, who seemed as centered and in control as ever. There'd been those two fleeting moments when he seemed close to tears, but he'd gotten himself back in check almost instantly. Maybe that was why Jenny suddenly felt inclined to take him up on his offer.

"Sam suggested I move to the ranch," Jenny said, keeping her gaze straight ahead.

Andi didn't respond right away. Finally, she asked, "Are you thinking about it?"

"I wasn't, but now I'm wondering if it might not be the best thing for Ida Jane. If she has a broken hip, she'll need weeks of physical therapy. That will mean trips back and forth to Merced. You can't take her and run the shop. I can't drag two babies everywhere. Sam's housekeeper would help."

"We could hire a baby-sitter or leave the twins in day care. Or get the Garden Club ladies to help."

Jenny considered the suggestions. They made sense, but they didn't solve her underlying problem. She wanted to escape to the ranch, to hide from the world. It might be a foolish, emotionally risky decision, but she needed to leave behind the image she had of Josh dying in the living room of their home.

"But when Ida comes home, we'll have to build ramps or put in an elevator or something at the bordello unless she stays with me. And my house is too small. Plus, there are ghosts there, too," she added under her breath.

Andi drove in silence for a few minutes then said, "We can't afford to build ramps, Jen. I haven't wanted to say anything because you have so much on your plate, but Ida Jane is just about broke. If I can find the money to hire a carpenter, it'll be to fix the stairs before someone falls and sues us. And then there's the roof. It leaks."

"So maybe moving to the ranch would be a solution. Sam suggested it. He said Ida Jane seemed depressed lately. She would have the guest suite on the main floor. The twins and I would be upstairs."

As they pulled into the parking lot of the hospital, Andi said, "This is going to sound selfish, but I'd like you to go. And take Ida Jane, too. I can't move a display case without getting in an argument with her. I know it's her business, and she's old and set in her ways, but she's driving me crazy."

"People will talk if I move in with Sam."

Andi sighed. "This is Gold Creek. Gossip is a fact of life. You have to decide how much other people's opinions matter. Are you Jenny Perfect? Or do you put family before your reputation?''

Jenny started to protest, but something stopped her. Was it that simple? Because if it was, then her decision was made. As far she was concerned, family came first. Always.

CHAPTER FIVE

As JENNY PULLED her car into a parking spot in front of the Anberry Rehabilitation Hospital in Atwater, she marveled at the difference a mere three weeks had made in her mental and physical health. She could take a deep breath without breaking into tears. Some days she went an hour or more without thinking about Josh. Of course, a whiff of his cologne could reduce her to sobs, but she knew she was healing.

So were those around her. Sam commuted to the ranch most days but continued to spend his nights in the travel trailer in her driveway. He used the baby monitor he'd once used for Josh to listen for the twins and was often at their crib before she could stumble to the nursery, a room the twins shared with Jenny's artwork and computer.

Jenny and Josh had planned to convert the guest bedroom into a nursery, but Diane had commandeered that room when Gordon left to check on things at the couple's Santa Barbara home two weeks earlier. He was due to return today to pick up Diane so they could continue their travels.

Jenny had tried to discourage Diane from staying, but neither subtle hints nor Sam's "Mother, the babies will be fine without you," worked. Perhaps she was worried about protecting Jenny's reputation—an issue that would become moot once Ida was released from the rehab center. Everyone had been apprised of the plan. Ida Jane, Jenny and the twins were moving to the Rocking M for the duration of Ida's recuperation…and possibly longer.

It was the *and possibly longer* that made Jenny nervous, but she was determined to do this for her family. Sam and his crew had revamped all of the entrances to accommodate Ida's wheelchair. The decks were now accessible, and Ida would even have a small private patio. The ranch house offered more mobility than the cramped quarters at the old bordello could possibly give, and the promise of Sam's housekeeper's help was a bonus.

"Greta is dying to get her hands on the twins," Sam had told Jenny. "Her grandchildren live in Alaska, so Greta and Hank don't get to see them often. And Greta was a nurse's aide before she married Hank and moved here, so she'll be a big help with Ida Jane, too."

Jenny felt a little guilty about unloading her problems on a stranger, but as Kristin said, "How would that be any different from letting Sam hire a nanny to help out?" The nanny had been Diane's idea, and she'd even gone so far as to put an ad in the paper, but no suitable applicants had shown up.

Grabbing her purse—she felt almost naked without a diaper bag—Jenny opened the Honda's door and got out. The air was warm and dry, but she detected a hint of autumn in the breeze. October was usually one of her favorite months. School was well under way but it was still too early for the holiday frenzy. Her class would have celebrated Columbus Day and the discovery of America by now and would be starting to make art projects for Halloween.

She missed teaching, but, except at odd moments like this, rarely had the luxury of thinking about it. She barely had time to eat, let alone pine for her old life.

Between visits to the pediatrician, the orthopedist and the obstetrician, every minute of Jenny's life was spoken for.

Thankfully, Ida Jane was healing with remarkable speed, given her age. The doctor said she could go home as early as Friday, just two days from now. The movers were coming tomorrow. And Jenny wanted some last-minute reassurance that she was doing the right thing for everyone.

"Hello," Jenny called out as she entered her aunt's room. "Aunt Ida?"

Ida Jane's bed—the one closest to the window—was empty and her roommate, a talkative woman who'd had knee surgery, had been released yesterday. Jenny knew where to look: the aviary—her aunt's favorite spot.

"Ida Jane?"

"Over here," came a loud whisper.

A responding flutter of wings and cooing filled the air. The air temperature was at least ten degrees cooler beneath the covered arbor. Jenny's heart tightened when she spotted her aunt in a wheelchair a few feet away. A white sweater enveloped her hunched shoulders, making her look sunken and withered; a knitted throw covered her legs.

"The doves spook easy," Ida Jane said, her voice croaking. "They're kinda simple."

Jenny smiled at her aunt's kindhearted appraisal of the dim-witted birds. She sat down on the park bench beside her aunt and took Ida's hand.

"Hello, dear heart," Ida said, squeezing her hand with remarkable strength.

Her smile was surprisingly bright and perky, and Jenny decided it was the wheelchair that made her look old and sick. *We'll get her up and walking when we get to the ranch.*

"Who did your hair?" Jenny exclaimed, reaching out to feather back a lock of silver. "I love it."

The simple cut was shorter than usual, but there was enough natural curl to keep it from looking austere.

"A gal comes in twice a week. I decided I needed something new because I get to go home soon," Ida said emphatically, as if daring Jenny to dispute the fact.

"I know. The day after tomorrow the doctor said. That's what I came to talk to you about. I want to be a hundred percent sure you're comfortable moving to the ranch. You won't be able to see your friends as often, you know."

Ida waved off the suggestion. "They know where to find me if they want to visit."

Jenny fought down a grin—very few of the old gals still drove. Ida Jane had stubbornly kept driving, despite her great-nieces' concerns. Whether or not she'd ever be able to get behind the wheel again was still up to debate. "I just don't want you to get lonely," Jenny said.

Ida smiled. "I'll have you and the twins. And Sam."

Sam. Jenny wondered if she should explain to Ida Jane about the twins' paternity, but decided against it. There would be time once they were settled.

"And Greta—Sam's housekeeper," Jenny added. "I think she's really looking forward to having some female company. She said it's been too quiet with Sam staying in town."

Ida's smile took on a wistful edge. "Suzy never liked living on the ranch. After she got married, she always found some excuse to go to town. But the Rocking M still feels like home to me."

Jenny looked down at the withered hand still holding

hers. Despite Ida's enthusiasm, Jenny had reservations. For one thing, it felt as if she was running away.

"You don't think this is the coward's way out?" she asked in a small voice. "That I'm dumping my problems in Sam's lap?"

Ida made a huffing sound. "That sounds like something Diane would say. You had lunch with your friends last Saturday. What did they tell you?"

She'd met five of her teacher friends at the Golden Corral for a "girls'" lunch. The school talk had made Jenny slightly blue, but she'd also walked away feeling better about her decision to stay home with the babies.

"You'll never regret giving yourself this time with the twins, Jen," Martha Rhodes had told her. "And if Sam's housekeeper is willing to help, I say go for it. My sister hired a nanny with her two—they were eighteen months apart, and it really saved her sanity."

"The change will do you good, Jenny," another friend had stated supportively. "Being away from the house will give you a break from the memories."

Jenny sincerely doubted that. Josh was everywhere, and he was very much a part of the ranch, but at least the well-meaning citizens who popped in and out of her kitchen ten times a day wouldn't be making the drive to the ranch.

"They were very supportive and didn't see anything wrong about taking help when it's needed and when it's offered," she said to Ida now. "And they understood when too much help is no help at all."

Jenny felt guilty about her feelings, but the plain truth was that the Good Samaritans of Gold Creek were driving her mad. She was tired of parenting by committee— arguing over how to feed, burp, diaper, comfort, bathe and dress the babies.

Ida Jane chuckled. "What now?"

This morning's debate had centered on whether or not Lara was fussy because she didn't stay on the breast long enough. "Breast-feeding," Jenny answered. "Lillian Carswell thinks Lara might be colicky because she stops nursing too soon and doesn't get enough of the hind-milk."

Lillian, the retired librarian, was sixty-nine and un-married, but she read a lot and was deeply concerned with the twins' welfare.

"Lillian's an old maid with too much time on her hands," Ida said, shaking her head. "She wouldn't know a teat from a hole in the ground."

Jenny sighed. "She showed me the article in a baby magazine. It had something to do with the amount of lactose intake from the foremilk and not getting enough hindmilk to digest the lactose."

Jenny had wanted to scream. She didn't question the article or Lillian's worry, but a part of her—a part she seldom had a chance to listen to—thought her daughter's problem might be something else.

"Could it be that Lara is just a little fussier by na-ture?" she'd asked.

"Heavens, no," Beulah Jensen had exclaimed.

"Absolutely not," Diane had chimed in.

"Lara is an angel," was Lillian's verdict.

An angel who had everybody wrapped around her tiny finger. Jenny loved her daughter, but she had a feeling the child was going to grow up to be a diva if they didn't get away from this opinionated crowd of do-gooders.

That was the Rocking M's most attractive lure. Soli-tude. Jenny wanted to be alone with her babies, her memories, her thoughts. No Garden Clubbers, no church ladies, no big-hearted friends, no mother-in-law.

"Am I being selfish by moving?" Jenny blurted out. "Diane thinks this is a huge mistake. She says I'm moving away from my support base. You know, the whole 'It takes a village to raise a child' thing."

Ida Jane made a sweeping motion with her hand, which startled the doves. A white feather drifted to the ground, settling at Jenny's feet. "Diane isn't exactly a font of maternal wisdom," Ida Jane said.

Jenny fought back a smile. "Aren't you being a little hard on her? Diane was a single mother most of the time the boys were little." An unpleasant thought struck her. "Like me. I'm a single mom. What if twenty-seven years from now Tucker's wife has this same conversation with her aunt?"

Jenny's temporary panic evaporated at Ida's merry giggle.

"Silly girl. You love others more than you love yourself. That's always been your problem. Diane, on the other hand, loves herself first. When she criticizes you about going to the ranch, it's probably because she knows she's never been invited there, nor is she likely to be."

Jenny sighed. "I've never understood Sam's antipathy toward his mother. Whenever I asked Josh why they didn't get along, he'd just say, 'Ask Sam. It's his business.'"

"Have you?"

"Asked him? No. Not exactly."

"Then do it."

"Now?"

"Why not?"

Jenny was caught off guard by Ida's succinct responses. The Ida Jane of Jenny's youth never used one word when fifteen would do.

"Are you tired?" Jenny asked.

"A little. They made me walk on a machine today. Sam doesn't have one of those machines at his house, does he?" Ida asked. "Because if he does, I'm not going."

Jenny smiled. "Do you mean a treadmill? No, he doesn't have a home gym, but he offered to buy anything we need. Stairstepper, treadmill, stationary bike."

Ida shuddered with mock severity. "Torture devices. That's what they are."

Jenny pictured Sam's response when she'd asked why he didn't have workout equipment. "If I need exercise, I go to the barn and lift bales," he'd said simply. And Jenny hadn't been able to keep from looking at his broad, well-muscled shoulders. She didn't know any man as fit as Sam.

Ida pushed back slightly with her toes so the wheelchair rolled an inch. "It's time for my nap. If you're worried about Sam and his mother, you should go ask him. No sense putting it off if it's stuck in your craw."

"You know, Auntie, that's a good idea. Maybe I will."

Jenny rose and took hold of the wheelchair handles. The apparatus was lightweight and agile, but Jenny felt more awkward than she did pushing the double stroller.

"Will you do me a favor when you're at the ranch?" Ida asked as they entered her room.

"Of course."

"Make sure my bed is under the window. That's what I hate about this place. I can't breathe at night if my bed isn't under the window."

Jenny hadn't been to the Rocking M for over a week. Ida Jane's room had been empty. "Okay. I'm sure that won't be a problem."

"Good. Do you know where my room is? It's on the first floor—just past the kitchen. Suzy's is upstairs beside Mama and Daddy's room, but it's my job to get the fire in the stove going in the morning so the downstairs is warm and toasty. I'm a good fire maker."

Jenny felt herself blanch. The original farmhouse that Ida and her parents had occupied before her father lost the ranch in a poker game had burnt down many years earlier, killing Suzy's husband, the triplets' grandfather. Some blamed the tragedy for pushing their grandmother over the edge.

Jenny cleared her throat. "Um, Auntie, you do know the old place is gone, right? We're going to be living in Sam's log home. He built it a few years ago. Remember?"

Ida blinked, owl-like, then frowned. "I know that. I just want my bed by the window if that's not too much to ask."

Her testy tone made Jenny blush with chagrin. "I'll check on that first thing." Jenny tried to make allowances for Ida Jane's mercurial temperament of late—no one liked being in a hospital. But Ida had changed radically since her fall, and Jenny couldn't wait to get them moved so she could keep an eye on her aunt.

SAM HAD JUST FINISHED the last screw on the mounting bracket, when he heard Jenny's voice.

"Sam?" she called.

"In the nursery."

He held his breath as her footsteps neared. She hadn't visited the ranch in nearly a week, preferring to let him handle the changes as he saw fit. He attributed her reluctance to take an active role on his mother.

Diane had made it abundantly clear what she thought of Jenny's decision to move.

"You're not doing that girl any favor, Sam. Jenny needs time to get over her loss. Imprudent change will just postpone the grieving process," his mother had said the evening before last.

"I'm grieving, too," he'd pointed out.

She'd made a scoffing sound. "Men don't know the meaning of grief."

Sam would have argued the point—some days it took every ounce of willpower he possessed to get out of bed. He was pretty sure he'd still be holed up in his room with a bottle if it weren't for two things: Tucker and Lara.

"Oh, my heavens!" Jenny exclaimed, stepping into the east-facing room. "Look at this place. Wow. Sam, who did this?"

A jolt of pure happiness—a feeling so rare it took him a second to identify it—made him grin. "I did."

She spun in a circle, head tilted back to take in the ceiling. "It's like walking in the sky. Look at that cloud formation—it's two horses rearing up, isn't it?"

Sam forced himself to remain composed. "It's whatever you see. The view changes when you step over this way."

She walked toward him, her chin lifted. "Now it's a camel on a biplane."

Sam hooted. "You've got some imagination, Jenny Perfect!"

Her eyes narrowed and she pointed to another spot. "Do you see that?"

Thinking he'd missed something, Sam stepped closer and followed the line of her finger upward. Squinting, he frowned. "What?"

"That tiny dot. It's a black hole where my ridiculous nickname is going to magically disappear."

Sam chuckled and moved away. Her scent was too appealing, too real. It made him want to loop his arm around her shoulder and— He cut off the thought. Leaning close to the newly painted wall, he took a deep breath. *Fresh paint.* Now, that was a safe smell.

"I had no idea you were such a gifted artist, Sam," she said, walking to the matching oak cribs.

FedEx had delivered the bedding earlier that morning. The design they'd chosen had black-and-white pandas peeking through bamboo stalks. The bright-orange accents added a cheery touch.

"It's just paint, Jen. Two colors. Couldn't get much simpler. I did the same thing in Josh's nursery when he was a baby."

"You were just a kid when Josh was born, and you painted a mural like this?" She picked up a stuffed panda and hugged it to her chest. The movement might have meant her milk was letting down, or she might have been trying to block his view of her ample bustline. Instead, it drew his attention to her outfit—khaki capri pants and a stretchy black top. He felt a very unwelcome flicker of desire.

"Maybe not quite as complex—it was a tiny house, but I tried." He turned back to finish snapping the blinds into their metal brackets. He'd vacillated between sunny yellow and plain white, which would have been more practical, given the possibility the twins might only be here for a few months. That was an issue he and their mother had yet to resolve. "Unfortunately, Diane made us move about six weeks later, so Josh never really got to enjoy it."

Sam pressed the hinged guides closed and then lowered the shades. "How do they look? I was going for that warm-sunshine look."

He glanced over his shoulder and saw her frown. "Wrong color?"

She shook her head. "No. It's perfect. The room is wonderful. The cribs, the layette…" She put down the bear and absently brushed her hand across her breasts. She was such a wonderful mother, just as Josh said she would be.

"Sam, why do you and your mother dislike each other?"

Sam almost dropped his power screwdriver. He started to deny her accusation but changed his mind. She had a right to know the truth.

He put the Makita back in its turquoise metal box then swept the shrink-wrap packaging from the blinds into a plastic bag. "How much time do you have?" he asked, facing her.

She stuffed her hands in the pockets of her pants. "If you don't want to talk about it, just say so. You don't have to be facetious. That was Josh's way of dealing with things he wanted to avoid."

Sam paused, befuddled, then he understood. "No. I meant, how soon do you have to leave? I can give you the long version or the short one."

She blushed and looked down to consult her watch— a slim gold bracelet–type that Josh and Sam had shopped for together in San Francisco the Christmas before last. Sam had advocated practical—"She works with fourth-graders." Josh had held out for sexy. Now Sam could see why—Jenny had delicate, very feminine wrists.

"I suppose I should head back in an hour or so. I stopped at the house on my way back from seeing Ida Jane. I left two bottles with Diane. We're mixing breast milk with formula, so the twins should be fine. Beulah was there, too.''

"Good. I don't suppose you packed your boots, did you?''

She shook her head, obviously puzzled.

He picked up his tools and clamped the trash bag under his arm. As he walked past her, he said, "I was going to suggest a horseback ride, but it's only been seven weeks. You probably shouldn't be on a horse yet.''

"Where are you taking me?''

"Josh's favorite spot. Come on. We'll take the quad-runner.''

Sam wasn't looking forward to the topic of conversation but he'd put it off long enough. It was time to tell Jenny about the past.

SAM WASN'T WEARING his hat. Sitting behind him and enjoying the ride on the padded seat of a vehicle that resembled a cross between a motorcycle and a tank, Jenny could see a few silver hairs glistening in the sunlight. They blended so nicely with his thick, wavy brown hair, she'd never noticed them before. Of course, she wasn't usually this close to him, either.

"We're not going too far, are we?'' she asked.

"No. Just to the top of the ridge.'' He patted the cell phone in his pocket. "Don't worry, we can check in at any time.''

Sam parked beside an area of lichen-covered slabs that she and Josh had named Stonehedge Unhinged. The long flat boulders resembled the mysterious circle laid flat, like dominoes.

She dismounted gingerly, acknowledging the reminder that she hadn't used certain muscles since the delivery. Nothing hurt, thank goodness, but she still moved with care as she followed him to a spot not far from an established fire pit. He dropped with careless grace to an armchair-shaped hunk of granite.

"When was the last time you were here?" Jenny asked, stretching to feel the cool breeze the altitude afforded.

Sam took a deep breath. "Josh and I camped here last May, remember?" he asked. "We came up right after he finished the second round of chemo. He was sicker than a dog." He cleared his throat. "You weren't real pleased, if I remember correctly."

Instead of sitting, Jenny leaned her hip against a waist-high formation and crossed her arms. "I was pissed as hell, actually. Josh was so weak. I thought he'd fall off the horse and break his neck."

"Maybe that's what he was hoping for," Sam said.

A flicker of pain wound through her ribs. "If I'd known how bad it was going to be for him, I wouldn't have minded. Truly."

His lips flickered sympathetically then he sat forward, hands linked together in front of him.

"I'll tell you what happened between me and my mother," he said, looking up at her, "but I need your promise you won't bring the subject up again. You can get Diane's side of the story if you want, but whatever excuses she gives you are of no interest to me. Deal?"

His serious tone made her hesitate. Not because she couldn't keep a secret but because this sounded like the kind of revelation that bonded people. Did she want to be the keeper of Sam's secret? Did she have a choice? Like it or not, they were already bonded.

"Deal," she said softly.

CHAPTER SIX

JUST START TALKING, Sam told himself. Should be simple enough. But the second he opened his mouth, his brain refused to cooperate.

He jumped to his feet and paced to the brink of the lookout. Below was the Rocking M. He gazed at the rolling pastures where his cattle grazed, the top-notch fences and the irrigated fields. The forest-green metal roofs that topped both his home and barn were easy to spot in the afternoon sun. He caught glimpses of vehicles moving, employees at work. He was proud of the fine working ranch he'd created. But none of it quite filled the void in his heart, left by a bitter betrayal.

He couldn't help wondering where he'd have wound up if things had worked out differently with Carley. No doubt he'd have stayed in Hollywood. Perhaps he'd now be rich and famous. There was no way to know. He probably wouldn't have grown as close to Josh. At least there was one saving grace to this saga, he thought.

He let out a long sigh. "I don't like to talk about what happened. It's old news, and Josh's death has taught me that bad things just happen. You can't dwell on them."

He swallowed against the tightness in his throat. "I fell in love when I was nineteen. I'd just gotten my first speaking role in a film and thought I was on my way. She was the director's daughter. Eighteen. Gorgeous. Dangerous as hell, but I was cocky and full of myself."

Sam closed his eyes to recall the pleasure of their first kiss. His palms had been so wet he hadn't dared touch her anyplace but on the lips. But within days, they'd moved beyond simple kisses to wild, sinful tangles of arms and bare skin and hot need. In empty dressing rooms, abandoned sets, the back seat of his car and on the sprawling private beach below her parents' million-dollar Malibu home.

"First love is unique, I guess. You feel like you invented something that could cure cancer or save humanity."

Jenny smiled at his wry tone and nodded. Sam was sure she and Josh had felt the same way. In fact, he'd been forced to listen to months of gushing details about "Jenny this, Jenny that" when he and Josh first moved to Gold Creek.

"Anyway, we talked about getting married, but she was sure her parents wouldn't approve since they wanted her to go away to college. I wasn't too concerned about what Diane would say. I'd moved out when she married a jerk named Frank and hadn't seen much of either her or Josh for a few months. I wasn't crazy about the idea of eloping—until Carley told me she was pregnant."

Sam rolled his shoulders against the tightness. He didn't look back often because the what-ifs always did a number on him. *What if I hadn't called Diane first?*

"Carley told her folks she was spending the weekend with friends in San Diego. I, unfortunately, told Diane the truth. Josh was just a little tyke, and I was afraid she'd pull some typical Diane stunt and I wouldn't be there to take care of him."

Jenny looked grave, her lips pursed. She was a good listener, Sam thought, momentarily distracted from his story.

"Did something happen?" she prompted.

Sam blinked. "Yes, but not to Josh." He put a little more distance between them. "Carley and I got married in some sleazy little chapel in Vegas. We stayed in the honeymoon suite—" he snickered to let her know it had been anything but glamorous "—of some joint on the Strip."

He looked at her and sighed. "That was twenty years ago. Vegas has spruced up a lot, but back then, the Golden Fleece was the best I could afford." He couldn't help but smile—the irony of the little joint's name never ceased to amuse him. He'd been fleeced all right—of his innocence.

He shook his head. "You get the picture. It wasn't what I wanted, but…we said our vows, paid the guy twenty bucks then stocked up on beer and fast food and hopped in bed." He caught Jenny's blush and bit down on a smile. "Wasn't quite the honeymoon you and Josh took, was it?"

There was a sad look in her eyes when she said, "I never understood why you were so adamant about us going away for our honeymoon. When you gave us tickets to Maui and a week in a hotel for a wedding present, my first thought was we could have used that money as a down payment on a house if you'd have given us a choice." She frowned. "Now I feel like an ungrateful brat."

"Don't. I should have asked you, but I was afraid something would happen to jinx things."

"Like with you and Carley?" she asked.

The memories rushed back. The chatter of a silly game show in the background. Carley's risqué parody: *I'll take door number one, Sam. Oh, Mr. O'Neal, what a lovely package—it's so much bigger than I expected.*

Slick bodies because the window air conditioner couldn't keep up. Naked giggles. Kissing Carley's flat, Malibu-tanned belly and trying to imagine what it would be like to hold his child in his arms. They'd teased each other with preposterous names: Lulu Blue, Xerce Cayenne, Rowdy Merriweather, O. Neal O'Neal.

Sam brushed away the wave of emotion that gripped him. "The morning of the second day, there was a knock on the door and three guys showed up demanding that Carley return with them to L.A. They said they worked for her father."

Sam's pacing picked up a notch. He couldn't contain the agitation this memory brought. Three hulking goons. Carley in pink baby-doll pajamas. Sam in jockey shorts. Two of the men pinned his arms while the third punched him senseless. He could still hear Carley's screams and the crowd of curious tourists pressing in the doorway to see what was going on. Sam fought back, but it was three against one. In the end, the lead guy landed a solid kick to Sam's kidney that knocked him out. When he came to, he was on gurney on his way to the hospital with a police escort. His wife was gone.

Suddenly, a soft hand touched his closed fist. "What happened? Can you tell me?" Jenny asked.

Sam jumped back. He needed space to tell his story. He didn't want its ugliness to touch her. "Sit down."

He hadn't meant to sound so gruff but her expression looked slightly wounded. She did as he asked. Instead of apologizing, he told her, "There was a fight. I landed in the hospital with a Vegas cop outside my door ready to haul my ass off to jail for a long list of charges including statutory rape."

Jenny gasped.

Sam looked away. He didn't need her sympathy or

outrage. Not now. Back then, he'd have given anything for a helping hand, a shoulder to cry on, some adult guidance, but the only person available was his mother—the one who'd betrayed him.

"When I got to L.A., after I'd used every penny I had on hiring a lawyer to talk the police into dropping the bogus charges against me, I found out Carley's parents had taken her to France."

He took a deep breath. "To make a long story short, Carley's dad managed to get our marriage annulled, me fired and my name on a studio blacklist. I was broke and out of work. A buddy of mine was heading out on the rodeo circuit, and I thought, Why not? Nothing like a two-thousand-pound bull stomping on you to give you a little perspective."

Jenny shook her head from side to side. "What about Carley? She just left? Without even talking to you?"

She would pick up on that first. Jenny—whose sense of honor would never allow her to act so callously. "I've never seen her since that morning. I heard she married a Frenchman a few years later. Probably still lives in France."

Jenny was silent a moment then asked the question he'd hoped might escape her notice. "What about the baby?"

"Aborted," he said simply.

Her gasp sounded like a wounded bird's cry. He tried to cover his own emotion. "It was a long time ago, Jenny."

"She did it without your consent?"

He made a dry, harsh sound in his throat. "Her father was rich and powerful. I was a nobody." He shook his head. "Save your sympathy. I probably would have given my permission if anybody'd asked." *Liar.* "I was madder than hell at the time, and there's no way I would have wanted any kid of mine to be raised in that kind of life.''

She rose and walked a few steps in the opposite direction. Sam understood completely; it was the way he felt about this story, too. He kept her in his peripheral vision. Her lips were compressed in a thoughtful frown. When she looked up and caught him staring, he turned away.

He heard her approach, and was grateful she didn't do something foolish like touch him. Even after all this time, these memories left him feeling splintered. One touch and he might crumple like a pane of broken safety glass.

''It's a tragic story, Sam. I'm sorry. You deserved better. But how does your mother figure into it?''

Sam closed his eyes and sighed. He'd almost forgotten about this part of the saga. ''Diane sold me out.''

''I beg your pardon?''

He faced her squarely and made eye contact so she would understand the significance of what he was telling her. ''Carley was flighty and headstrong but she also had every intention of marrying me. I know she did. She knew her parents would try to stop her, so she didn't tell anyone—even her best friend—where we were going. The only person I told was Diane.''

The look of comprehension on Jenny's face made Sam swallow thickly. This wasn't something he'd shared with anyone else, even Josh.

''She accidentally let it slip?'' Jenny asked in a small, hopeful voice.

Sam shook his head. ''She went to Carley's parents and told them. She admitted it.'' He closed his eyes, trying not to remember the horrible argument that had followed his mother's revelation.

He wasn't proud of the way he'd acted, but he'd been crazy with anger, frustration and disappointment, not to mention the pain of three broken ribs and a bruised kidney. He'd truly loved Carley and his unborn child, and as far as he could see, the only one to blame for this situation was his mother.

"A few days later, Diane took off with Josh for Mexico with enough money to spend the next couple of years there," he said, leaving Jenny to draw the same conclusion Sam had twenty years earlier.

"Oh, Sam, that's awful. There must have been some reason. Did she tell you why?"

Sam turned to look at the view. Usually, he could escape to this vista to find peace, but today its serenity was lost on him. "She said Carley's father had planned to have me arrested as soon as we returned. She claimed Carley had lied and was only seventeen. Even if that were true, they would have had to prove that our association was forced, which it wasn't. But Diane said she didn't know that. She did what she thought was best— for me."

How simple and logical the words sounded, given the cushion of time, but Sam hadn't believed them then and he didn't believe them now. He had no idea which side Jenny would take.

She was silent for several minutes. "I feel terrible for both of you," she said. "But the person I'd really like to get my hands on is Carley's father. What a bastard!"

Sam smiled. She seldom swore—another reason Josh called her by her unwanted nickname. "He did what he thought was best for his daughter. Maybe I'd make a similar choice if Lara's future was at stake."

He'd spoken candidly, realizing too late what his words implied. Fatherhood. His connection to Jenny's child.

"We should go back," he said, not ready to get into another heavy subject. That could wait until he had his paperwork assembled.

JENNY WAS PUTTERING in the kitchen, just finishing up the last of the dishes when the thought hit her. *No wonder Diane is so mean to Sam—he's her guilty conscience.*

"Hey," Kristin said, flopping onto the padded stool at the counter across from Jenny. She'd driven down from Oregon for a quick visit and to help Ida Jane move. "That Lara makes it so darn hard to put her down. She's such a lovebug."

Jenny smiled. Lara liked to cuddle; Tucker was a miniature action figure. When he was in your arms, he wanted to see everything; Lara was content to be the center of your attention. "Is she asleep?"

"Yup. But Tucker's a bit restless."

Jenny poured the last of the coffee into a cup for her sister and put it in the microwave then turned on the gas under the teapot. She missed coffee but was still watching what she ate and drank. She hadn't eaten anything with peanuts in it because Sam mentioned reading something about the peanut enzyme causing future allergy problems in nursing babies. His fascination with the birth process made more sense to her now.

"Ida told me you went to the ranch today," Kris said conversationally. "I stopped to see her on my way here."

Jenny removed the coffee cup from the microwave and put it in front of her sister. "Wait till you see what

Sam's done with the nursery. It's amazing. I didn't realize he was that...creative.'' The significance of the word took on new meaning when she saw Kristin's impish grin.

Jenny let out a low growl. "You know what I mean.''

She turned around to fill her cup with boiling water then added a chamomile tea bag. The aroma riding on the billow of steam eased her tension. This was a crazy time, some might say she'd made a crazy decision, but in many ways, Jenny felt more relaxed than she had in months.

"Let's sit in the living room,'' Jenny said, carrying her mug to the recliner. She still avoided the couch, which had been returned to its usual position under the window. To her, that couch would forever be associated with Josh's dying. It was on her list of things to give away once the house was rented. But there were a number of minor repairs that would need to be done before that could happen. A window Josh broke the summer before last. The screen door that didn't latch. New vinyl flooring in the bathroom.

Sam had told her to make a list, but she hadn't gotten around to it yet.

Kristin sat across from her. "What did you think of Diane's offer to rent this place? I noticed you nearly choked on your egg roll, but I thought you recovered quite nicely.'' She spoke softly, her voice a near whisper.

"Why are you whispering?''

Kris blushed. "I don't know. Diane has a way of popping in when you least expect it. Are you thinking about her offer?''

Jenny sighed. "Like I told her, there's a bunch of work to be done before the house is ready to rent, but I suppose I could rent it to her. She seemed sincere about wanting to be close to the twins, and I know Sam wouldn't want her staying at the ranch.''

Jenny's mind was still caught up in the sad story of his mother's betrayal. It had taken every bit of willpower to be nice to Diane during dinner. Jenny kept telling herself there were two sides to every story, but her instinct was to take Sam's side unequivocally.

Thankfully, Diane and Gordon would be heading off on their travels in the morning. Canada, Gordon said. Maybe even Alaska.

''I probably shouldn't say this, but I'm glad she's leaving,'' Kristin said. ''I know she's been trying to help, but it really irks me the way she treats Sam.''

''I know. Sometimes I want to shake her. She's lost one son, and she seems to have no feelings for the one she has left. Why can't she see what an incredible person he is.''

Kristin looked at her. ''You like him, don't you? I don't blame you. He's damn attractive. But, Jen, things could get even more complicated if you two—''

Jenny took a gulp of too-hot tea. ''There's never been anything inappropriate between us,'' she snapped.

''Of course not. We don't call you Jenny Perfect for nothing,'' Kris said lightly. ''However, we both know he adores you. He thinks you're better than perfect. But he's far too much of a gentleman to overstep his bounds, especially now with the babies.''

Jenny felt a funny warmth in her belly; she chose to blame it on the hot tea. ''What does that mean?''

Kris gave her a don't-be-dense look. ''Jen, this arrangement is going to take a lot of finesse. Sex would only complicate things. You're both grieving. You both loved Josh. You share two babies. Living together might work out nicely or the whole thing might blow up in your faces. I think Sam's smart enough to know that—which is why he's not here tonight.''

Jenny had been puzzling over Sam's earlier call but now understood. She'd thought he was embarrassed about having shared his secret. Now, she realized he was giving her a chance to rethink her decision.

''Am I making a mistake, Kris?''

Kristin shook her head, her fair curls dancing. ''No. I told you what I think—this has Josh's fingerprints all over it.'' Kris had been the first to say she thought Josh would not only approve of the move but probably had it in mind all along.

In the back of her mind, Jenny agreed. Josh liked to see people happy. He once drove a young couple all the way to Tuolumne Meadows to watch the sunset because that had been their honeymoon dream, but they'd run out of funds and couldn't afford another night in Yosemite.

Jenny looked around. ''You know, sis, what I'd really like is for you to move in here.''

Kristin sat back stiffly. ''I already have a house. In Ashland.''

''I know that, but we need you closer. Even if Ida recovers to the point that she can walk, it's doubtful she'll ever drive again. With Andi running the shop and me at the ranch, we could really use your help.'' Andi had been the one to suggest this, but since she and Kristin still had some issues between them, she hadn't wanted to put it to Kris.

''Is there any reason you can't hang up your shingle—or whatever they call a massage therapist license—here in Gold Creek?''

''Yes.''

"Why?"

It was Kristin's turn to sigh. "I have a life in Oregon, Jen. I make good money. Besides, I'm a pariah in Gold Creek. The girl most likely to screw up. How much business would I get from locals?"

Jenny scowled. She didn't understand why her sister insisted on thinking of herself in such negative terms. "That's ancient history, Kris. Nobody cares about some stupid fight between a bunch of kids."

"I do. And I know other people—Gloria Hughes, for example—who feel the same way. I feel their looks, Jen. They tolerate me when I'm here to help you, but that's because you're their golden girl. You can do no wrong. Even moving to your bachelor brother-in-law's house is okay because you're Jenny Perfect."

Kristin rose abruptly and walked to the kitchen. Jenny admired her sister's slim build and graceful movement. Kris was the prettiest and most feminine of the sisters, yet she seemed to have the least amount of self-confidence. Jenny had never figured out why. Nor did she understand why Kris seemed fixated on something that had happened in high school.

Unfortunately, Jenny just didn't have the energy to make another soul-searching trip down memory lane. Sam's tortured past was quite enough for one day.

"Well, you don't have to decide right away, Kris. Diane and Gordon will be gone for a couple of months."

Kristin nodded. "I'll think about it, but I can't promise anything. There are...other considerations." She walked to the back door. "I'm kinda wound up from the drive. I think I'll go for a walk."

Secretive, as usual, Jenny thought as the door closed behind her sister. She'd given up trying to second-guess

Kristin's motivation. But Kris had been there for Jenny in the delivery room, and Jenny would never forget that.

A couple of minutes later a car pulled into the driveway. It wasn't the rumble of a diesel engine, so Jenny knew it wasn't Sam. Disappointment washed over her, but she didn't have time to examine her reaction before her mother-in-law opened the door and walked purposefully to the couch. She sat down facing Jenny.

"We need to talk."

Before Jenny could reply, there was a faint cry from the bedroom and she jumped to her feet. "I'll be right back."

Diane followed her to the nursery. The twins shared a crib—an arrangement that worked out just fine except when one woke the other. Jenny swooped in and grabbed Tucker before he could work up a howl. His tiny face scrunched up angrily, and his fists were tightly locked.

"Shh...hush, little man," Jenny soothed. "Mommy's here."

She carried him to the changing table and quickly unsnapped his terry-cloth sleeper. His feet kicked when the cooler air touched his skin, but he kept quiet. Diaper changing still left her feeling as graceless as a fourth-grader handling papier-mâché, but she was getting better. Sam was much more efficient.

"Practice makes perfect," he'd claimed. "Even as a baby, Josh was full of you-know-what."

"I think you're making a mistake," Diane whispered.

Jenny glanced at the baby wipe she'd just pulled from the plastic container. "What?"

"Don't move to the ranch," Diane said bluntly.

Jenny looked around at the crowded conditions— desk, easel, bookshelves crammed with art books, children's books and baby paraphernalia, then pictured the cloud-adorned walls and ceiling that Sam had prepared for his children. "I want to move."

"Aren't you concerned about what this will do to your reputation? I know things were different in my day, but this is a small town. People will talk."

Her day? Josh had told Jenny all about the men his mother had lived with without benefit of marriage. Still, what Diane said touched the very core of Jenny's self-image.

She swallowed. The move made sense at so many levels. And as long as there was nothing between her and Sam—other than the twins—where was the harm?

"I'm sorry you feel that way, Diane, but I'm moving. Sam has the space. Greta is anxious to help with Ida Jane *and* the twins. It may sound selfish, but I need some time to get back on my feet, both financially and emotionally. If people can't accept that, then..." Her throat closed.

She pressed the sticky diaper tabs round Tucker's pudgy belly then slipped his feet back into the fitted sleeper. She picked him up. He fit so perfectly against her chest, his head right beneath her chin. A tidal wave of love welled up from her toes and swept through every particle of her being. She'd never expected to feel anything this powerful.

"Your dad would have loved this," she whispered against Tucker's temple. "He would have loved you, sweet boy."

Diane made a low keening sound and rushed from the room.

Jenny started to put Tucker back in his bed, but he seemed too wide-awake. "You're just like your father— he couldn't stand to miss a thing," she whispered, catching her mistake after she said it. With a sigh, she went in search of her mother-in-law.

Diane was standing in front of the grouping of framed photos on the wall near Jenny's bedroom door. "We all miss him, you know," Jenny said, joining her. "We always will."

"I know," Diane said, her voice tearful. She lifted her chin and pointed to a photo of Sam and Josh. Jenny had taken it while she and Josh were in college. Sam had visited them in Fresno, and they'd gone to the fair one afternoon. The brothers were standing, arms linked, in front of a display proclaiming Hybrid Bull Semen.

"Josh worshiped Sam," Diane said. "From the minute he was old enough to walk, he followed Sam everywhere."

Jenny nodded. "And Sam loved Josh just as much."

"Then he shouldn't try to take over Josh's family the minute his back is turned," Diane said.

Jenny fought down a strangled laugh. "Diane, dead is a little more serious than *turning your back.* Josh left me alone with two babies and no set of instructions on what to do next. I'm doing the best I can here."

Diane nodded. In the harsh yellow light of the hall fixture, her features showed her age. Black mascara was blotted under her eyes. "I know you are, Jenny. This isn't your fault. It's Sam's."

Jenny started to defend Sam, but Diane walked away. She motioned for Jenny to follow. Jenny lifted Tucker up so she could whisper in his ear, "I don't want you to pay any attention to what's said here, okay?"

He opened his mouth in a big yawn.

Once seated opposite each other, Diane took the lead. "It's easy at this age, you know," she said, nodding to the baby in Jenny's arms. "You can't go wrong. All you have to do is love them, and they love you back. Only when they get older do things get tricky.''

Jenny didn't argue. She knew that raising a child wasn't easy—especially for a single parent.

''It's when you make a mistake and they can't forgive you, that everything really starts to go to hell in a handbasket.'' Diane's ominous tone made Jenny clasp Tucker a little tighter.

''I was young when Sam was born—too young, I suppose, but try telling that to a girl in love.'' She smiled fleetingly. ''I tried to be a good mother. The thing about Sam is—he was born serious.'' She made a nervous gesture. ''Sam never cooed and smiled like other babies. It was like he was judging me right from the very beginning. And I was never good enough. Never.''

Jenny looked down at Tucker who blinked twice and opened his mouth. Would he judge her harshly for what she did...what she was about to do?

''Josh, on the other hand, was Mr. Sunshine from the minute he was born. That's what I called him when he was little. Mr. Sunshine.''

Tears suddenly materialized in Jenny's eyes. The name fit. He'd been the sunshine of her life, and now he was gone. Forever.

Diane seemed too wrapped up in her own memories to notice Jenny's distress. ''Anyway,'' she went on, ''I did my best to raise those boys. There were men in my life off and on. A few—like Clancy—stuck around longer than others, but mostly it was just me and my boys.'' She looked at Jenny imploringly. ''Until I did something that drove Sam away.''

Jenny gulped. Sam had told her she could get Diane's side of the story, but Jenny wasn't sure she wanted it. Still, something made her ask, ''What did you do?''

"I saved his life—not that he ever saw it that way."
Jenny waited for Diane to go on.

"When he was nineteen, Sam got involved with a spoiled little brat who set her sights on him." Diane gave Jenny a knowing look. "You'd have fallen for him, too, if you could have seen him then. So handsome. Those eyes. And shoulders out to here."

She held up her hands to about the width that Sam's shoulders were today. Jenny ignored the funny little hum in her belly. "Sexy, huh?"

"Tom Cruise and Daniel Day-Lewis rolled into one. The girls flocked to him, but he was very picky—until this little rich girl came along. She was beautiful and willful and she managed to get pregnant so Sam would marry her."

Jenny didn't point out that Sam must have taken an active role in that matter. "I did my student teaching in a high school in the Valley and I saw that happen all too often. Usually, the girl gets stuck being a single parent."

Diane looked at her sharply. "Sam's an honorable man. He offered to marry her. But the little twit was only seventeen. She lied to Sam—told him she was eighteen. She begged him to elope with her to Las Vegas. Sam stopped by my house on his way to pick her up. He told me what he was doing and where he'd be. He didn't ask for my advice—or my blessing." Her tone was surprisingly hurt. "So, when her father called, threatening to have Sam arrested, I decided to cooperate—for Sam's sake."

Jenny looked at Tucker. As much as she didn't want to sympathize with Diane, she couldn't help wondering how she'd react if Tucker's whole future was in jeopardy.

"I take it Sam didn't appreciate what you did?"

Diane threw up her hands and let out a cry of exasperation. Tucker, who was starting to doze off, startled as if pinched. Jenny hugged him close and murmured softly in his ear. "It's okay, sweetie. Go back to sleep."

"Appreciate," Diane muttered ruefully. "God, no. He came home madder than heck. Only stayed long enough to tell me off. He didn't want to hear my side of the story. When I mentioned that I was leaving, he stormed off. Josh and I caught a bus to Mexico a few hours later."

Using the payoff money. Jenny's heart started to harden, but suddenly Diane burst into tears. "That's where we were living when Josh got sick. I didn't even know he'd missed those booster shots until we were back in the States," Diane cried. "Immunizations weren't that big a deal back then. How was I supposed to know he might get cancer from the infection in his gonads?"

"Why'd you go to Mexico, Diane?"

She took a deep breath and clasped her hands together in her lap. "To get away from Frank, the man I was married to at the time. He claimed I'd embezzled a bunch of money from the travel agency he owned." She shook her head and said softly, "I took some money, but it was only a fraction of what it should have been."

Jenny thought she heard her add, "After what he did," but she couldn't be sure. Diane stood and walked to the door.

"Do what you want, Jenny, but never forget that Sam has his own agenda. He's an unforgiving, humorless man with ice water in his veins, but if you choose to live under his roof, there's nothing I can do about it. Gordon and I are leaving in the morning."

After she was gone, Jenny continued to rock the warm, now-sleeping bundle in her arms. "Cold and humorless?" she repeated. "Sam?"

She kissed her little son's forehead. Jenny might not know much about mothering, but she knew Sam O'Neal—a whole lot better than his mother did, apparently.

No man who painted white clouds on a blue-sky ceiling could have ice water in his veins.

CHAPTER SEVEN

THE NEXT MORNING, Sam handed out assignments like an army general. "Hank, I need you and Bill to move Jenny's things into the spare room. Kristin will meet you at the house to show you what goes and what stays. Jenny and I will bring the baby stuff with us. Andi's bringing Ida Jane's things after work."

Jenny and the twins were moving in today. Ida Jane would join them tomorrow—provided her doctor signed the release papers. Jenny had told him on the phone a few minutes earlier that Ida was trying to strong-arm her doctor into letting her go a day ahead of schedule. "She really wants to be with us when the twins and I move in," she'd said.

Sam understood and respected that, but there were a few things he and Jenny needed to iron out before anyone moved anywhere. Sam regretted leaving this until the last minute but his lawyer had been out of town until Monday. His office hadn't called to say the documents were ready until after Jenny had left the ranch yesterday. He'd thought about taking the papers to her last night, but with his mother still there, he'd opted to wait until today.

Shifting gears, he looked at his housekeeper. "Greta, if you need any help inside grab one of the cowboys."

She blushed as if he'd suggested something dirty. "I

can handle everything that needs to get done in here. You just worry about your own problems."

Sam chuckled at her tone. Greta could be quite bossy—after all, she'd been the woman of his house for nearly nine years—but they'd had a long talk the night before, and she'd seemed optimistic about having Jenny and Ida move in.

"We could use some new life in this place," she'd said. "And I'm sure your brother would like the idea of Jenny and the twins being here. He always loved the ranch."

That was true. Sam was positive his brother would have approved of the move, but he wasn't sure how Josh would feel about what Sam was about to propose.

Hank walked up and laid a hand on Sam's shoulder. In his late fifties, Hank retained the lean, beanpole body of many professional cowboys. Lanky legs and extra-long arms that could pitch both a rope and horseshoes with surgical accuracy. "You 'bout ready, boss? We can follow you with the trailer."

Sam took a deep, calming breath. He'd been up since four making East Coast calls and returning e-mail. His business had picked up just at the wrong time. The next two weeks were going to be jam-packed with sales, breeding schedules and prior commitments he couldn't change.

"Go ahead and take off. I need a couple of things from my office." He turned to leave and caught the look that passed between his housekeeper and her husband. Sam knew Hank had reservations about this move.

But unlike Jenny, who cared what people thought, Sam had long ago learned it was impossible to please everyone, so he'd given up trying. As long as he felt right about what he was doing, then to hell with what

other people—including his foreman and his lawyer—
said.

He retrieved his briefcase from his office then fished
in his pocket for the key to the new minivan he'd purchased the day before. Smiling, he walked around to the
driver's side and climbed in. Despite the leather seats
and new-car smell, something didn't feel right. He
glanced in the rearview mirror and saw his cowboy hat
atop his head.

Chuckling, he took it off and sent it sailing toward
the back. It bounced against the window and dropped
into the rear storage compartment. A part of him—the
cowboy, he guessed—never pictured himself behind the
wheel of anything that didn't have four-wheel drive and
a gun rack. But Jenny and the babies needed reliable
transportation and more room than her little compact afforded.

Ignoring the howls of mirth from three cowboys
mending fence, Sam reached over to engage the CD
player. The salesman who'd delivered the car yesterday
had included six of his favorite CDs in the package. As
Diamond Rio started to play, Sam relaxed. The vehicle
might be a bit lower to the ground than a sporty SUV,
but it would be more practical for Ida Jane and two
infant seats. He wondered what Jenny was going to say
when he handed her the keys.

How she'd react to the van worried him almost as
much as how she'd react to the papers in his briefcase.
He'd had weeks to think about this, but hadn't actually
sat down and faced the reality of their situation until he'd
met with his lawyer.

"Are you sure this is what you want to do?" Dave
Dunningham had asked.

They'd been friends for years; business associates

even longer. Dave's uncle, Jasper Lancaster, was the Realtor who sold Sam the Rocking M.

Sam hadn't hesitated when he outlined his plan to Dave, but now his stomach was in a knot. He had to sell it to Jenny, and although he was pretty sure she'd understand the rationale behind the arrangement, he knew better than to second-guess what another person would do.

I'll find out soon enough, he thought, turning his focus to the music.

The melody was beautiful, the harmony soothing, but the words made his throat tighten. The song was about love that ended too soon, the wish for more time to spend together. Another sunset, another chance to say, "I love you."

Sam saw a turnoff and took it. The minivan gave a little shudder as it pulled to a stop on the dusty shoulder. Sam reached into the molded console between the seats and picked up the plastic CD cover: One More Day, it read. The title of the song that was playing. *What would Jenny give for one more day with Josh?*

He closed his eyes and let the music wash over him. The words brought back the pain of the goodbyes in his life—the one with his brother, the one he never had a chance to share with Carley. He told himself he wasn't expecting a miracle with Jenny. He didn't expect her to fall in love with him or give up her future to make him happy. He was only postponing the inevitable. Sam knew that. He just couldn't handle another loss in his life at this moment. Not yet. Maybe with time.

When the music ended, Sam pushed the eject button and tucked the disc into the case. He dropped it into the allotted space, then turned on his blinker. He'd have an answer to his grand plan soon enough.

"YOU'RE CRAZY, aren't you?" Jenny shouted, pointing first at him, then at the shiny new vehicle. Her animation brought a smile to his lips. It was good to see her as vibrant and engaged as she'd been when Josh had been alive. Sam had wondered if that feistiness had died with his brother.

"A new minivan? What were you thinking?"

Sam was certain she didn't want to know that. "Josh called *me* a spendthrift? The kid who had to have every new gizmo and gadget ever made? He'd have had you in bankruptcy court if you hadn't cracked down on him. I know, he told me so."

The diversion worked. Jenny stopped staring at the desert-sand-colored van long enough to roll her eyes skyward. "So, it's genetic, huh? Does that mean I'm going to have to break your check-writing fingers, too?"

The teasing tone let Sam relax some. Maybe buying the car had been an uncharacteristically impulsive move on his part, but it stemmed from seeing Jenny squeezed between two infant seats in the back of the Honda when she and her sisters had taken the babies to visit Ida Jane.

"I really did it for Miss Ida," he said, using what he hoped would be the deciding argument. "She's going to be needing the wheelchair at first and a walker for another month or so after that. How are you going to carry a wheelchair in your little car? And why subject her to that kind of indignity?"

Sam's heart made a funny wiggle when he saw her face soften. Jenny loved her aunt and would do anything to make life easier for the older woman. She looked at him a moment then shook her finger like a teacher. "You are as sneaky and manipulative as your brother. But just because it makes sense doesn't mean I'm going to let you pay for it." Her forehead crinkled. "I'll get a loan just as soon as I have all the hospital bills figured out.''

Sam stifled a sigh. Money was only one small part of what they had to talk about. ''Are you ready to go?'' he asked.

She turned on one heel and dashed back into the house without answering him. With her hair in a ponytail and her black jeans and white, man's-style shirt with the tails hanging out, she looked about sixteen. He clamped down on his gut reaction—which was also reminiscent of age sixteen—and followed. *Business. Think business. Jenny's going to be your new partner in the business of bringing up the twins.*

He ignored the other voice that snidely said, *Right.*

To Sam's surprise, Gordon and Diane were in the living room, each holding a baby. He'd been under the impression they were leaving at sunrise to beat the traffic in Sacramento. In the corner by the telephone stand were two plump diaper bags and an assortment of boxes labeled Twins.

''Hi there, Sam,'' Gordon called out cheerfully.

Sam smiled. ''Hello, Gordon. How's the golfing?''

''Shot a two under yesterday. Couldn't believe it,'' he said, shaking his head. ''They wanted me back today to prove it wasn't a fluke, but your mother has her heart set to leave.''

Diane passed the baby in her arms to Jenny. ''You take good care of this little boy, you hear me?'' she said with mock ferocity.

''I will,'' Jenny said gravely. Then she looked at Sam and added pointedly, ''We will.''

Sam's heart nearly fell out of his chest. He sucked in a breath and didn't let it out. What did that mean? Had she told Diane about the babies' paternity?

Diane looked at him a moment, her lips pursed. "Josh would have expected nothing less."

Well, that answers that. He let out the breath he'd been holding then took a step closer to Gordon.

"Here's your little angel," Gordon said innocently. "I'm going to miss these punkins more than I would a hole in one."

Sam knew the feeling. He wanted to spend as much time as possible with his children, which was why he'd made his lawyer spell out the terms of his relationship in the documents in his briefcase. Now, all he had to do was get Jenny's signature on the dotted line.

JENNY RAN HER HAND across the plush leather upholstery one more time. She still couldn't quite believe that Sam had purchased this beautiful new car for her. Now they were on their way to Atwater to see Ida Jane, after which they would return to the ranch to begin... *What? Playing house?*

"Um...Sam. The car's wonderful. Really. You've done so much. I'm really grateful, but..." She swallowed, trying to find the right words.

"Jenny, I'd planned to bring this up at the house, but I didn't want to start anything with Diane and Gordon there. Do me a favor and open my briefcase." He nodded toward the floor. "That antique by your feet."

Jenny reached down and picked up an amber-colored leather satchel, so old it had that soft feel of a well-traveled suitcase. She set it on her lap, inhaling the almost-smoky quality of it.

"It was Clancy's. He gave it to me before he died. Still smells like cigar smoke, doesn't it?" The fondness in his tone made Jenny run her hand across the embossed initials on the flap. S.S.O.

"I don't know your middle name," she said, oddly disturbed by the fact. Sam was her brother-in-law. She should know that about him. Why had she never bothered to ask? What was wrong with her?

Sam chuckled. "Probably because I never use it. Sam Stuart O'Neal—sounds too much like a distress call."

"Stuart?" The name was familiar to her.

"It's Diane's maiden name."

"Oh. That's right." Jenny felt her tension abate... until a few seconds later when Sam said, "Open it. I had my lawyer draw up a couple of things for us—just to be safe."

Safe? Oh, God, here it comes.

As if reading her panic, Sam turned the van sharply to the right, pulling into a fruit stand that Jenny had never stopped at before. He drove to the far corner of the parking lot and turned off the engine. With his hands on the steering wheel, he said, "It's not what you think."

"How do you know what I'm thinking?"

His lips flickered. *Has he always had such compelling lips? Josh's lips weren't like that. Were they?* She couldn't remember. She couldn't bring her dead husband's face to mind and the fact made her start breathing too fast, too shallowly.

She pushed Sam's heavy leather satchel off her lap and clawed around blindly for her purse, which had fallen to the back. She sensed Sam watching her with growing alarm, but she had to see Josh's face. Right this instant. Finally, her fingers connected with the strap of her shoulder bag. She dug inside for her billfold.

She caught the look of confusion on Sam's face. She whipped open her wallet and flipped past the driver's license and insurance cards to the photo section. *There,* she thought with instant relief. *There he is. Happy eyes. Smiling lips. Not Sam's lips—Josh's lips. The lips I kissed good-night for ten years.*

Heaving an unintentionally loud sigh, she sank back in the soft seat and closed her eyes. "Sorry about that."

Her heartbeat was almost back to normal when Sam said, "What happened?"

"I don't know. I just couldn't remember what Josh looked like for a second, and it scared me."

"Oh. I said 'papers' and you got that deer-in-headlights look. But you don't have to be afraid, Jenny. Not of me. This isn't a custody issue," Sam said, leaning over to pick up the papers that had spilled to the floor. "It's for your protection, in case anything happened to me."

Jenny swallowed the restrictive lump in her throat. "I see."

He shook his head. "No, you don't. You can't. Not until you read the documents."

His tone was sharp, but Jenny thought she understood why. Sam had had to deal with the many loose ends after Josh's death, and he'd said several times that he planned to do things differently with his estate.

She took the papers from his hand and tried to focus on the legalese. Sam leaned between the seats to check on the twins, who seemed to associate automobile travel with sleep. His shoulders barely fit between the opening. His bulk made it hard for her to concentrate. His smell— something clean and fresh with a hint of outdoors— made her want to lean up against him and inhale deeply.

She tugged on her seat-belt strap and put her right shoulder against the window. The sunlight highlighted her reading material, making it impossible to miss the words *beneficiaries of his estates*. She gasped. "Oh my God, Sam. This is your will."

He pulled back sharply, facing her. "It's a codicil to my will."

"You've put my name on everything. The ranch, your patents, your life insurance. Everything. Why?"

He sat back, his shoulders against the door. "You're the mother of my children, Jenny," he said simply. "I know you didn't plan to be. And it seems like some cosmic farce that you wound up with me—a man eleven years your senior—instead of the love of your life. But, we don't have any control over that, Jen. We do have control over how we proceed, and if you read a little further, you'll see that all of those material things come with a price."

Jenny's heart sped up, a low roar hummed in her ears. She didn't dare look down at the papers in her lap; her hands were shaking too badly. "What is it?"

He swallowed first then said, "Five years."

Jenny squinted. Maybe the hum had blocked her ability to hear. "What?"

"I want you to give me the next five years. Live with me, at the ranch—basically, until the twins start school."

"Five? Why five?"

"To be honest, I really want eighteen, but that wouldn't be fair to you. You're young and beautiful and at some point you'll want a real life—dating, a new husband, more kids. I understand that. And I can live with it, if I can have the early years with Tucker and Lara."

There was something so sad about what he was saying Jenny wanted to cry, but he was acting very businesslike and she tried to do the same. "That's all?"

He shook his head. "I also want to be named as their father, legally. We don't need to broadcast it, but it's the smart thing in case anything happens to you. I will always be their father, but I only expect you to stay with me five years."

"What happens after that?"

"I'll give you child support, and you can move back to Gold Creek. Maybe by then your writing will have taken off, but if not, you could probably teach again."

"What about you?"

He showed his first sign of vulnerability. "I go back to the way my life was before this happened, except that I will have established a bond with my children. They'll know me. And I won't have missed out on the early years."

Like I did with Josh. And with my own child that was never born. Jenny heard the unspoken words, and her heart melted. She knew this man better than he thought. His businesslike facade hid a very fragile heart.

"I think I can do this," she said. "Although I'd like to think about the arrangement for a while before I sign anything. But even if I do it, you don't have to make me heir to your ranch. Put the twins' names on the deed."

He smiled for the first time. "I trust you to pass my estate on to them when I'm gone. You're not like my mother."

"What does that mean?"

"When Clancy was dying, he instructed his lawyer to sell the ranch and put the money in a trust for me until my twenty-fifth birthday—he said I'd be smart enough by then. He knew if he left it to Diane, the whole thing would have been gone by the time I was old enough to vote. You, I trust."

Jenny was honored, but saddened, too. "You know,

Sam, I talked to your mother. She told me her version of what happened.''

He swung about sharply and reached for the key. ''Good. Now you know both sides of the story, but I don't want to discuss it.''

He started the car. ''One more thing. I think we should tell Ida Jane today. About the babies.''

Jenny closed her mouth and sat back, arms crossed. At times, Sam could be even more bullheaded than his brother had been, but he was right about one thing—Ida Jane needed to know the truth.

''YOU AND SAM DID IT in a laboratory? That doesn't sound very romantic.''

Ida Jane's response to Jenny's revelation almost made Sam burst out laughing. Jenny's mouth dropped open but no words came out, so Sam said, ''What's worse is neither of us was even in the room at the time. But look what we have to show for it.'' He held Lara up like a blue ribbon won at a fair.

Ida looked from Lara to Jenny, who was nursing Tucker in the armchair across the room, and grinned. ''And you got two for the price of one.''

The elderly woman was sitting in her wheelchair, looking quite regal in her purple jogging suit and bright-white sneakers. Sam wasn't certain Ida Jane understood the mechanics of what they'd just told her, but she didn't seem particularly scandalized. However, she had yet to give her opinion of Sam's five-year plan.

''So, what do you think about Jenny staying with me for five years?'' he asked. ''Is that unrealistic?''

Ida Jane took a breath. ''If I were you, I'd just marry her and get it over with, but you young people have a different way of looking at things, I guess.''

Sam's stomach did a little flip-flop. He'd purposely avoided using the M word in his contract. He would have offered to marry her in a heartbeat, but Jenny was still in love with Josh. You didn't just turn that off when the person you loved died.

"That's right," Sam said, forcing a lightheartedness he didn't feel. "We like to keep our options open. Jenny is free to do anything she wants, as long as she lives at the ranch so I can spend time with the twins."

Ida Jane frowned. "For five years. But what happens then? Won't it break your heart to give them up?"

Sam looked down at the child in his arms and couldn't keep from flinching. "It won't be easy," he admitted, trying to keep his pain from showing in his voice. "But I want to do what's right for Jenny and the twins. I suppose it'll be like a divorce, but, at least, Jenny and I will be able to handle it amicably since we don't... I mean...we won't have a lot of baggage to throw at each other, like some people. We're doing this for the good of the children."

Ida gave him a look that called him a liar, but she didn't say the word out loud.

Sam was grateful, because they both knew he was one. His fancy legal contract was a sham—in every way that counted. He might have agreed to five years on paper, but in his heart he wanted much more. Ida Jane was a sharp old gal. She'd no doubt guessed Sam's ultimate goal was to get Jenny to fall in love with him, or, at the very least, to marry him and provide their children with a stable, loving home.

Sam was no fool. He accepted that Jenny would never love him the way she did his brother. First love was too special, too perfect to compete with. Sam knew he could never take Josh's place.

Lara made a cooing sound, startling Sam. The babies seemed to change every time he looked. She waved her tiny fist and he gave her his finger to grab. Her grip amazed him, as did the way her gaze seemed focused on his lips when he spoke her name.

"Hello, Lara, love. Are you ready for lunch?"

He pressed a kiss on her knuckles. She blinked twice as if surprised by the movement. "Do you want Ida to give her a bottle, Jen? Or does she get the other side?"

He'd gotten over his embarrassment about helping with breast-feeding. Once Jenny and Lara had worked out the kinks in their nursing relationship, the little girl seemed to enjoy the time and nourishment her mother gave her as much as her brother did.

"There's a bottle in the bag," Jenny said. "She won't mind if Ida Jane feeds her."

After placing the baby on Ida's lap, Sam found the plastic bottle and handed it to the older woman. He watched his daughter suckle in bliss, her hand gripping the slick fabric of Ida's jogging suit.

"Well, since everyone is busy here, I'll go find that doctor and see if he plans to sign your get-out-of-jail-free card." He draped a receiving blanket over the arm of Ida's wheelchair then left.

His gaze met Jenny's as he walked past. Her smile seemed slightly troubled, but he hoped a private chat with her great-aunt would help ease her mind. At least Ida hadn't accused him of trying to steal his brother's family—the way his mother would have if she'd been privy to the agreement.

Thankfully, Diane would be gone for two months. Her parting words to Jenny had been, "We'll be back in time for Christmas...maybe even Thanksgiving. Take good care of those babies."

Sam paused in the hallway, trying to remember which way to turn. He hated the sounds and smells of hospitals. He hated seeing people confined to beds. An image of Josh wheezing for each breath made his knees wobble and he touched the wall until the moment passed.

The Hospice nurses had warned him to expect a full year of mourning. They were wrong. Sam would mourn his brother for the rest of his life, but Sam also knew that he couldn't live in the past. He had to move on. For Tucker and Lara who needed a father. And for Jenny, too.

Even if his grand scheme didn't work out, Sam planned to make the next five years as happy as possible for Jenny. She deserved nothing less.

TUCKER HAD FINISHED nursing a full minute before Sam left the room, but Jenny had waited to move until he was gone. It was difficult listening to him talk so dispassionately about their living arrangements. True, theirs was a passion-free relationship, but there was something so one-sided about his proposal, it made her want to cry. He was doing all the giving, she, the taking. It was almost as though he didn't think he deserved anyone to love him.

He was offering her his life, but only long enough to bond with his children. The whole concept boggled her mind. And there were so many questions she needed to ask. *Will we be roommates, relatives or what?* And what would happen once Ida Jane was back on her feet? If Ida returned to town to live, wouldn't that make Sam and Jenny's living arrangement look suspicious—even if they were just friends? They were friends, weren't they?

"What do you think, Auntie? Am I crazy to say yes? Or would it be more crazy to say no?"

Jenny rebuttoned her blouse, stood and walked to her aunt's bed to change Tucker's diaper. He liked nothing better than to fill up on one end and discharge on the other. She laid him down then fished in the bag for a disposable diaper. He'd just moved into a bigger size; Lara still had a couple of pounds to go.

As she worked the snaps on the crotch of his sleeper, she looked at her aunt. "I'm serious, Auntie, I need your advice. Should I sign Sam's papers?"

Ida Jane seemed intent on feeding Lara, who was happily batting the bottle with her fist. She liked to slug Jenny, too, when she was nursing. "Sam's taking me home today."

Jenny's heart made a funny, fluttering sensation. There was something odd in Ida's singsong tone, as if her mind was somewhere else. "By *home* you mean the Rocking M, right?" Jenny asked, trying to keep her alarm from showing.

Ida nodded as if hearing something Jenny hadn't intended. "I used to live there, you know. Before Daddy lost it in a poker game. Gambling is a terrible vice."

Jenny braced herself for the "horrors of gambling" lecture. She'd heard it a million times.

Instead, Ida sighed and said, "But what in life isn't a gamble? Sometimes, you just have to do what feels right, regardless of the risk."

Jenny watched her gently brush one gnarled finger against Lara's plump cheek. "If you hadn't taken a chance, we wouldn't have this little gal, would we?"

Jenny couldn't argue with that logic. She wouldn't trade Lara and Tucker for anything. Even another fifty years with Josh? a voice in her head asked. The answer that flitted through her mind left her a little shaken.

"Life has a strange way of working out the way it's

supposed to," Ida Jane said. "Did I ever tell you about the night you and your sisters were born?"

"Your friends still talk about it like it happened yesterday," Jenny said.

"It was a big deal to this little town. A terrible tragedy—two lovely young people killed in a senseless car wreck, and at the same time, three precious little miracles were born. You spent twelve days in the hospital, then you and Andi came to live with me. Poor little Kristin didn't join us for nearly a month. We almost lost her, but the doctors and nurses never gave up."

Jenny smiled. Kris had always loved that part of the story.

"I became a mother at age fifty-four," Ida said, her tone bemused. "An unmarried spinster. A dried-up shell of a woman, and I suddenly got my dream come true, three times over."

She shook her head, obviously musing over fate's little trick. "Some gifts are too wonderful to question, Jenny girl. But you know deep in your heart, they come with a price." Her eyes filled with tears. "My poor Lori. She and Mick should have been the ones to raise you. That's the natural order of things. But it was probably best they went together. They were so much in love."

Jenny heard the sadness in her aunt's voice and hastily finished diapering Tucker, who fussed a little because he much preferred being naked.

"I'm so glad you're coming to the ranch with me."

Ida looked confused. "To my daddy's ranch?"

Tears welled up in Jenny's eyes. She didn't understand Ida's sudden slips in clarity and it scared her.

"The Rocking M was your family's ranch, but it belongs to Sam now. Some of Sam's workers are moving your things out there today, remember?"

Ida looked unperturbed. She lifted Lara to her shoulder and burped her with efficiency. "Sam's a good man, and he'll be a good father to these little tykes. Josh knew that."

Jenny knew it too, but she was still nervous about signing Sam's papers. *Why?*

She didn't get a chance to raise the question aloud because Sam entered a minute later with a nurse in tow.

"All set, Ida Jane. Just need your John Hancock on the bottom line and we're out of here."

"Good," Ida said, motioning him to her. She signed the three sheets of paper, then the nurse left.

"I'll pull the van around to the front. What do you want me to carry out, Jen?" Sam asked.

For some reason, his voice sounded very much like Josh's. Either that or Josh's voice was fading from Jenny's memory. The possibility robbed her of her ability to speak.

"My suitcase is right by the door," Ida Jane said. "We'll be ready as soon as Jenny finishes changing the baby."

Jenny felt Sam's gaze on her, but she didn't look up. She couldn't. Not when Josh was out of touch.

Once Sam was gone, Jenny glanced at Ida. Her great-aunt smiled. "Don't fret, child. The people we love are obliged to stay around as long as we need them, but they have a journey to make, too, you know."

"They do?"

Ida Jane nodded. "We all do." She sighed. "I'll be getting on with mine, too, pretty soon. But not before I see each of you happily settled."

Jenny smiled. She'd heard that line before. "No wonder our lives are a mess. We want you to live forever."

Ida shook her finger at Jenny threateningly. "Don't

say such a thing. We all have to go sometime. Besides, you girls are making progress.''

"We are?"

Ida nodded. She turned her head to gaze out the window. "You're leading the way, Jenny. Just like always. All you need is a little time.''

Time. Jenny wished it were that simple. *If time's all it takes, then I'm in luck. I'm about to sign up for five years. Maybe by then, I'll have a clue.*

CHAPTER EIGHT

JENNY WASN'T SURE if she'd actually heard Tucker's cry or just anticipated it. In the two and a half weeks that she'd been living at the ranch, she and Sam had discussed the merit of letting him cry himself back to sleep as a way to eliminate the middle-of-the-night feeding, but in all honesty, neither of them could do it. Jenny really cherished the peaceful interlude with her son.

She was out of bed at the first muted whimper. She shrugged on her heavy robe—November had brought with it a couple of light showers and even some frost. Shoving her feet into her alpaca slippers, she dashed through the bathroom to the nursery. Two strategically placed night-lights guided her way.

In the shadows, the white clouds of Sam's painted-sky ceiling looked like friendly angels smiling down on her. After picking up Tucker—who blinked at her and smiled with such Joshlike charm her eyes misted—Jenny peeked into the hallway. It surprised her that Sam wasn't on the scene. He often beat her to the punch, sometimes delivering Tucker to her in bed so she didn't have to get up.

Sam was hands down a gracious host. If Jenny still felt a little tentative about their relationship, she could place none of the fault on Sam's shoulders. He was a perfect gentleman every evening and spent most daylight hours either in the fields or in his office.

That first Sunday after she'd moved in, he'd invited Jenny's sisters to a barbecue, which he'd prepared. During dessert, he explained, line by line, his five-year plan, as Jenny had come to think of it.

After what Jenny thought amounted to very little discussion, Kristin and Andi had endorsed Sam's plan. Ida Jane gave her blessing by nodding off in the lawn chaise.

The following morning Sam had escorted Jenny to his lawyer's office to sign the papers. They then stopped by the bank to add her signature card to Sam's checking and savings accounts.

"You'll need to buy things for the house, for the kids, for whatever," he'd told her. "Think of this as a job, if you like."

A job with very long hours, Jenny thought, smiling at her little son. *But one I wouldn't change for anything.* She yawned, then after waiting a minute to see if Sam would appear, she strolled to her room and sat down in the padded rocking chair in the alcove. She kept the curtains open at all times to enjoy the panoramic view.

Tucker fussed impatiently.

"I know. I know. Mommy's slow tonight." She fumbled with her robe and the buttons of her gown. "It's because your daddy's still asleep, and I'm not quite awake."

Somewhere along the way, Sam had become the twins' daddy. Jenny wasn't conscious of making the switch in her mind; it had just happened. And although still a bit conflicted, Jenny accepted it. There would be time to tell the twins about Josh's role in their lives.

And he was never far from her mind. Or Sam's, either, it would seem. Just that morning, Sam had strolled into the breakfast nook where Jenny and Greta were experi-

menting with the twins' first taste of solid foods—
mashed ripe banana.

Sam had pulled up a chair and watched with rapt attention, applauding when Lara successfully swallowed a
tiny dollop, but Jenny had sensed he was distracted. A
few minutes later, after each baby was finishing off the
meal with a bottle, Jenny asked what was on his mind.

"The school called yesterday and asked if I could put
together something outlining the goals and requirements
for the Josh O'Neal scholarship. I prepared a rough draft
and I'd like your feedback."

Sam's rough draft would have put most finished prod-
ucts to shame. He'd scanned a photo of Josh standing at
Glacier Point with Half Dome in the background and
had incorporated it into text that summed up Josh's phi-
losophy of life: "Respect nature as the gift it is and work
toward lessening man's impact on the environment." In
addition, Sam had attached a list of the donations that
had been received to date, including a ten-thousand-
dollar gift from the Rocking M Ranch.

"By next spring when they start passing out schol-
arships, the Joshua O'Neal Scholarship Fund will be able
to award two each year to students—one male, one female—interested in studying forestry, earth sciences or
conservation," he said. The quiet pride she heard in his
voice had touched Jenny, and she'd had to blink back
tears.

Fortunately, Ida Jane had chosen that moment to enter
the room pushing the high-tech walker, which she'd
graduated to earlier that week.

Tucker's warm little body wriggled against her. Blinking, she sat up a little straighter to get settled and was
just about to put the baby to her breast when an odd
flickering light in the distance caught her attention. The

glow—whatever it was—was too far to see distinctly but close enough to be on Rocking M land.

"What's that? Taillights? A police car?" Rising, she walked to the window. Putting her nose to the glass, she squinted into the blackness.

Red. Yellow. White. Dancing. The answer hit her like a slap across the cheek. "Fire."

Tucking the startled baby under her arm like a football, Jenny raced out of the room and down the hall. Sam's door was partly open; she stiff-armed it, making it explode against the wall.

"Sam," she cried. "Come quick. Fire."

He sat up. "Where?"

"Outside. Toward the road."

He was out of bed by the time she reached the light switch. He dashed into the adjoining bathroom, but not before Jenny got an eyeful. A lean back tanned to the waist. Rock-hard buttocks, pale white. Wide, powerful thighs adorned with sparse dark hair.

"How far away?" he asked, emerging a second later wrapped in a white terry-cloth robe that reached to his calves.

His tone was all business, but Jenny stuttered, trying to get her brain to cooperate. "I don't know." She pointed in the direction of her room. "I could see it from my window."

He grabbed the portable phone from its cradle beside his bed and hurried past her. Jenny sagged against the wall, pressing Tucker to her chest like a shield.

He returned a few seconds later, handing her the phone. "Call Donnie. It looks pretty close to the hay barn. Hank's rounding up the men."

Without giving her a second glance, he dropped his robe and opened a drawer in the built-in wardrobe. Jenny flattened her back to the wall, juggling both child and phone. In the reflection of the French doors opposite them, she had a clear view of Sam dressing. Jeans, no time for underwear. Socks and boots followed. He grabbed a gray-and-green plaid flannel shirt as he turned around.

"Hurry."

His voice was low and calm, but Jenny's fingers wouldn't cooperate. Tucker, undoubtedly picking up on his mother's agitation, started to cry. Finally, she punched in 911.

Sam disappeared into the bathroom. He returned just as she gave the information to the dispatcher. Her voice sounded strained and brittle. "And can you patch me through to Donnie Grimaldo? Please."

Sam paused for a millisecond then brushed his knuckle against her chin before dashing off. A blur of plaid flannel and denim, he took the stairs three at a time. "Be careful," she called from the top of the staircase. She didn't know if he heard because the front door slammed but a heartbeat later.

"Oh, Tucker, I don't like this," she whispered, feeling her baby son's tears on her cheek. Or were they hers?

"Jenny?" a thin, reedy voice called from the first floor.

Ida Jane. Always a light sleeper, her great-aunt would want to know what was going on. Soothing Tucker's sobs as she went, Jenny trotted down the staircase.

"There's a fire out in the field, Auntie. Sam and the men are headed there now. I think I heard him say something about a hay barn, so it could be bad," she added hoarsely.

Ida Jane was already out of bed by the time Jenny reached the first-floor bedroom. She angled her walker past Jenny and started toward the kitchen. "They'll need coffee when they get back. Come along."

"Let me get Tucker fed and in bed, then I'll be right down."

Half an hour later, Jenny returned to the brightly lit country kitchen to find Ida Jane and Greta working side by side making biscuits. The smell of coffee made Jenny's stomach growl.

"Emergencies build appetites. Might as well be prepared to feed 'em," Greta said, glancing over her shoulder. Her thinning brown hair stood up in back; and over her jeans she wore a shirt that had to belong to Hank.

"Let me do that for you, Auntie," Jenny said, rushing to help. "You should sit down and rest your hip."

Ida put up a small fuss, but Jenny could tell she was grateful to sit in the padded armchair Sam had moved into the kitchen just for her. Jenny knelt down and pulled the ottoman over so Ida could elevate her feet. "How's that?"

"Just fine," Ida said a trifle breathlessly. "All this commotion reminds me of the first fire out here."

"When was that, Miss Ida?" Greta asked.

Ida let out a sigh. "The actual date escapes me, but it wasn't long after your mother was born, Jenny. I remember thinking it was a good thing Suzy and Lorena were in town at the time. I was living in Oakland, working for the telephone company, when I heard about the fire."

Jenny finished placing the last of the dough cutouts on the cookie sheet Greta had prepared. The sprinkling of cornmeal made her fingers slick. She inhaled deeply, enjoying the comforting smell of flour, salt and water.

"What was the old house like?" Jenny asked. "I don't think I've ever seen a picture of it."

"You wouldn't have," Ida said. "Daddy destroyed every picture there was of it. I truly thought it would kill him when Suzy married Bill Scott, the man he claimed cheated him out of his family's homestead."

Jenny knew the story well. Suzy, Ida's younger sister, was a beauty who could have had any man in the county. For reasons no one seemed to understand, she chose to marry Bill Scott, her father's archenemy. A man sixteen years her senior.

"Suzy was in town, visiting Mama when it happened. She only visited when she knew Daddy was going to be away. The night of the fire, Daddy was at his lodge. Those were the war years and things were rationed, but Bill was quite well off, and Suzy always had gas coupons. She would have returned to the Rocking M before Daddy got home, but the sheriff came and told her the ranch house had caught fire with Bill in it."

Even though Jenny had heard this story a hundred times or more, tonight she had a sudden image of Sam caught in an inferno, blazing timbers crashing about him. Her hands started to tremble and she almost dropped the cookie sheet. She quickly deposited the pan in the prewarmed oven and walked to the window. She heard the sound of the dogs' frenzied barking. Cupping her hands to the glass, she looked into the distance.

"Headlights," she said, her heartbeat speeding up. "Someone's coming."

She beat Greta to the door and hurried out to the porch, clasping her arms about her against the cold. She'd changed into sweatpants and a bulky sweatshirt, but the night had turned bitter.

The yard lights helped illuminate the arrival of a patrol car. Donnie Grimaldo leaped from the driver's seat and rushed around to the passenger door. His obvious haste heightened Jenny's fear. Her fingers closed around the fabric at her throat as she watched him bend to help someone stand. *Sam.*

Jenny grabbed a post for support. Her knees suddenly had less substance than the dough she'd just handled.

As Sam and Donnie neared the porch, she spotted burn marks and a long rip on the sleeve of Sam's jacket. "Oh my God," she cried. "Is he okay? Should I call an ambulance?"

At the sound of her voice, Sam lifted his chin. His eyes were watery, his face blackened and streaked. He pushed away from Donnie. "I can manage," he said, his voice an unrecognizable growl that was followed by a gut-wrenching cough.

He wavered on wobbly legs before Donnie grabbed his arm. "Shut up and hang on."

Together they stumbled up the ramp that Sam had recently built for Ida Jane.

"Smoke inhalation," Donnie barked, brushing through the door she held open. "Damn fool won't let me call the paramedics."

"I'm fine," Sam muttered, his voice three tones deeper than usual.

Donnie helped Sam to the armchair at the head of the table—his usual spot. In the bright light of the kitchen, Jenny could take stock of the damage. His hair was plastered to his head with sweat. Soot streaked his face and hands. His canvas jacket was charred and looked like a rag. A red gash dissected the top of his hand, but it was hard to see how deep the wound was because Sam kept tucking it out of sight. Other bloody spots had already crusted over—a cut on his neck, another at the top of his ear.

"What the hell happened?" Jenny demanded to know.

Sam looked at Donnie, not her. Something in their silent exchange told her that Sam knew how close he'd come to adding to her problems. She was hit by a melange of emotions so powerful she almost collapsed to the floor.

Luckily, Greta took charge. "Jenny, run out front and break off a few stems of rosemary for me. I'll get a pot of water boiling. We need to make a steam bath for his lungs."

Jenny glanced at Donnie for one brief second. The deputy's grim expression revealed more than she wanted to know. It had been close, too close.

SAM USED the tented towel above a pan of steaming water as an escape. If he breathed deeply enough and closed his eyes tight enough, he could almost block out the look of fear he'd seen in Jenny's eyes. Only a fool would take the kind of risk he'd taken tonight. An idiot. A moron. He wanted to kick himself but couldn't work up the energy.

"How's the water, Sam?" Ida Jane asked. "Hot enough?"

Not as hot as it's going to get when Jenny learns the truth, he thought. He nodded and pulled the towel a little tighter. He could sense Jenny hovering behind him, as if afraid he might keel over.

You risked everything for a cat. What the hell kind of fool are you?

Sam tried to reconstruct the series of events that led to his impulsive act. He'd raced off to the fire in his truck while Hank and the rest of the crew loaded another truck with shovels, a generator and hoses.

By the time he got there, the fire was less than a hundred feet from the shed that housed his well pump and secondary-holding tank. The dried grass snapped and crackled as the flames snaked forward.

Sam had grabbed a shovel and started to create a firebreak between the shed and the hay barn, which if it ignited, would create an inferno of horrific proportions.

The men were making progress—and they could hear the sound of the California Department of Forestry fire trucks in the distance. Sam had been in the process of hooking up a portable generator to a pump, when a pile of straw and windblown leaves that had collected against the wall of the pump house caught fire.

Shovel in hand, he raced toward it, knowing instinctively it was too late. The wind was fanning the flames. No thin stream of water from a garden hose was going to put that out.

From the corner of his eye, he saw a silver streak enter the hay barn. A barn cat. One of several that lived in this compound. Periodically, Sam visited the SPCA to purchase mousers to rid his barns of pesky critters. This particular tabby was a shy sort that spurned human contact.

For reasons Sam couldn't explain, the thought of that cat being burned in his hay barn was not acceptable. He left Hank to work on the pump and raced to the spot he'd seen her enter the building. A thin meow was his only guide. He scaled the ten-foot wall of bales. A layer of smoke, which had become trapped under the metal roof, blinded him. His lungs burned. He was about to give up, when he spotted her in the far corner.

He reached for her and was rewarded with a stiletto-like gash on his hand. He caught her by the scruff of the neck and stuffed her under one arm while he tried to figure out an escape route. His heavy canvas jacket took a beating but gradually she quieted.

Through the building's lone window, Sam saw that the flames had branched. Time was running out. Unfortunately, the wind had shifted and smoke was pouring in behind him, forcing him to crawl arm over arm, without squishing the cat, to the far side of the building. He couldn't rappel down the face of the bales with a cat in one hand, so he shimmied between the stack and the wall with his back against the building's metal skin.

A small secondary grass fire on the north side of the building scorched his jacket through the metal siding. Sweat blinded him, and his foot slipped. In a desperate attempt to fling the cat to safety, he twisted sideways and his head collided with a steel beam.

Sam didn't recall losing consciousness, but the next thing he remembered was Donnie calling for help. "Over here. Get him to my car."

Sneaking his hand under the towel, Sam eyed the four-inch red streak on the top of his hand. There's going to be hell to pay when Jenny hears about this, he thought.

Ida Jane's voice brought him back to the present. "Is the steam helping?"

Sam inhaled slowly, deeply. He had to fight to keep from coughing, but managed to keep the breath inside for almost a second. "Yes," he said, exhaling. "It's worked magic. I'm gonna go clean up."

"Wait," Jenny cried, placing her hand on his shoulder. The touch held a charge that tingled all the way to his arches. "Aren't you going to tell us what happened? We barely got two words out of Donnie before he left."

"We lost a couple of outbuildings, but Hank and the boys saved the barn."

A burning sensation at the base of his throat made him cough. Jenny passed him a mug of something hot; Sam thought he tasted lemon and honey. It soothed the seared lining of his throat. "Thanks," he muttered, not making eye contact.

Jenny gently touched the red stripe on his hand. "How'd you get cut?"

Sam was prepared to lie in order to postpone the inevitable, but Ida Jane rescued him. "Tall tales are best left till morning," she said firmly. "Jenny, help the poor man to bed—although I'd suggest a shower first. He smells like the main course at a pig roast."

JENNY HURRIED to do her aunt's bidding. "Let me help you," she said, putting out her hand.

She didn't like the way it trembled, but Sam didn't appear to notice. He grabbed the edge of the table and hauled himself to his feet. He seemed just as tall and in control as usual—until he stumbled against a chair.

Jenny looked at his face, which was still streaked with soot. "You can lean on me," she said softly.

"I can make it by myself," he replied gruffly.

"Quit being cantankerous. It doesn't become you," she said, sliding under his arm so it was looped over her shoulder. "I'm going upstairs anyway. You might as well let me help."

He made a grunting sound but didn't pull away.

"Your sharp eyes saved the ranch," he said when they were about halfway up the stairs. "Jenny Perfect to the rescue."

His tone was dripping with sarcasm, which momentarily threw her, until she figured out that it was his way of keeping her at her arm's length.

When they reached the landing, he started to push her

away, but Jenny dug her fingers into the softer flesh at his waist. Sam wasn't reed thin like Josh, but he wasn't fat either—just substantial. "Let me get your shower started."

He let out a sigh, but didn't object. Jenny knew why. She'd felt the slight tremor that passed through his body and knew he was reaching a state of exhaustion. She guided him to the master bathroom, decorated in Santa Fe tile and turquoise accents. The shower was the size of Jenny's walk-in closet in her old house. There wasn't a shower door.

After closing the lid on the toilet so Sam could sit down, she pushed up the sleeve of her sweatshirt and leaned into the stall to turn on the water. The gush of warm water was almost instantaneous. She fiddled with the adjustment, getting a bit damp in the process. Water beaded up on her arm.

Pulling back, she used the end of the towel that was still draped around Sam's neck to wipe off her arm.

"Do you need help getting undressed?"

He shook his head from side to side. He was hunched forward, his elbows on his knees, fingers linked.

Jenny squatted in front of him. "Sam, I've been a wife. I'm not a prude. I can hel—"

Whatever platitude Jenny had been about to spout was ripped from her mind the second Sam lifted his head to look at her. The bright light of the bathroom revealed what had been hidden before. Sam's eyebrows were nothing more than tiny shriveled wisps, his lashes appeared to have melted and the soot on his cheeks and forehead cloaked red welts that looked like burns.

She grabbed his right hand—the one with the red sliver of blood across it. The hair on the back of his hand was gone.

''Oh my God,'' she cried, rocking back so suddenly her feet gave out and she landed on her butt on the cold tile floor. ''You...you're hurt. Burned. You could have been killed.''

He closed his eyes and sighed but didn't try to refute her charge.

Panic made her lash out. She kicked her heels against the slick floor trying to scoot backward. One slipper popped off. ''You put yourself in jeopardy for a few lousy bales of hay?'' she cried. ''You selfish bastard.''

Sam heard her fury; he understood her fear. He wanted to comfort her, console her, even refute the argument, but he couldn't. His brain felt full of smoke. His nostril hair was singed; all he could smell was smoke. He sure as hell didn't need Jenny yelling at him to know he was a screwup. He'd heard that all his life from Diane.

Desperate for some relief, he put his hands on his knees and pushed himself up. Through a blur of watery haze, he turned toward the sound of running water. Barefoot—he'd managed to get his socks off while Jenny was turning on the faucet—he stumbled toward the big open cavern.

He didn't bother undressing. The water offered a refuge. The clean mist was warm and healing.

''Dammit, Sam, I'm not done talking to you,'' she said, following on his heels.

''Fine.''

He turned just enough to grab her arm. With one quick tug, she stumbled after him, propelling him deeper into the shower stall. His foot slipped and she wound up plastered to his chest, her chin brushing his shoulder.

Water cascaded over his head. It ran into her face when she looked up at him, her mouth open. She spit out a mouthful of water like a swimmer surfacing, then arched back as if to scold him more.

The last thing Sam wanted to hear was a lecture. He wanted someone to hold him and tell him things were going to be okay, but he'd settle for a pair of lips on his. Jenny's lips.

Ducking his head beneath the cascade, he kissed her.

She struggled against him for the space of a heartbeat then her fists went flat. Her eyes closed—against the emotion she was feeling or the water he didn't know. Or care. Separated by a sopping sweatshirt and saggy flannel—two of the least sexy materials known to man— Sam's body reacted as if Jenny were modeling the latest fashions from Victoria's Secret. The steam finally loosened the knot in his chest, but now another knot built— lower.

A voice of reason tried to push past the greedy, life-affirming rejoicing in his mind. But she felt so good in his arms, so right, he couldn't quit.

And somewhere in the middle of his pheromone-saturated brain, a truth solidified. Jenny was kissing him back. Her lips parted to give him freer access. A tiny sigh passed between them, and he swallowed it like a balm to his parched soul.

She tasted of mint toothpaste and herbal tea. Her tongue started out shy but quickly dived into a passionate exchange that made Sam think about where he might have stashed his condoms. It had been so long since he'd needed them, he couldn't remember.

That tiny foray into reality sucked Sam into a big white room with a warning beacon flashing: *What the hell are you doing, O'Neal? Think.*

Reality hit like a bucket of ice water. *Too much. Too soon.* He wasn't a hormone-driven kid the way he'd been with Carley; this wasn't any ordinary lustful urge. This was Jenny, the woman he loved. And if he didn't stop now, he might never get a second chance to prove how much he loved her.

CHAPTER NINE

JENNY WASN'T PREPARED for the sensation to stop. For one heart-stopping moment—the second Sam's lips touched hers—she'd been transported to a safe place, a place where the loneliness of the past months was replaced by heat and need. A place where she wasn't just a mother or a niece or a sister or a widow. Where she was Jenny. A woman. Desirable. Alive.

Her response may have been fueled by months of deprivation—Josh had been in too much pain those last few months to tolerate touch of any kind—but all Jenny knew was that whatever Sam was offering, she wanted more of it. She needed the reassurance that Sam was alive. And so was she.

"No," Sam said, breaking the lock she had around his neck.

Jenny blinked away the moisture beaded on her lashes. The mist that enveloped them was steamy and smelled of smoke and Sam. Her fingers clung to the scruff of his soaking-wet collar. Although he'd pulled away with his upper body, she was still pressed against him from the chest down. His hardness, his desire, was muted only by the layers of wet clothing between them.

"Please," she whispered. The neediness in her voice resonated in the tiled stall.

"No. This isn't right."

She knew that, but it didn't stop her from reaching up

to cup the line of his jaw. His beard was rough, and she wanted to feel its abrasive quality against her skin.

Sam shifted them sideways so the water slanted between them like a silver diagonal from shoulder to hip. A fine mist clung to his melted eyelashes. Jenny noticed for the first time a small scar that would normally have been hidden by his eyebrow. She put her index finger on it and asked the question with her eyes.

His upper lip pulled back in a look Josh called Sam's run-for-cover smile. "A tribute from my ex-wife's father," Sam said, adding an extra couple of inches to the space between them.

Despite the warm water and the steam, Jenny shivered.

Sam dropped his arms, accidentally knocking Jenny's hand away. "Go to bed, Jenny. It's been a long day, and tomorrow's going to be worse."

"Why?" she asked, folding her arms across her chest. The emotional charge between them had triggered a release of her milk, which reminded her all too vividly who she was—Tucker and Lara's mother. Sam's dead brother's wife.

"Why what?" Sam asked, coughing. He turned into the steamy water and let it wash over his upturned face. He continued to cough, a loud rattle that echoed acoustically.

The smart thing would be to leave, but she couldn't get her legs to move. "Why will tomorrow be bad?" she asked.

He leaned one shoulder against the wall and started to unbutton his flannel shirt. The rush of water combined with fatigue made him fumble like a drunk.

Jenny brushed aside his hands. "Let me do that. Then I'll go. Why is tomorrow going to be so tough?"

He let his head loll back. "Because you're going to find out what really happened out there, and you'll pack your bags and leave."

Jenny's heart knocked erratically. "What do you mean?"

"About the cat," he swore, turning away just as she finished the last button. "Go, Jenny. I..."

He turned his back to her and slowly took off the shirt. Jenny stepped away, needing the space to keep from touching him. His broad tanned back was corded with muscles; faint whorls of hair were flattened by the torrent of water cascading over his shoulders. Red welts—scrape marks, she'd guess—marred the sleek perfection.

When he started to unbutton the waistband of his jeans, she retreated, recalling all too vividly the lack of underwear beneath those pants.

She grabbed a big thick towel from the bar opposite the shower and fled. Heedless of the wet footprints she left behind or the trail of water dripping from the hem of her sweatpants, she ran down the hallway to the safety of her room.

She dashed into her bathroom and quietly closed the door to the nursery. After stripping off her wet clothes, she toweled dry as briskly as her skin could tolerate.

Fool. Idiot. She turned on the overhead light and looked at herself in the unflattering brightness. Her wet hair hung in scraggly lengths—it really needed a cut. Her eyes were red from the water, her skin blotchy. Her breasts were large and unfamiliar and her belly sagged in unattractive folds.

If Josh were alive he'd have teased her out of her funk. He'd have reassured her that she was beautiful, desirable. But he wasn't here and she was so pathetically needy she'd turned to the only man around for comfort.

She leaned across the counter, careful not to disturb the baby paraphernalia. "You are a miserable excuse for a human being," she told her reflection. "Sam has enough problems without you throwing yourself at him for reassurance that you're not just a pair of mammary glands with feet."

A chuckle made her turn sharply. Andi stood in the doorway that connected to Jenny's bedroom. "Naked and talking to yourself. Not a good sign," she said, grinning.

Jenny let out a low groan and reached for her terry-cloth robe hanging beside the bathtub. "What are you doing here?"

"Ida called to tell me about the fire. I came out to see if I could help. Wanna tell me what all that muttering was about?"

Snugging up the fabric belt, Jenny reached for the hair dryer—anything to postpone the inevitable. As she feathered her damp tresses with her fingers, she looked at her sister's reflection in the mirror. Jenny and Andi hadn't talked about anything besides Ida Jane and business for so long, she didn't know where to begin. Would this sister understand? Jenny had a feeling Kristin would, but she was in Oregon and wasn't scheduled to visit for another couple of weeks.

"It's nothing. I was upset with Sam. He put himself in danger and…" Jenny turned off the dryer. *And what? He kissed me? Or I kissed him? Which was it?*

"Yeah, sure. Like I believe that. Come on. I'm sleeping with you, and you're going to tell me everything. I learned how to interrogate people in the marines. You'll be putty in my hands."

Andi's teasing laugh made a shiver course down Jenny's spine. She'd been just that and more in Sam's hands. Sam's wonderful hands. Even now, that one thought was all it took to make her hungry for more.

You're in bad shape, girl. Bad, bad shape.

Minutes later, the two sisters were snuggled together in the down mattress of Jenny's double bed. A yellowish glow from the night-light in her bathroom cast long shadows across the walls and ceiling.

"So?" Andi asked. "What's gives with you and Sam?"

Jenny shook her head. "It was no big deal."

Andi pinched the fleshy part of Jenny's upper arm. "Ouch!" she hissed, batting Andi's hand away.

"I told you. I know torture."

The silliness of the comment made Jenny giggle and within seconds she was consumed with laughter that quickly segued to tears. Andi watched, her obvious mirth turning to concern. Jenny grabbed a tissue from the box beside the bed and blew her nose. "Sorry."

Andi turned on her side, placing head on hand to look at Jenny. "Okay, then, the truth this time. I heard that anguished plea in the bathroom mirror so don't even think about lying."

Jenny stared at the ceiling. The semidarkness made it a little easier to confess. "I was helping Sam into the shower and I sort of stumbled and wound up in the shower with him—fully dressed, of course—and we kissed. I'm sure it was just a close-brush-with-death kind of thing for him." She didn't add, *But I liked it. It felt wonderful.*

Andi ran her free hand back and forth in front of Jenny's eyes. "Are you smoking crack?"

Jenny turned her head. "What?"

"Drugs of some sort? I've met a few delusional drug

addicts over the years. They're good at building elaborate fantasies…like that one.''

Jenny frowned. "It was just a kiss.''

Andi made an impatient snort. "I know Sam O'Neal, Jen. If he kissed you, it was because he wanted to, not because you were handy." She snickered. "I know because I've given him ample opportunities over the years to kiss me and he never did. Not once. Well, *once*. On the forehead. When I was particularly persistent, but that was it.''

Jenny pulled the covers over her head. "I kissed him back," she mumbled. "It was really good.''

Andi's chuckle made the mattress jiggle. "Way cool. Can I tell Kris?''

"No.''

She shrugged. "She'll find out. You'll blab sooner or later. You always do. Jenny Perfect has to confess, otherwise she's not perfect.''

Jenny sat up sharply. "Dammit, would you quit with that name? Would someone so perfect be attracted to her own brother-in-law when her husband has only been dead two and a half months?''

The words, once spilled, seemed to take on a life of their own, echoing in the big room like a yodel.

"Wow," Andi whispered in hushed awe. "This is serious? You've actually got the hots for Sam?''

Jenny sank back down. She felt sick to her stomach admitting it, but there was no use lying. Andi was right—Jenny always blabbed. "Maybe. I don't know. I don't think I want to know.''

Andi snuggled close and patted Jenny's cheek. "It's okay, kiddo. You're young, you're alive. Sam's a sexy guy.''

Jenny closed her eyes and sighed. Those sounded like

weak excuses for what was surely immoral behavior. Jenny owed Josh more loyalty than two and a half months of mourning. She owed it to herself, too.

"That kiss was an aberration, Andi. It's not going to happen again. I'll talk to Sam in the morning and make it clear that we can't be attracted to each other. Period."

Andi flopped back. "Yeah, that'll work."

Jenny ignored the sarcasm. It *would* work. It had to.

SAM PAUSED beside Jenny's door. At first, he thought he heard her crying, but the instant his hand touched the doorknob he knew the sound was laughter. And a second voice was evident. *Andi.*

He relaxed. His apology could wait.

He had no excuse for his behavior. He just hoped it wouldn't ruin the fragile balance they'd created the past couple of weeks. He'd planned on slowly courting Jenny over the course of the next year or two. Instead, he'd lost his mind and attacked her in the shower.

Turning, he headed downstairs to get a drink. Maybe whiskey would help, he thought. The scrape marks on his back hurt and his right shoulder ached, but that was nothing compared to the knot of dread in his belly.

Sighing, he trotted down the stairs in stocking feet. His exhaustion had vaporized the instant they'd kissed. Unfortunately, the encounter had left him recharged in more ways than one.

After struggling out of wet jeans that had stuck to him like melted plastic, he'd lathered and scrubbed until his skin hurt, but no amount of mental gymnastics could minimize his body's longings. Finally, a blast of cold water had done the trick.

With teeth chattering, he'd dried off and dug through his drawer for his lone pair of flannel pajamas, last year's

Christmas gift from Ida Jane. Normally, Sam was such a light sleeper he'd never had to worry about being awakened accidentally while sleeping in the buff. But he should have known better with guests in the house.

He went to the liquor cabinet beside the fireplace. The orange glow of the fire burning in the hearth filled the room with a warm, pleasant homey quality—a far cry from the raging blaze he'd encountered a few hours earlier. After downing a shot of single malt, he poured a second then wandered toward the east-facing glass doors at the far end of the room.

"Are you here to watch the sunrise, too?"

Sam jumped a full foot to the right before his brain registered the voice. Ida Jane. Patting his chest until his heartbeat returned to normal, he faced his guest, who was sitting in the recliner, a woolen throw gathered across her legs. "Miss Ida, you almost gave me a heart attack. What are you doing up?"

He sat down on the matching mahogany leather sofa across from her. He'd picked the furniture because it fit the decor, but he seldom sat here, preferring instead the solitude of his office or the coziness of the reading nook in Jenny's bedroom. Jenny and Ida Jane had made more use of the great room in the past weeks than he had in twelve years. The addition of two baby swings and a playpen made it look like a real home.

"I like to watch the sunrise. I'm a bit early, but when you get to my age, you don't take anything for granted."

Sam smiled. He liked this old woman more than he could say. He'd never known a grandmother, only having met his mother's mother once when he was seven or eight. He vaguely remembered the experience as a tedious bus ride winding up in a busy town with rows and rows of brick houses so close together they almost touched. They didn't stay long at the skinny building with the planter box outside the window.

Sam couldn't picture his grandmother, but he vividly recalled the flowers in the box—purple and white with round faces that looked like little men with black mustaches and bushy eyebrows. On the bus home, Sam had asked about the flowers, but Diane had cuffed him, saying, "I don't want to talk about it. Or her. Ever again."

And they hadn't. That was Diane's way. When Josh was old enough to ask about his heritage, Sam had said, "All dead. Don't bother asking."

"Quite the adventurous night, wouldn't you say, Sam?"

To put it mildly. "Definitely."

"It got me thinking about our old home. It burnt down, you know."

Sam knew. The people who'd owned the ranch before Sam had lived in the mobile home Hank and Greta now occupied. When Sam had expressed an interest in placing his house on the flat area across from the barn, they'd told Sam the story of the original homestead.

"You lived here growing up, didn't you, Miss Ida?"

She nodded. Her hair looked a bit wild in the dim light. Her face seemed amazingly alert. "Up until I was sixteen. That's when Daddy lost the place in a poker game."

Sam blinked in surprise. He'd always pictured her as a child, not a young woman, when her family moved into town.

"Suzy was eleven at the time. It almost broke my heart, but I think Suzy preferred living in town. She was the social one." Ida made a swishing motion with her hand. "She loved action. I was content with the animals and the quiet. She was bored to tears."

Sam pondered that point a few seconds. "And yet, she wound up marrying the man who won the place from your father, right?" he asked, trying to recall all the pieces of the story he'd heard over the years.

"That's true," Ida Jane said. "Of course she sold the place after Bill died. Said it held bad memories for her."

Sam sipped his drink, savoring the slow burn that eased the harsh tightness in his throat.

"Bill was her husband? The man who was killed in the fire that destroyed the farmhouse?" Sam asked. He felt a little strange asking—after the close call he'd experienced, but he couldn't deny his curiosity.

"Poor Bill," Ida Jane said sadly. "He and Suzy had only been married a short time when he died. Less than two years, I believe. From what my mother told me, it was a difficult period for him. He loved Suzy and adored Lorena, but Suzy was a bit high-strung, she could exhaust a person. Especially someone as quiet and laid-back as Bill."

"Did you know him well?" Sam was curious about the man—Jenny's grandfather.

"Heavens, yes. He was our neighbor the whole time I was growing up. The Rocking M was much smaller than it is now. After Bill got this property, he deeded the two parcels together." She chuckled. "He kept the Rocking M name and brand instead of his own. Daddy always said Bill did it just to annoy him."

"I take it your father was something of a poor loser?"

Ida Jane sighed. "Truth is, Daddy liked gambling a whole lot more than he liked ranching. Bill was a good rancher, Daddy wasn't.

"The ranch had belonged to my mother's family. She inherited it when her parents and brother passed away in an influenza epidemic. Daddy tried to keep it up, but his heart wasn't in ranching. The only reason he risked the deed in that poker game was because the back taxes had come due and he couldn't pay them. He'd have lost the place one way or the other, but he'd never admit that.''

Sam smiled. He'd always been charmed by Ida Jane's ability to tell a story. ''So how'd your family end up with the old bordello?''

She gave a small laugh. ''When we moved to town, Daddy started working in real estate. He made good money—the man could sell fleas to a dog, and Mama put her foot down about the gambling. We were living in a nice little place not far from Jenny and Josh's house when the old bordello went on the market. It had been used as a boarding house for a number of years and was in pretty bad shape. Daddy snapped it up. He planned to turn it into a hotel and was in the process of fixing it up when Mama got sick. Cancer.''

''That's too bad.''

Ida nodded. She seemed caught up in the past and went on as though he hadn't spoken. ''Suzy was working at the diner, and Mama was worried about her, but there wasn't anything she could do. I was in my last year of college in Missouri. I came home for Suzy's graduation, then the next thing I know she's run off to Reno and married Bill Scott.

''Daddy didn't take it well. Suzy had always been his little princess, and Bill was quite a bit older than her. Daddy went on a bender and threatened to kill Bill.''

Ida sighed. ''The trouble with old grudges is they make you a prime suspect when the person you hate dies under mysterious circumstances.''

Sam sat forward, resting his elbows on his knees. ''The fire wasn't an accident?''

Ida Jane made a who-knows motion. "I was living in Oakland at the time. But there was a lot of talk. You know how small towns are."

"Did the sheriff name your father as a suspect?"

She shook her head. "I don't think so. There wasn't any proof. But there was gossip. Some speculated Daddy did it out of revenge, others said Suzy did it for the money."

"People thought your sister killed him?"

Ida frowned. "You have to understand. Suzy was a bright shiny penny in a bowlful of nickels. She didn't have a lot of friends. The other girls didn't trust her with their boyfriends. She had a bit of a reputation."

She paused in thought. "Bill wasn't the most handsome fellow around, but he was one of the richest. Mama told me he'd come into town almost every day to eat lunch at the diner where Suzy worked. Leave big tips. Treat her nice. I think my sister was looking for a way out of Gold Creek and she thought Bill would give it to her."

Sam didn't like the uncomfortable feeling in his midsection. *Must be the booze.* "Why do you think she married him?"

Ida Jane sighed. "Suzy and I were never real close. When I came back for her graduation, I brought along my beau—the man I thought was going to ask my father for my hand in marriage."

Sam heard a tangible sadness in her tone.

"But he took one look at my sister and fell out of love with me and in love with her. I was pretty bitter at the time. I blamed Suzy, but the fact is, she couldn't help being pretty any more than Kristin can."

She sighed. "We didn't speak for years. I dropped out of school and took a job in Oakland. Daddy chased off my beau, threatening to have him shot. And a few months later, Suzy ran away with Bill.''

"What happened to your boyfriend?" Sam asked, caught up in the story. "Did you ever hear from him?"

"Yes, I did. He joined the army after he left here. He wrote me from Fort Benning, Georgia, right before he was shipped out. He apologized for breaking my heart and hoped we could still be friends. A month or so later, I got a telegram from his mother telling me he'd been killed in action.''

Sam reached out and took her hand. Her paper-thin skin was cold, and he chaffed it between his palms. "That's a sad story, Miss Ida. I'm sorry I brought it up.''

"It was a long time ago. Every one of them is dead. My mother passed away right before Lori's third birthday. Daddy lived another six years, but he'd failed a lot by then. Suzy died the year Lori graduated from high school.''

Neither spoke for a minute, then Sam asked, "Do you think Suzy cared for Bill when she married him? Or was he just a means to an end?" He hated the tentative tone of his question. What did any of this matter to him?

Ida thought a moment. "Well, there was a lot of talk in town about *why* she married Bill. Particularly when Lori was born two months prematurely. The gossips had a field day. Snickering behind Suzy's back. They didn't make it easy for her.

"But I think they felt badly about the way they treated her when she and Lori came back here to live. You could tell Suzy wasn't right in the head. And Lori was the sweetest little girl that ever lived—all sunshine and sugar. That could be why people tried so hard to help when the triplets were born.''

Sam had heard a number of tales about the night of

the triplets' birth and the heroic efforts that had gone into trying to rescue Lorena and Michael Sullivan when their Volkswagen bus slid off the road in a snowstorm and crashed down a steep embankment.

"But to answer your question—I get a little side-tracked sometimes—I do think Suzy cared for Bill. He was a bit of a hermit and set in his ways, but he was kind to her, and generous to a fault. He bought her a new car for a wedding present—one of the first con-vertibles in the county. It was a thing of beauty."

"But they never determined how the fire started?"

Ida shook her head. "Some thought Bill might have been drinking and fallen. Perhaps hitting his head on something and somehow the log fire sparked the blaze."

Sam made a steeple with his fingers and stared at the flames dancing behind the protective screen.

"I never believed the gossip about Suzy," Ida Jane said softly. "People said it was suspicious that Suzy had Lori with her when the fire broke out. They wondered why a mother would take a toddler out on a cold winter's night instead of leaving her home with Bill."

"Did you ask her why?"

Ida looked away. "No. I never did. But I had a hunch it was because Bill was drinking. Suzy never said so, but that's what I think."

"And you're not sure Bill was the baby's father, are you?" Sam was just speculating, but by the look on Ida Jane's face he knew he'd guessed correctly. "I'm sorry, Ida Jane. I shouldn't have said that."

Ida lifted her hand wanly. "Looking back at the past is like turning over a rock. All the dark critters scatter, and you see things you don't really want to know exist."

Sam lifted her hand and kissed the back of it. "Es-pecially late at night."

Her fingers closed around his, her grip surprisingly strong. "What you should know is that Lori—the triplets' mother—was lightness and love. She and Suzy showed up on my doorstep when Lori was about ten. They moved in with me, and I knew right away that Suzy was sick. She'd spend weeks at a time in bed. The doctors couldn't find anything wrong and labeled her a hypochondriac. After a while, she refused to leave the house. Eventually, she stopped talking. I was afraid she might hurt herself. Or Lori. So I had her committed.

"But Lorena would ride her bike to the Pine Glen Rest Home every week to visit her mother. She never complained, never whined about how unfortunate she was. She was a sweet girl, and everyone in town loved her. That's why it hurt so badly when she died."

Like my brother. Sam squeezed her hand supportively. "But she left behind three wonderful gifts."

Ida Jane nodded, tears spilling over her eyes. "They were my blessings. A reward I never deserved. Oh, Sam, if you only knew—"

"I do know, Ida Jane," he said. "You're an amazing woman and you did a fabulous job raising those girls. Look at how incredible Jenny is. What a terrific mother she is to the twins."

"And you're a good father, too, Sam. I hate to say it, but you're probably a better father than your brother would have been."

When Sam started to protest, she looked at him sternly. "I don't mean to speak poorly of Josh. I loved that boy to pieces, but he reminded me of Suzy in some ways. Like the world revolved around him. You're just the opposite. You put others first. Even cats."

Sam blanched. "You heard about that, huh?"

She nodded, a wry smile on her lips.

"Well, believe me, I'll never do that again," he said, rubbing the scratch on his hand.

Ida Jane snickered. "Yes, you will. That's just the kind of man you are. And, Sam, two words of advice—don't apologize."

He blinked. "I beg your pardon."

"Don't let anyone—even my niece—make you feel badly about doing the right thing. You saved that poor creature's life. You deserve a reward."

The whiskey in Sam's belly somersaulted. He felt his cheeks burn. "Thanks, Ida. I'll…ah…tell Jenny you said so." *Right after I apologize.*

"You do that. Now, help me up. I'm plumb tuckered out. Would you hand me my walker?"

Sam did as she asked and accompanied her to her door. "Get some sleep, Sam. The babies will be awake soon, and both you and Jenny will be crying the blues."

Sam nodded. The twins were never far from his thoughts. They were the reason he had to cool his ardor. Gossip was destructive, as Ida Jane had just reminded him, and he refused to do anything that might compromise Jenny and the twins' futures.

Sam started away, but paused. "Miss Ida, do you think Jenny and I…never mind."

Ida's chuckle eased the knot that seemed permanently lodged in his chest. "Jenny is a lot like her mother, Sam. She loves easily and is easy to love. Things will work out the way they're supposed to whether we worry about them or not."

Sam blew her a kiss then walked upstairs. Ida was a wise old woman. Worrying wasn't going to change a thing. Sam could only hope things would work out the way he wanted them to.

CHAPTER TEN

"AND THEN OUT FLIES this bag of bones with fur. Butt over ears, hissing like an old tire with a pinhole in it. Scared the devil out of me."

Sam caught just enough of Hank's impassioned speech to know he was never going to live down the story of his encounter with the barn cat. Bracing himself for the worst, he squared his shoulders and entered the sunny kitchen.

He'd overslept and wasn't moving too friskily thanks to the ache in his lower back, but he'd figured his tardiness might work to his advantage—obviously, he'd been wrong.

"'Morning, everyone," he said from the doorway. He nodded at the group sitting around his table then made a beeline for the coffeepot.

Greta had a cup poured for him by the time he got there. "The least I can do for a hero," she said, grinning.

With her hair pulled back in its standard bun, Greta looked all business—except for the twinkle in her blue eyes. Sam vaguely remembered seeing her last night—well past midnight. Was he the only one who felt as though he'd been trampled by a fire-breathing dragon?

He focused on the window ledge just past her shoulder. Something new caught his eye. A series of mismatched jars with cuttings from plants in them. Tender white roots were spinning tangled webs. *Jenny's touch.*

Her house in town was filled with plants. Sam had helped with the rigorous watering schedule toward the end of her pregnancy. It suddenly occurred to him that she hadn't brought any plants with her.

Sam took a sip of the scalding liquid then looked at his foreman. "Have you been telling lies again, Hank?"

The man chuckled and shook his nearly bald pate. "Just expounding on what I saw. Not everybody would put his life on the line for a mangy barn cat. Might be some cat-lover society that would give you a medal or something. Ain't that right, Miss Jenny?"

The coffee lodged in Sam's throat, making his eyes water. Without waiting for Jenny's answer, he turned to Greta and asked, "What's for breakfast?"

"Griddle cakes and eggs." She stepped to the stove and fiddled with the burner. "I was getting worried— you're usually such an early riser, but Jenny said to let you sleep in."

Jenny. Sam stared at the black abyss in his cup. Jenny was as much to blame for his sleepless night as the fire. He'd replayed the incident in the shower a hundred times and couldn't forget the moment she linked her arms around his neck and sighed against his lips. That was more than capitulation—it was exaltation. Sam knew because he'd felt the same way.

He took another sip of the hot, powerful brew before turning to face the group at the big pine table. Ida Jane was sitting in Sam's usual place. Andi and Jenny flanked her; each was holding a twin. Ida Jane had her hands folded in her lap and was looking around like a spectator at a hockey game. Hank lounged near the hat rack, his long, lanky frame as relaxed as a human could be without falling over.

When they made eye contact, Hank nodded ruefully

and raised his mug in acknowledgment. That was when Sam spotted a white bandage on Hank's hand. "Is that a burn?"

"Naw. Got a scratch moving that darned generator. Thought the fire truck was gonna run over it."

"Have you had a tetanus shot recently?"

Hank gave Greta an inquiring look.

"Year before last," she said, cracking three eggs into the pan. "When he tangled with that rusty fence."

Sam smiled. He knew Hank hated to be reminded of the ignoble landing he'd made into a pile of old barbed wire.

Hank scowled. "What about you, boss? Had your rabies shot yet?"

Sam glanced at the mark on his hand. Before he could say anything, Jenny said, "Good point, Hank. Maybe we should find the cat and get her tested. The only other choice is for Sam to have those shots. I've heard that's pretty painful."

Sam didn't like the way that possibility brought a smile to her lips. *Her lips. I kissed those lips last night.* "The cat's fine," he said shortly. "She had all her shots when I got her. I get all my cats from the SPCA and I make sure they're vaccinated and fixed."

He couldn't read the look Jenny exchanged with her sister, but whatever the coded message, it made Andi grin. Had Jenny told her sister about their encounter in the shower? Sam wondered.

Andi looked at him just then and winked.

I'll take that as a yes, he thought, stifling a moan. He turned away, ostensibly to retrieve some silverware from the drawer, but mainly to hide his embarrassment.

"Here you go. Sit down and eat while it's hot," Greta ordered.

Sam took the empty chair directly across from Ida Jane. As he smoothed his napkin in his lap, he glanced from one sister to the other. Even though he'd known them both for almost twelve years, he'd never really realized how different they were. Andi was an attractive woman—a live wire, Josh called her. But not his type. *Not the way Jenny is.*

He knew better than to focus on that thought. He dropped his chin and tried to concentrate on the perfectly cooked eggs on his plate. Using his fork, he hacked into the first yolk and mopped it up with a hunk of griddle cake. The tacky texture of the egg mingled with the sweet flavor of maple syrup. "Mmm, good, Greta," he mumbled, his mouth not quite empty.

Jenny leaned forward and pushed a glass of milk his way.

"Were you able to save the hay?" Ida asked.

Sam had talked with Hank on the phone before turning in last night and he knew the answer, but he gave his foreman a nod to fill them in.

"Yes, ma'am. The pump house is a goner, but the hay is safe and nobody got hurt outside a few scratches."

"You and the boys did real good last night, Hank," Sam told his foreman. "We'll talk later about some bonuses."

Hank pushed off from the door and carried his cup to the sink. "Still a mess of mopping up to do," he said, giving Sam a nod. After shrugging on his western-style jacket, he walked to the door. "See y'all later."

Before Hank could make his exit, a visitor arrived— Donnie Grimaldo. In uniform. Greta offered him coffee, which he accepted. After he sat down, he looked at Sam and said, "You got lucky last night, my friend. Real lucky."

Sam's appetite disappeared. He knew how close it had been. He'd awakened periodically with the smell of fire in his nose and the sensation of heat pressing against his back. The metal siding of the wing walls had felt like a frying pan against his skin.

"Do you know what caused the fire?" Jenny asked. "Hank said he thought it might have been set off by an electrical spark in the pump."

Donnie planted his elbows on the table. "The arson team from Sacramento is on its way down. I'm not an expert in this field, but even I know a setup when I see it." He paused and looked at each person sitting around the table.

Sam grabbed the glass of milk to help dislodge his last bite of egg that had become stuck in his throat.

"How can you tell?" Andi asked.

Sam looked at Jenny. He recognized the whiteness around her lips. Fear. He'd seen it often those final few weeks before Josh died. Now he'd inadvertently brought it back into her life.

You invited her to live with you so you could take care of her, not put her life in jeopardy, he thought.

"…buckets," Donnie was saying.

Sam coughed. "What about buckets?"

Five-gallon buckets weren't an uncommon feature on a farm. Everything from motor oil to disinfectant came in them. Sam discouraged his employees from leaving them lying around, since any vessel that caught moisture could become a breeding ground for mosquitoes, but he didn't remember seeing any near the barn.

"We found some half-melted buckets near the site where the fire began. There appeared to be traces of kerosene in them. We won't know for sure until we get the lab tests, but that's a working guess.''

The four women gave a collective gasp. Sam pushed his plate away and took a sip of coffee. "Let me get this straight. You're saying someone came on to my property with the express purpose of setting it on fire?" Sam shook his head. "Nope. Couldn't happen. The dogs—"

"Whoever set it knows your dogs don't range that far," Donnie argued. "He or she stayed at the boundary of your land. The person started the fire then banked on the wind pushing it to your barn before you could react."

Sam's sick feeling intensified. He rose. "Let's talk about this in my office."

Jenny jumped in. "I don't think so. We all need to hear what's going on. Donnie, even if someone dumped those buckets of kerosene, what makes you think the barn was the target. Maybe they were just stupid. Or careless."

The look Donnie gave Sam said he didn't believe that scenario. And neither did Sam.

"Sam, I hate to say this, but somebody tried to burn you out. Or, at the very least, hurt you financially. This wasn't a sophisticated setup, so I'm guessing that it was a spur-of-the-moment thing. Someone trying to get back at you for something."

Jenny let out a small squeak.

Sam wished they were alone so he could put his arm around her shoulders and reassure her that everything was going to be okay.

He gave Donnie a look he hoped conveyed his displeasure at the fact that Donnie had brought this up in front of Jenny. "I'll have to see some evidence before I believe it. I don't have any enemies."

Donnie shrugged his broad shoulders. "It was arson, Sam. The who, how and why are up to the investigators to determine. But my gut feeling is this was someone with a grudge and a match. If a pro had set it, believe me, the hay would have been a complete loss."

Sam repressed a shudder. The hay was a valuable item, but it was secondary to the sense of violation he felt. Fire fighting was dangerous business. Someone had deliberately put the California Department of Forestry crew and the men working for Sam in danger. Sam knew they were damn lucky nobody had been seriously hurt.

"But who would do such a thing?" Jenny asked the question that was on the tip of Sam's tongue. "Everyone knows how dangerous and unpredictable a range fire can be. If the wind had shifted, it might have doubled back on the town."

Or headed toward the house, Sam thought, his stomach heaving.

"I don't know, Jen, but we're investigating. And we will find the person who did this," Donnie said.

Jenny sat forward, lifting Lara to her shoulder. The baby was starting to fret—no doubt picking up her mother's agitation. Sam started to suggest Jenny take the babies upstairs, when Jenny looked at Donnie and said, "This doesn't make any sense. Sam can't be a target. He's a great guy. He helps sponsor youth rodeo teams and he opens up the Rocking M for the fund-raiser every year. It just isn't possible."

Her support warmed Sam from the inside out.

Donnie shrugged. "Everybody pisses off someone at some time or another. Even Sam," he said with a congenial wink. "Anybody from your past that might want to give you a hard time, Sam?"

"The only person who regularly tells people I'm a

jerk is my mother—and this doesn't seem like Diane's style,'' he said, trying to inject a little humor into the group.

Andi laughed, but Jenny frowned. "What about those two guys who were fighting the day Ida Jane fell and broke her hip?'' she said, patting Lara's back vigorously. "The one I saw didn't look very happy about getting fired.''

Donnie pulled a wire notepad from his breast pocket. "That was Tim Collier, right?''

"Yes.'' Sam frowned. He hated to believe that any of the men who worked here could be that vengeful. "I suppose it's possible that Tim could be responsible, but it doesn't seem likely. Cowboys come and go all the time. A job is just one of those things you do till you get your stake together for your next go-around. It's not like I blackballed either one of them.''

"He's got a reputation for being a hothead,'' Donnie said. "Maybe he's vindictive, too.''

Sam sighed. It was possible. Tim was a troubled young man with an arrest or two on his record. Sam had never let something like that stop him from giving a man a chance, but now he couldn't help wondering if Tim was a danger.

"I'll bring him in for questioning,'' Donnie said. "Until we get some answers, you should be extra careful.''

Sam planned to be. He'd start by making sure his family was safe. "You're right. That means, Jen, you, Ida and the twins need to move back to town.''

"What?'' Jenny asked.

Donnie rose. "Guess I'll be going.'' He looked at Andi. "Andi, do you want to walk me out? I wanted to talk to you about the last town council meeting. There's something going on you aren't going to like. Someone has reintroduced the idea of a by-pass around town."

"I thought that got shot down years ago," Andi responded.

Donnie shrugged. "Maybe it was only wounded."

Sam cleared his throat. "Actually, Donnie, if you don't mind seeing yourself out, Andi could help Jenny pack." A residual scratchiness made it that much harder to say what he had to say. He looked at Jenny. "Just the stuff you need to get by. I'll move the rest later on."

Her expression went from bemused to incredulous. She looked at Ida first, then her sister. Sam might have smiled at the disbelief he read in her eyes, but he was serious. There was no way he could allow Jenny and the children to live here while the Rocking M was the target of an arsonist.

"Move?" she repeated slowly, as if the word had more than one syllable.

"Yeah. Back into town where you'll be safe." He looked at Ida Jane for support. The older woman's eyes sparkled as if he'd just won a prize.

Momentarily confused by Ida's impish grin, he added, "Your aunt told me last night your grandfather died in a fire in this very spot."

"Did I say that?" Ida asked.

"So what?" Jenny shrugged.

Sam pushed back his chair and rose. "So, I'm not about to risk your life or the twins' lives. And we can make arrangements at one of the lodges or a motel for Ida Jane until we can get ramps built at the old bordello."

His speech done, he picked up his plate and walked to the sink. He noticed Greta slipping out the door just when he could have used some moral support. He was about to call her back, when he felt a tap on his shoulder. He turned to find Jenny a foot away. Her hands were on her hips, and her eyes were blazing. She was obviously pissed off.

"If you want to give me grief about the damn cat," he said, "it'll have to wait. We've gotta get you moved first."

He glanced over Jenny's shoulder to see Ida holding Lara. Andi was bouncing Tucker on her lap; his chubby legs wobbled like a newborn calf's. Sam's heart twisted. He couldn't believe how much the twins had grown in just ten weeks. God, he'd miss not having them here.

"May I speak with you a moment?" Jenny asked, her tone formal and tight. "In your office, perhaps?"

Sam didn't recognize the look in her eye, but it made him feel like a student in her class—a student who'd been caught cheating. "All right. But I really think you should be packing. If we hurry, we might be able to get Donnie to escort you into town."

Jenny turned and looked at Andi, her eyes rolling in obvious disbelief. "Give me a break, Sam. This isn't an old western with bad guys perched on bluffs with rifles. Jeez."

Sam's face heated up. Maybe he was overreacting a little, but that didn't mean Jenny shouldn't return to town. That was nonnegotiable. Period.

He stepped aside to let her lead the way to his office. He'd have given anything to be able to span her trim hips with his hands and spin her around to face him. If things were different, they could sneak a little necking in the hallway. *Wake up, Sam. You're a responsible adult—act like one.*

Jenny opened the door, walked in then closed the door

behind him. She didn't give him time to put the desk between them.

"Let's get one thing straight," she said. "Either I'm a houseguest or I live here. Which is it?"

He blinked, totally unprepared for either her response or her attitude. Without waiting for him to reply, she continued. "What is it with you O'Neal men? Are you throwbacks to some other age? Maybe it's Diane's influence. She was always looking for a man to take care of her, right? So you think all women are like that. Well, here's a tip, Sam. That doesn't work for me. I can take care of myself."

Sam took a step back defensively, but she closed the gap. "We made a deal, Sam. Five years. Now, at the first sign of trouble you're trying to get rid of me."

Temper darkened her eyes to a rusty brown. The sunlight streaming in through the windows highlighted little gold flecks that hinted at passion. "No. Yes," he stammered. "It's for your own good, and the babies'."

She jabbed her finger right below the button at the center of his chest. "Let me tell you what's not good for babies, Sam. Being carted back and forth like so much baggage is not good for babies. We're just getting settled into a routine. Tucker didn't even wake up for a second feeding last night. In another week or two, he'll be off the midnight feeding all together. Do you want to ruin that?"

I like that feeding best, he thought, but shook his head. "No, of course not. But we're a long way from town, Jen. We were lucky last night. What if—"

She interrupted him. "No. *You* were lucky. I heard the whole cat story from Ida Jane, and frankly, I'd send you to detention for a week if you were one of my students. That was a totally unacceptable risk, Sam, but I'm willing to cut you some slack because you're not used to thinking like a married…like a father," she amended.

Was she going to say *married man?*

Sam didn't have time to consider her slip. Jenny paced to the far side of the room and stared out the window. The midmorning light added such vibrancy to her hair he ached to touch it.

She'd been in his dreams again—dreams that had moved to a new level of intimacy given their encounter in the shower. That memory made her attitude all the more baffling. Why wasn't she grabbing at the chance to leave? Surely she knew things were bound to come to a head between them if she stayed.

"I don't understand," he admitted, walking around his desk to his high-backed chair. He dropped into it and rested his elbows on the desk. "Why the hell aren't you hightailing it back home? I just don't get it."

Jenny didn't reply immediately. She knew that Sam meant well. She even sympathized with him to a point, but she was sick and tired of O'Neal men making decisions for her. Josh had picked their town, their friends, when Jenny should get pregnant, who the father would be. True, she'd agreed to everything, but often her capitulation came after relentless lobbying on Josh's part.

The decision to move to the Rocking M had been at Sam's suggestion, but it was Jenny's choice. This was her home—for the next five years, at least, and she wasn't letting some punk with a pack of matches scare her away. The sooner Sam understood that, the better off he'd be.

She left her spot by the window and marched to Sam's desk. He looked so powerful and in charge. His western-style shirt, open at the throat, showed the white edge of an undershirt. Such a cowboy thing, Jenny thought. And why is that the least bit sexy? She couldn't explain why, but it was.

"Jenny," Sam said, his tone patient. "Think about it. That fire was virtually in our backyard." *Our*. He said, *Our*. "If the wind had been stronger, there's no telling where it would have wound up. I'm not willing to take that risk. Not where you and the twins are concerned."

She placed her hands on the desk and leaned on them. She watched as his gaze was drawn to her breasts. His reaction gave her a small, womanly thrill that she couldn't deny. And she liked the feeling, even if it scared her a little. "Well, I am."

He gave his head a shake. "Why? I'm not saying this is forever. Once they catch whoever did it, you can come back."

Could she? Maybe this was Sam's way of getting rid of her. Last night had obviously affected him, too. Sam was a loner, a guy who didn't need a woman in his life. He was probably just as shaken up over the shower incident as she was. She had a feeling that was the real reason he wanted her to leave.

Her heart picked up speed as if she were about to take a leap across a vast abyss. "Listen, Sam, I'm not a coward." She looked him squarely in the eye. "But you are."

He blinked as if she'd hit him on the nose. "What?"

She took a deep breath. "You're having second thoughts about me being here. I can understand that...especially after what happened between us last night."

She hated the way her skin tone always betrayed her feelings. To hide what had to be a flame-red face, she walked to the window again. In the three weeks that she'd been living at the Rocking M, she'd grown to love its solitude, serenity and beauty. She wanted all that it had to offer, including, quite possibly, the man behind the desk.

She wasn't blind to the attraction percolating between them. Maybe fear and loneliness had triggered some of what she was feeling. Maybe it was something more. But that didn't mean she was ready to act on her feelings.

"Jenny, I apologize for last night. It was crazy—*I* was crazy. I felt like I'd cheated death and—"

She turned, suddenly furious. "Don't say that. Josh always talked like that—as if life was a game and he had an extra ace up his sleeve. But it's not, and he didn't."

Sam sat back. "I'm sorry."

"Are you sorry you kissed me?"

He looked like a man with two choices—neither appealing. "I would never deliberately do anything to hurt you, Jenny. You're grieving, and I don't want to screw that up. Maybe I was being selfish when I asked you to move here. Maybe I should have given you more time."

Jenny let out a low squeal of frustration. "Time," she spit. "Don't talk to me about time, Sam. Josh promised me time—it was the only thing we ever argued about. Every May, he'd tell me, 'This is your summer, Jen. Three months to devote to your writing.' But something would always come up."

She swallowed against the bitterness in her throat. *If you'd teach summer school, we could pay off the car, Jen, but I promise next summer is all yours,* Josh had said.

"That's how you got me to agree to this move, Sam. You promised me time to mourn, to write. Remember?"

He nodded, his expression grim. "Well, I've used it for both."

She looked at the floor. It wasn't easy to admit that she'd finally put words to paper. Twice that week she'd found herself with a few free minutes on her hands and she'd escaped to the gazebo to enjoy the solitude. And to her surprise, words and thoughts had pressed against her mind until she'd jotted them down.

"Just free verse," she admitted, feeling her blush intensify. "Nothing wonderful, but thoughts. Images. Memories."

She'd come to the conclusion that before she could write a children's book, she needed to write Josh's story—the legacy he'd left behind for the children he would never know. But she couldn't do that if she left this place. Josh was linked to the Rocking M, and somehow, her creativity was centered here, too.

"I need to be here, Sam. You're right about one thing, though. I wasn't ready—emotionally—for what happened in the shower. It's too soon...I owe Josh...I can't...."

She didn't know how to ask for the emotional distance she needed without giving up the routine and peace she craved.

The look on his face told her he took her plea seriously. His singed eyebrows were knitted, his lips pressed together. Andi was right—Sam was a very sexy guy. To distract herself she turned sideways and sat on the desk.

"I suppose we could beef up security," he said gruffly.

Jenny's heart gave a little leap. "I'll volunteer for the night shift," she said, smiling. "I'm up half the night anyway."

His chuckle rumbled in his chest—and echoed in

Jenny's. "I didn't mean you. You have enough to do—Ida, the babies…your book."

Jenny felt her cheeks ignite again. "I've got a long way to go with that."

Sam rose. He leaned forward and put his hands flat on the desk. "You have to start someplace. Might as well be here."

Jenny was close enough to smell his just-showered scent. His damaged eyebrows made her yearn to touch them, but she controlled herself. She'd never tell Sam, but his heroic efforts on behalf of the barn cat touched her deeply. However, since she was the one setting the limits, she had to make sure they both lived up to them.

"Does that mean we can stay?" she asked, hopping off the desk.

"Against my better judgment." He shook his head. "Maybe that talk about your grandfather's death got me spooked."

Suddenly anxious to put this behind them, Jenny walked to the door. "It was a long time ago, Sam. And Ida always told us it was an accident."

She waited for him to join her in the hallway. Shoulder to shoulder they walked toward the rear entrance of the house. The cedar logs still gave an inviting smell of permanence that made her feel safe, just like Sam did.

He had his hand on the doorknob, when he paused. He tilted his head in a way that was pure Sam and asked, "Did you give Josh this much trouble when you were married?"

Jenny bit down on a grin. She liked this man, more than she dared admit. His rare flashes of humor made them all the more precious. "Of course not. I'm a very acquiescent wife." Then she grinned. "Too bad we're just living together."

She batted her eyelashes coquettishly.

Sam's soft hoot made her think of Josh. She missed his playfulness. Suddenly blue, she walked into the kitchen and kept on going, right past her sister, her aunt and her babies.

She stopped when she reached a safe spot around the corner of the living room. Hauling in a deep breath, she fought the pain that suddenly engulfed her. Sam. Josh. Josh. Sam. If anyone had told her she'd be facing this kind of emotional dilemma so soon after Josh's death, she'd have been furious. She loved Josh, she still cried for the future they would never share. But she genuinely liked Sam. And at some level she desired him.

Maybe I should have taken the out he gave me, she thought. *Played it safe.*

Oh, Jenny Perfect, there's no such thing as safe, she heard Josh say. *You know that.*

She closed her eyes against the tears that clustered. Sweet tears for a man who'd played hard and played well but had never played it safe.

ONCE SAM DISCLOSED the verdict to Andi and Ida Jane— she won't budge—he returned to his office to think. Jenny had leveled with him, and he appreciated that. She hadn't said how she felt about him, but she liked what he had to offer. His home. A routine. Time.

It was a start.

As he pictured her finger poking him in the chest, his lips twitched. Damn, he liked her.

Don't kid yourself, buddy, you love her.

Sam heard the words as clearly as if Josh had spoken them aloud. He closed his eyes and tried to feel his brother's spirit, but it was gone—a wisp of his imagination. Somehow he knew Josh wouldn't object to Sam loving Jenny, but at the same time, Sam was certain that he was on the verge of blowing it. Jenny needed more time. If she was determined to stay, he'd let her, but there'd be no repeat of last night's performance.

He stood up abruptly. He needed to talk to Donnie about the investigation. The more he thought about someone deliberately starting that fire, the madder he got. He'd been an active member of the Gold Creek volunteer fire department for years. He knew firsthand what a huge toll range fires extracted on the land and on the firefighters who battled them.

The first thing on his agenda was to find the guy who'd done this. Then he planned to make sure people knew about the dangers of grassland fires. Maybe a public service campaign—a sort of ''Wild Fires Cost You'' kind of thing.

A meaningful challenge was just what he needed. Something to keep him from thinking about Jenny. Or more specifically, about being in love with his grieving sister-in-law.

CHAPTER ELEVEN

JENNY PAUSED beside the open nursery door. She closed her eyes a moment and listened to the sound of Sam chatting with the twins, who, at four months, loved to talk. Both babies were making cooing sounds and smiling, even laughing when tickled. She loved every single moment with them and could barely keep up with the changes, which seemed to happen hourly.

She smiled as she caught bits and pieces of Sam's one-sided monologue. "...traffic was abominable... maybe they'll have flying cars by the time you two learn how to drive...saw the Washington Monument...take you there someday...breathe history so you don't have to study it..."

He'd returned home a few hours earlier after a meeting in Washington, D.C., with the National Park Service. Since starting his wildfire awareness efforts six weeks earlier, Sam had traveled to Wyoming, Colorado and, now, the capital. He'd also met with a nonprofit group about sponsoring a publicity campaign before next year's fire season.

Jenny was proud of how much Sam had accomplished, but she was glad to have him home. Although he was seldom gone more than two or three days at a time, Jenny missed him.

He'd returned from D.C. a day ahead of schedule at her behest. She'd wanted him to attend Andi's Christmas

Open House at the Old Bordello Antique Shop and Coffee Parlor this evening. The coffee idea was yet another attempt to save their great-aunt's business. Since attention from the "haunted bordello" brouhaha had died down, Andi hoped she might increase traffic and profits by selling fancy coffees in the building's front parlor.

"This town needs a place where you can get a good latte," she'd explained to Ida Jane, Jenny and Sam at their very quiet Thanksgiving dinner. How she'd pulled off the conversion so fast was pure, ex-marine determination, and something called a grandfather clause. Apparently Ida's father had operated a diner in the front parlor years ago, which allowed Andi to expedite the application with certain upgrades to meet new health codes.

Jenny looked down at her floor-length black velvet skirt and ivory satin blouse. Not exactly sexy, but elegant, she thought. Andi had been critical of Jenny's choice. "How are you going to entice Sam with an old-lady outfit like that?" she'd asked.

An hour later, Kristin had phoned to suggest something less "teacherish." "How about a short skirt with your red boots and that sparkly sweater?" *Josh's favorite.*

"This isn't a date," Jenny had argued. "Sam's just being supportive of Andi."

"Oh, right. He flew across the continent for a cup of Andi's espresso. That's it. I'm sure it's not because he misses you and is waiting patiently for you to admit that you're interested in him, too."

I'm not! she'd wanted to yell. But it would have been a lie, so she took the high road.

"He also came back because his mother is in town,

and he needs to prepare himself for Christmas with the whole family.''

''Uh-huh.''

Jenny had ignored her sister's sarcasm. Sam was an astute man. He'd sensed that Jenny needed time alone with her grief, her confusion, her guilt. He'd given her that by taking on an ambitious project that kept him so busy their paths barely crossed—except when the twins were involved. He was at her side when Lara spiked a fever—a result of an ear infection. He'd accompanied the three of them to the pediatrician for immunizations.

And although Jenny missed having other times with him, she'd kept busy, too. She had something she couldn't wait to show him. She switched the manila folder from her right hand to the left and walked into the room.

''Hi, there. You must have slipped in while I was helping Ida dress. I'm glad to see you're home safely.''

Sam stood upright from the table where he was changing Tucker's diaper. Keeping one hand on the wiggly baby's tummy, he looked over his shoulder.

Jenny felt the look he gave her clear down to her toes.

''You look very beautiful,'' he said. His gaze went to her hair, which she'd arranged in an upsweep. She'd liked the old-fashioned style, but her neck felt exposed, especially when his gaze settled on the antique choker Josh had given her the Christmas before last.

Sam picked up Tucker, whose red flannel sleeper resembled long johns. Sam held the baby's chubby fist to his lips and pretended to give a wolf whistle.

''Are you teaching him sexist behavior?'' she teased.

''You're never too young to appreciate beauty,'' Sam said, his gaze following Jenny as she walked toward him.

Swallowing the sudden moisture in her mouth, she lifted her chin. "You look pretty good yourself. How'd you manage a shower so fast?"

"I tried to get back in time for a haircut, but Mel's Barbershop was closed when I got to town," Sam said, lifting Tucker overhead in a way that made the little boy squeal with delight.

Jenny's heart constricted at the sound. She loved to watch Sam interact with the children. He was a natural parent, and the twins loved him. He needed to be around more; maybe it was time to talk about what was between them.

After the holidays. After Diane leaves.

"Beulah Jensen called Ida Jane and told her Mel had emergency gallbladder surgery," she said. "He was giving Ron Campbell a crew cut and suddenly collapsed in pain. You know Ron. Music teacher at the high school, choir director at the Methodist church. A nice guy, but no muscle man by any means. Still, according to Beulah, he carried Mel—who's a good two hundred eighty pounds—to his car and drove him to the hospital."

Sam looked impressed. "That's what I love about this town. People aren't afraid to get involved. You wouldn't believe the apathy I've encountered since I started this campaign. It's disheartening."

He walked to the crib where Lara was attempting to push herself up on her elbows, her bottom bouncing up and down. Sam scooped up his little daughter with his free hand. "Do we have time for a story?"

Jenny's fingers clutched the folder behind her back so tightly she was sure there'd be imprints on the paper inside. "We have half an hour. Ida would like to see the twins before we go, then Greta's going to put them to bed."

He gave her a puzzled look. "What's wrong?"

"Nothing."

"Jenny."

She took a deep breath and produced the folder. "I have this...um, it's nothing important. You can look at it tomorrow."

"Why don't I look at it right now?"

Her heart started to race. "No. That's okay. Tomorrow will be fine."

His chin dropped, and he gave her a look that told her he didn't believe her. She wished now she'd left the damn pages in her notebook where they belonged. She should have waited, but the story had been done for days, and it was killing her not to share it with someone. *All right, with Sam.*

He nodded toward the rocking chair in the alcove. "You rock. I'll read."

With a little maneuvering, the kind that involved arms brushing breasts and shoulders touching chests, they exchanged twins for folder. Jenny was practically breathless after the encounter, but Sam seemed to handle it with ease. Tucker immediately reached for the beads on her necklace and tried to pull himself close enough to taste them.

"Read fast," Jenny said in a strangled voice.

Smiling, Sam handed his son a purple frog rattle that Tucker waved, delighting in the sound it made.

Sitting on the nearby window seat, Sam opened the folder. "What is it? Tax stuff?"

Jenny shook her head. Her heart was beating so quickly she felt a little light-headed. "It's for a children's book. The sketches are really rough. The text is probably too adult." Her voice rose and picked up speed; she forced herself to take a breath. "I'm sure there's no market for this kind of thing, but we can always give it to the twins. Someday.''

"This is your work? You wrote this?'' His tone was hushed with awe. "And you're letting *me* read it?''

"You really don't need to read it now. It can wait till we get back,'' she said, stalling. What if he hated it?

Sam sat forward, cradling the open manila folder between his hands like a hymnal. Two sheets of heavy white watercolor paper were exposed. In the overhead light, the sketches looked stark and crude, the block printing childish. Jenny fought the urge to snatch it back.

"*The Green Cowboy Hat* by Jennifer Sullivan O'Neal,'' he read aloud.

Jenny's face filled with heat. "It's sort of free verse mixed with prose. A cross between Robert Frost and Dr. Seuss,'' she said, forcing a laugh.

"Two of my favorites.'' His earnest smile made the butterflies in her stomach stop flitting about. "Shall I read it aloud?''

"God, no!'' she exclaimed so loudly Tucker dropped his rattle and started to cry. "Oops. Sorry, sweetie,'' she said.

Lara, picking up on her brother's woes, joined in, her wails escalating in volume.

Sam closed the folder and rose. He set the folder on the cushion then took Lara from Jenny. He made soothing sounds that distracted the baby from her impassioned sobs.

"Is someone hurting my little angels?'' Greta asked, standing in the doorway.

"Just sympathy cries,'' Sam said, brushing away his daughter's tears with his thumb. "I think these two are tired.''

He looked at Jenny. "Why don't we take them downstairs for good-night kisses then let Greta give them their bottles.''

Jenny nodded and rose. This wasn't exactly the way she'd planned his return, but having children required flexible scheduling.

Ten minutes later, he helped her into her wool coat, then handed her the keys to the van. ''Can you walk Ida Jane out? I forgot something.''

He charged upstairs, his western-style raincoat flapping against his calves. She watched for a second, struck by how handsome and fit he was. When she felt Ida Jane's gaze on her, she blushed and took her aunt's arm. ''Are you ready? This will be the first time you've been to the bordello since your accident, isn't it? I hope you're prepared for a few changes. Andi's been a busy little beaver.''

Andi had tried to keep Ida informed, but Jenny wasn't sure how much her aunt had taken in. Despite the weekly visits from her Garden Club friends, Ida seemed disinterested in what was happening in Gold Creek or the changes Andi was making to her beloved bordello.

''Yes. Yes. I know. The ice-cream parlor. Won't that be tasty,'' she said, wrapping both hands around Jenny's forearm.

Jenny fought a grimace. ''She's selling espresso and cappuccino, Auntie. Those are kinds of coffee. Andi looked into selling iced drinks, but she's decided to hold off until after the holidays.''

''Oh, yes, I forgot.''

They slowly walked down the well-lit ramp to the van. Jenny had already stowed Ida's cane and their purses in the back of the vehicle. Today was the winter solstice, the first day of winter and the shortest day of the year. The chilly temperature reflected the light smattering of snow they'd received last night.

Sam caught up with them just as Jenny opened the sliding door to the back seat. "Let me help," he said. His closeness, the wonderful woodsy smell of his cologne, made her almost drop the keys. "Miss Ida, would you mind riding in front with Jenny? I have something important I'd like to read on the way in."

"Sam," Jenny hissed. She hadn't mentioned her story to either her aunt or her sisters. "Can't it wait?"

"Nope. I don't think so." His face was shadowed, but his tone was dead serious.

The trip to town was the longest of her life, Jenny decided as the lights of Gold Creek, decorated for the holidays, came into view.

"Doesn't it look pretty?" Ida Jane exclaimed. "I just love this town at Christmas. Did somebody put up my lights? I meant to do it, but I can't remember if I did."

The panic in her voice made Jenny reach out and squeeze her hand. "Andi hung them, dear. The old bordello looks like a fairy palace."

Ida Jane let out a long sigh. "Oh, good. I don't want people to think we lack holiday spirit."

Jenny glanced into the rearview mirror. Were those tears on Sam's cheeks or a trick of the van's lighting?

Ida Jane suddenly yanked on the steering wheel. "Jenny girl, I'd just as soon get there in one piece, if you don't mind."

Stricken with chagrin, Jenny gripped the wheel with sweaty palms and focused on her driving. As she turned into the parking lot, she barely noticed the multitudes of tiny white lights that encircled the turret, outlined every gable end and wrapped around the porch. The pine in the front yard was gaily festooned with colored bulbs and ornaments crafted from old pie tins.

"Oh, my, it's just lovely," Ida Jane exclaimed.

Jenny pulled to a stop in front of a sign marked Ida Jane Montgomery ONLY. She looked behind her and saw Sam sitting motionless, his face turned toward the window. Jenny exchanged a look with Ida then got out and hurried around to help her aunt.

"Is he okay?" Ida asked when they were standing.

Jenny closed the door. "I think so. Probably just tired."

Jenny quickly fetched Ida's cane from the rear compartment then walked her to the steps. Impatient to hear Sam's impression of her story, Jenny hurried her aunt along.

"What was he reading?" Ida asked.

Jenny gulped. "Something I wrote. About Josh."

Ida moved along the uneven concrete with exaggerated care. "Sam's opinion matters to you, doesn't it?"

"Of course. He's Josh's brother."

Ida stopped at the foot of the steps. Her mink coat, an antique with three or four bald spots where Jenny and her sisters had gotten carried away grooming it when they'd played dress-up, smelled of cedar and White Shoulders perfume. "He's also…Sam," she said to her niece.

Before Jenny could reply, a threesome—Linda McCloskey and her son, Bart, a local roofing contractor, and his wife—joined them. After a few seconds of pleasantries, Bart gallantly offered Ida Jane his elbow, and the four ascended the steps and disappeared inside.

Inviting smells of coffee and pine lingered in the air, and the faint sound of Christmas carols and laughter beckoned, but Jenny turned on the heel of her sensible black pumps and dashed to the van.

She yanked open the sliding door and hopped inside, closing the door against the chilly night air. She tugged the lapels of her wool coat together; her fingers felt numb, but she barely noticed the discomfort.

Sam was sitting with his back against the window, legs stretched on the rear bench seat.

"Well?" she asked, sitting sideways in the middle seat.

He looked at her. His expression somber. "You said not to read this aloud, but you were wrong. It deserves to be read aloud. It's wonderful."

Tears rushed to her eyes. "Really?"

He shifted position, sitting forward so Jenny could see the page as he read.

"'*Josh was not a cowboy, but he loved his big brother, Sam, who was one. Every spring Josh would ride with the other cowboys to round up the cattle. He couldn't ride as well as the others, and sometimes he'd fall behind and get lost, so Sam bought him a special hat—a green cowboy hat. This made Josh easier to spot.*

Josh loved his hat even though it was a little tight.

He wore it to bed.

His wife was not amused.

This was not a good thing, but it wasn't bad, either.'"

Sam smiled and turned to the second page.

"'*One day, Josh got sick. Real sick. The doctors told him he had cancer. He'd had the same thing once before when he was a little boy, and he thought he would get well with medicine. He took the medicine, but it made him too weak to chase cows. He still wore the green hat, though, when he sat on the fence and watched Sam and the other cowboys round up the herd.*

The medicine made Josh's hair fall out.

His hat fit better.

This was a good thing, but it wasn't perfect.'''

Sam took a deep breath. Jenny knew he was remembering all the chemo and radiation treatments. All the questions. The fear of not knowing what would happen next. Would Josh rally? Would the next round of chemo send him into remission? Would herbs help keep food in his stomach? Would he live long enough to see the twins?

Sam turned the page. Jenny saw him tilt his head to study her drawings. His lips flickered, and she knew which image he was looking at—Josh playing poker with four aces stuck in the band of his green hat.

Sam cleared his throat then started again.

"'As sometimes happens, the medicine didn't work. The doctors couldn't think of anything else to do to help Josh's body fight the disease. And Josh was getting very tired of fighting, anyway. He wanted to rest and laugh and remember all the good times in his life. His friends dropped by to play cards, and he always won. His family came to see him. Sam brought Josh's favorite horse to the house. Some nice nurses made Josh very comfortable in a special bed where he could watch the birds and hear the sound of the wind in the trees.

Josh died early one morning when the dew was on the grass, so you could see his soul's footprints as he left.

His family cried. Sam cried. The other cowboys cried, too.

But Josh wasn't in pain anymore.

That was a good thing, but it was hard to say goodbye.'''

When he lifted his chin, Jenny saw tears. He blinked

them away before they could fall, but she saw them. After a moment, he turned the page.

"'Time passed, as time does. The green hat sat in a closet, getting dusty. But one day, a little boy named Tucker found it. He put it on and it fit just right. Like it had been made for him. He ran to his cowboy daddy and said, "Look what I found. Can I have it?" Sam smiled and told him, "It belonged to a special person. He was the best cowboy of all. He wore this green hat so everyone could see him doing his job. His name was Josh, and he was my brother."

Tucker wore the hat with pride.

He wore it to bed.

His mother was not amused.

But Josh's spirit looked down from above and smiled.

This was a good thing. A very good thing.'''

Sam passed his hand across his face, then closed the folder. "I don't have the right words, Jenny," he said gruffly. "It's Josh. His spirit. The love he had for us. Thank you."

Jenny couldn't swallow. She felt slightly faint. "Do you really think so? Really?"

He nodded. "I'd never lie to you, Jen. About anything. Especially something as important as this."

His empathy gave her the courage to say, "It came to me right after you left for D.C. As you were driving away, I had this image of Josh last year at the St. Patrick's Day party. Sitting on the fence wearing that silly green hat. You were mad at him, remember?"

"I thought he was going to wear himself out. I wanted to cancel the party, and he wouldn't let me."

Jenny reached across the distance to touch his shoulder. "That wasn't Josh's style. He loved life, Sam. That's what I wanted to show in this story."

She'd never forget the feeling that had come to her after writing these words. She'd wept. Not out of grief, but from a sense that finally everything was going to be okay.

"I'm glad you liked it."

He looked as though he had something say, but before he could speak, there was a knock, then the door slid open. "Jenny? Are you okay?"

Diane.

Sam let out a harsh sigh and lunged to his feet, hunched slightly to exit the car. "I'll be inside. I'm suddenly dying for a cup of coffee." Once he was standing, he adjusted his coat then said, "Hello, Diane. Merry Christmas." Then he turned and walked away.

Jenny glanced furtively toward where he'd been sitting, hoping he hadn't left the folder behind. She wasn't ready to share her story with the world—especially not with Josh's mother. The seat was empty.

"Hi, Diane. Sam and I were catching up. He just got back and there hasn't been time to fill him in on all the holiday plans."

Diane and Gordon had arrived three days earlier for a two-week stay. They'd missed Thanksgiving because of engine trouble with their motor home, which they'd finally sold. Since Jenny had been too busy to do anything about renting her house, she'd gladly handed the key to Gordon and Diane for their visit.

"Did you tell him we'll be at the ranch on Christmas morning?"

"Of course. Everyone wants to be there for the twins' first Christmas."

Diane moved aside to let Jenny out. "I would have preferred you to come to Santa Barbara. The weather's so much nicer, but I know traveling is hard on Ida Jane.

She looks marvelous, by the way. She's inside flirting with my husband.''

Jenny laughed. ''Then we'd better go rescue him.''

''Or her. Ever since we got here, Gordon has become fixated on the old bordello's history. He and Andi have been poring over the old photos. They're both talking about historical preservation.'' She made a clucking sound. ''As if the town needs to celebrate *that* aspect of its past.''

Jenny hid her smile. She knew that some of the town matrons had from time to time begged Ida Jane to change the name of her antique shop, but Ida had flatly refused.

''Well, it *was* a house of ill-repute at one time, Diane. That's public record. The red light above the old bordello sign used to hang beside the door. I think it makes us unique.''

''Perhaps,'' Diane said, following Jenny up the steps. They entered the hall together. The low hum of voices filtered through the door leading to the store. Jenny felt a twinge of sadness as she looked toward the kitchen.

''So,'' Diane said, hanging her coat on the old-fashioned hall tree, ''when are you coming to Santa Barbara? I'm dying to show off those babies to all my friends.''

''Possibly Easter. We can't do it before then because we have the St. Paddy's Day party to plan.''

Diane's forehead creased. Her lips pursed in a flat line. ''You're doing that? Without Josh?''

''Diane, everything I do is without Josh.'' Jenny didn't mean to be hurtful, but she was losing patience with her mother-in-law's effort to thrust Josh into the center of every conversation.

"Besides," she quickly added, "Josh would want us to do it. He loved to party."

Jenny took off her coat and hung it on top of Sam's. She happened to see a corner of the folder sticking out of his sleeve and made sure her coat covered it.

"Well, you knew him best," Diane said, studying her image in the ornate beveled mirror hanging opposite the door.

Jenny touched up her lipstick, then put the tube in her pocket. Lately, she'd been wondering just how well she had known Josh. They'd come of age together, but there were questions Jenny didn't have answers to. Like what Josh would think about her feelings for Sam.

She touched the necklace at her throat, then opened the etched glass door that separated the family quarters from the store. "We should go inside. My sisters are going to wonder what happened to me."

Suddenly, she wished Andi had decided to open a bar instead of a coffee parlor. She could really use a drink.

SAM OBSERVED the action from a secluded spot behind a potted palm. The dusty fronds were adorned with tiny twinkle lights like the ones on every pinnacle and cornice of the bordello's roofline. He liked the festive quality it gave the place.

He knew that some townsfolk resented the idea of celebrating the bordello's sinful past, but they were in the minority. Unfortunately, the vocal contingent was headed by Gloria Harrison Hughes, author of "Glory's World." Gloria considered herself the moral adjutant of Gold Creek. Fortunately, most people considered her a narrow-minded gossip.

"Gloria's had it in for the triplets ever since—according to Gloria—Kristin led her son astray in high school," Josh had confided last summer when Sam had read him something spiteful from the amazingly biased column. "Don't you remember the girls' eighteenth birthday party? Donnie and Tyler Harrison got in a big fight. Ty left town a short while later and didn't graduate with his class."

Sam vaguely recalled the incident.

"Ever since then, 'Glory's World' has been very snippy toward Ida and the girls," Josh had said indignantly. "If I felt stronger, I'd give that old witch a piece of my mind."

Unfortunately, by then, Josh barely had enough energy to walk to the bathroom.

Sam shook off the troubling memory when he spotted Jenny enter the room with his mother following. The two looked somber, but Jenny's pensive frown changed to a smile the moment she made eye contact with him. Sam's heart turned over in his chest.

She was so beautiful. And talented. He'd never guessed she was such a sensitive, gifted writer. Her words had touched him deeply.

"Nice party, isn't it?" a voice asked beside him.

Sam glanced down and saw Ida Jane smiling up at him. Thanks to Jenny's gentle prodding to do her daily exercises, Ida was showing amazing improvement. "Has anyone told you how lovely you look tonight, Miss Ida?"

Ida batted his arm with the paper menu Andi was passing out. "Save all that sweet talk for Jenny. She's the one who's been pining for you." Her words made Sam's heart jump—particularly when she added, "'Bout time you got home."

"D.C. was my last stop. The rest is up to the people."

Ida looked at him shrewdly. "It always was, Sam.

You can't legislate against human perversity. There will always be that careless fellow who tosses a cigarette out the window. But, at least Donnie caught the fellow who set your field on fire."

Sam nodded. Tim Collier had been arrested in Reno. He'd admitted starting the blaze, but claimed he was drunk at the time. Drunk and mad at Sam for firing him. Sam wished Tim's arrest had been enough to ease his fears but he still worried every time he was away from home overnight. No one had been apprehended in the other cases.

"May I get you a refill?" he asked, lifting his cup.

Ida Jane shook her head. "No, thank you. I've had enough caffeine to keep me awake till Christmas."

The word reminded Sam that in three days he'd be entertaining his mother and Gordon and Jenny's family at his home for the first time since he'd bought the place. He was scared spitless.

"Are you looking forward to the festivities?" she asked, as if reading his mind.

"I'm anxious to see how the twins react to all the hoopla," he told her truthfully. "I've bought them way too much junk. Jenny's going to shoot me."

She chuckled. "You can't help it. You're a generous man. Always have been."

Something about the twinkle in her eye made him wonder what she was getting at. "Not really. I just made the mistake of going into FAO Schwarz when I was in San Francisco."

She gave him a look. "I was referring to the bonus you gave Hank. Greta told me about it. Quite magnanimous. They're planning a cruise to Alaska next summer."

Sam took a sip of the powerfully fragrant coffee. "I

learned a long time ago you pay for what you get—one way or another.'' Because that came off sounding a bit harsh, he added, ''They've earned every dime. Hank helped tremendously with the fire and he's practically had to run the place single-handedly with me gone so much, and Greta is a huge help with the twins.''

Ida nodded. ''Some men would make Jenny hire a sitter when she's doing her writing. Your brother would have.''

Sam frowned. ''I beg your pardon?''

Ida shrugged. ''Don't get me wrong. I loved Josh as much as anyone, but he wasn't terribly supportive of Jenny's dreams. In fact, he was a little jealous of them.''

Her words bothered Sam, but she went on before he could say anything. ''You may not believe me, but it's true. Ask Jenny. Why do you think she's never written anything before now—when she's so busy with a crippled old aunt and two babies.''

Sam didn't know the answer to that, but he was curious to find out. ''Maybe she just didn't have the right space.''

Ida smiled. ''You mean like your office?''

''Excuse me?'' *Jenny works in my office?*

''It's her favorite spot,'' Ida said offhandedly. ''I see her go past my room after the twins are asleep. She uses that walkie-talkie thing of yours to listen for them.''

The baby monitor. But it didn't answer the question why Jenny would choose to work in such functional surroundings. ''Why my office?'' he wondered out loud. ''Oh, to use the computer, I bet.''

Ida made a scoffing sound. ''To be close to you.''

Sam choked on his coffee and doubled over coughing. Ida shook her head. ''Men. You can't help but love 'em, but, Lord, I've known dogs that had a better understanding of the human heart."

Sam straightened and scanned the room. This wasn't a conversation he wanted his mother to overhear. He knew how she would react if she found out about Sam's feelings for Jenny. He spotted Diane standing with Jenny talking to a group of women.

"Jenny looks good, doesn't she?" Ida Jane said, apparently drawing her own conclusion about the object of his focus. "Your mother certainly missed the mark this time."

Sam turned his chin. "What do you mean?"

"Diane visited me when I was getting my hip fixed. She wanted me to talk Jenny out of moving to the ranch. Told me Jenny wouldn't last a month in that kind of isolation. I told her, 'Hogwash.' My sister wasn't made for ranch life. And Josh wouldn't have been happy there for long, either, but Jenny's more like me. We don't need whole bunches of people to be happy. Just the few we really care about."

Her broad hint was almost enough to make Sam blush. "Miss Ida, are you trying to play matchmaker?"

"Somebody should," she muttered.

Sam leaned down and kissed her cheek. She startled, then batted him with her menu again. "Save that for my niece. She's the one who needs kissing."

Sam wished that were true, but he knew better—especially after reading the story she'd written about Josh. Jenny was a long way from over Josh. Despite Ida Jane's attempt to play Cupid, Sam needed to keep his distance from Jenny. Especially with his eagle-eyed mother in the room.

AFTER A QUICK CALL to check on the twins, Jenny wandered through the house that had been her home for so many years. It smelled of furniture polish, mildew, coffee and Christmas potpourri. She'd missed the place, but it was no longer home. Neither was the house she'd shared with Josh.

She'd stopped by earlier in the week to make sure the furnace was running, and she'd been struck by how empty it felt even though Gordon and Diane were staying there. In truth, Jenny felt closer to Josh when she was sitting in Sam's office than she did wandering through the rooms of their old home.

Maybe, she thought, *he moved with us. He'll always be a part of our lives, no matter where we live.*

In no hurry to return to the party, Jenny decided to check out the changes Andi had completed on the second floor. To her left were the two large rooms that faced the street. She and her sisters had shared one room as a bedroom; the other was for studying, talking on the phone and painting their nails. Ida had called it their playroom when they were little. It was where Jenny had lost her virginity to Josh—on a bed of beanbag chairs, with a Sting song playing on the radio.

Jenny poked her head inside. Empty except for some boxes. Andi had been lobbying Kristin to move home and set up shop there, but Kris refused to consider it.

"Oh, sure, just what one needs to achieve a peaceful, therapeutic environment—the threat of a ghost popping up during the massage," she'd argued the last time she'd visited.

Jenny didn't understand why her sister was so resistant to moving back to Gold Creek, but Kris insisted this wasn't the place for her. She tried to visit Ida Jane every couple of weeks but seldom stayed longer than a day—two at the most.

Jenny closed the door and backtracked down the long hallway that led to the six remaining bedrooms. Rooms that had at one time accommodated the ladies of the evening, then later housed railroad workers and miners.

Just last week, Jenny and Ida Jane had talked about Andi's advertising campaign. Sadly, interest in the ghost story had died out not long after it was introduced, but Andi hadn't given up on the idea. She was in the process of designing an old bordello Web site, which would include a "ghostly" apparition displaying the items up for sale.

Jenny hated to think what Gloria Hughes would make of it. If rumors were correct, the columnist was anxious to put the old bordello out of business so her hotshot builder son could buy the land.

"She wants the old bordello closed and the building torn down to make way for some civic center Tyler Harrison is promoting," Andi had explained just minutes earlier to Jenny and her teacher friends. Andi had started attending meetings of the Gold Creek Chamber of Commerce in their aunt's absence.

Jenny knew Gloria still harbored a grudge against the Sullivan sisters, but she couldn't believe the woman would go so far as to have the old place bulldozed. It was a historical landmark, for heaven's sake.

Sighing, Jenny wandered along, listening to the cheerful sounds coming from the first floor. The volume increased momentarily then faded. Someone had opened the door leading to the living quarters. She heard footsteps ascending the stairs.

Jenny put on her "public" face, as Josh called it. He alone knew that she played the role of gracious hostess under duress. He'd been the social one in the family; she'd gone along with it because she'd known it made him happy to entertain people, throw dinner parties and get together with friends. But secretly, she was happiest when they were alone.

Maybe that was one reason she felt so comfortable living at the ranch. Visitors were few and far between. The Rocking M's employee Christmas party would be her first attempt at entertaining since August, but the ever-efficient Greta seemed to have that under control.

She heard voices, male and female. Suddenly feeling guilty about avoiding the party, she hurried toward the stairs. Two people were almost at the top, apparently caught up in a serious conversation, because neither of them noticed Jenny.

Sam and Kristin.

Sam looked up as if sensing her presence. His smile almost robbed her of breath. "There you are. Kristin was leaving and wanted to tell you goodbye."

Jenny wasn't sure she believed that explanation, but before she could say anything, Kristin cleared the three steps between them and gave Jenny a hug.

"We haven't talked all evening, but I heard there's a storm coming and I don't want to get stuck in Redding and not be able to get over the pass."

"Why don't you stay? I still don't understand why you aren't going to be here for the twins' first Christmas. You were with us in the delivery room. You're a part of their lives."

Kristin's eyes filled with dismay and…guilt, but the emotions were replaced by stubbornness. "I have prior commitments, Jen. People who need me more than you do. I can't let them down."

Jenny looked at Sam for help but he moved his shoulders as if he didn't understand her reasoning, either. "I invited her to come to the ranch Christmas party. We have a new employee. Lars dropped him off last week. He's a good-looking guy. Probably single.''

Jenny and Kristin exchanged a look. *"Probably?"*

"Lars said he found him wandering around up near the mine. Apparently the guy suffered a head injury in a motorcycle accident during the big storm that came through last month. Doesn't seem to remember much about his past. Lars named him Harley after the emblem on his jacket. He let him recuperate in his cabin at the Blue Lupine for a few weeks, but you know how suspicious Lars is.''

Jenny had visited Lars's old mine once years before with Josh. She knew the crusty old miner's reputation as a pot-smoking hermit. Sam was practically his only friend.

Kristin made an impatient gesture. "Well, thanks for the attempted matchmaking, Sam, but you'll have to introduce him to Andi. Or Jenny, for that matter. I'm not in the market for a man.''

"Me neither,'' Jenny said.

Sam flinched—just barely, but Jenny noticed. She'd been referring to the new man. But she'd spoken the truth. *Hadn't she?* She wasn't in the market for *any* man. To hide her confusion, she stepped down to hug her sister goodbye. "Drive safely. Especially if there's a storm coming.''

Kristin squeezed her fiercely. "I will. Give Tucker and Lara a big kiss for me. 'Night, Sam. Merry Christmas, and remember what I told you.''

She turned and dashed down the stairs, slipping into the antique store a second later. Jenny took a breath, deliberating on what to do next. Go back to the party or stay here. With Sam. Alone.

"What did she tell you?''

Even in the dim light, she spotted the discomfort on his face. "I'd rather not say."

"Why? Was it about me?"

"In a way."

She stepped to stand directly in front of him, bringing them eye to eye. "I hate secrets. Tell me."

"She said you weren't going to need a year to mourn."

A blush heated her cheeks. "Really? Is that all?"

He shook his head, then took a breath before adding, "She said if I waited too long, you'd get scared and run away."

Her sister knew her well. She was probably right, but that didn't make Jenny any less furious. "I'm going to kill her."

"No, you're not. You love her," Sam said, touching her cheek with the back of his hand. "Like I love...Josh."

Had he meant to say *Jenny?* She didn't ask. Instead, she kissed him. And Sam responded as though he'd been kissing her all his life. He tilted his head and started to deepen the kiss, but she stopped him. "This is a very public hallway."

"And you're worried about what people will say."

Jenny was embarrassed to admit that she cared about public opinion, but she did.

"Would it make a difference if I told you we have a perfectly good excuse?" he asked, drawing her hand to his lips. His lips kissed her fingers.

"We do?"

"Look up. Your sister went crazy with mistletoe."

Jenny glanced up. Sure enough, hanging from the old-fashioned light fixture was a straggly clump of mistletoe adorned with a red ribbon. Laughter bubbled up from deep inside.

"You're as bad as Josh," she said, but the words seemed to come from a long way off. The light quivered and suddenly Josh's shimmering image superimposed itself over Sam's body.

"Jenny?" Sam said.

His voice sounded as if he were speaking through a block of ice. Which made sense, because the hallway had suddenly turned cold. Deathly cold.

Panic flooded her veins. A blinding fear possessed her. Without conscious thought, she struck out at the image that didn't belong there.

"No," she cried. "You're dead. Leave me alone."

One minute Sam was standing in front of her; the next he was gone. So was the vision of Josh. All that remained was an odd groaning sound.

Dizzy, Jenny grabbed the handrail until the vertigo passed. She looked down and spotted Sam sprawled at the base of the staircase. Jenny let out a terrified scream. "No. Sam." *What have I done?*

CHAPTER TWELVE

SAM DIDN'T MOVE for a good four or five seconds. *What the hell happened?* One minute he was kissing Jenny, the next he was cartwheeling down the stairs.

Jenny pushed me.

Thank God for years of stunt work, he thought. A fall like that could have broken something. Bad enough his pride was in pieces. At least nobody had seen it happen, he thought, opening his eyes.

The angles of the walls in the dim hallway shifted two or three times before finally coming into focus. He was about to move, when a piercing scream made him freeze. Almost simultaneously, the sound of footsteps snapped on the staircase beside his cheek. Rolling his eyes as far back as possible without lifting his chin, he saw Jenny flying down the stairs, her long skirt flowing.

A door opened somewhere behind him. "Good heavens," a voice said from the opposite direction. "What happened?"

Sam slowly turned his head. *Neck seems fine,* he silently gauged.

Warren Jones, Sam's tax accountant, stood frozen in the doorway leading to the antique shop.

"Sam, Sam, are you okay?" Jenny cried, dropping to her knees beside him. Her hands skittered over him, sending shock waves in all directions. "I'm so sorry. I didn't mean to...I don't know why... God, tell me you're all right.''

Her plea fell like sparkling drops of honey on Sam's ear. *She cares.*

"Call 911," she ordered Warren.

Sam pointed at the hapless man. "Do and you'll regret it," Sam threatened. He started to sit up, but Jenny pressed both hands flat against his chest, rendering Sam immobile. "Don't move. You could have a neck injury."

"I'm fine, Jen."

"You don't look fine." She ran the tips of her fingers down his torso then his legs as if checking for broken bones. His response was the kind that would have proved to anyone looking that he was healthy—and horny.

"Jennifer. Stop it. I'm fine."

He rolled to his side. Twinges zinged him from hip to lower back. Apparently his grimace showed.

"Is it your back?" She slid her fingers beneath his shirt at the small of his back and gently probed his spine. Her touch was agony, but not for the reason she assumed.

"Believe me. Nothing's broken," he muttered through clenched teeth. "Can we go home now?"

Suddenly the door flew open, and a dozen people poured into the tiny anteroom.

"What happened?" a familiar voice asked. "Sam, you okay, bud?"

Donnie. Sam had never been as glad to see his old friend. "Just peachy," Sam said, pushing into a sitting position. He gingerly rubbed a tender spot on his elbow. He must have clipped the banister on his way down. "I lost my footing and fell."

Jenny made a squeaky sound. "He's lying. I pushed him."

"No, she didn't. I slipped," Sam stressed.

Jenny's gaze met his, and through her tears he could read her confusion.

Before either of them could say anything more, the crowd parted to let Diane and Gordon past. Donnie backed away. "I'll see if I can catch Kristin before she leaves."

Sam wasn't sure he understood the reasoning behind that, but maybe a good masseuse could help.

"How'd this happen? Were you feeling dizzy before you fell?" Gordon asked, his tone professional.

"He didn't—" Jenny started.

Desperate to prevent a second impassioned confession, Sam said the first thing that came to mind. "There's a board loose on the stairs. It made me lose my balance."

The crowd gave a collective gasp and murmurs started to build. Sam caught a few words like "liability insurance" and "litigation." He stifled a groan.

His elbow was starting to throb, and he could feel a painful area under the knee of his jeans that was probably bleeding. He needed a hot bath and a couple of aspirin. "I'm okay, Gordon. Really."

"I don't like that goose egg on your head," Gordon said, gently probing a spot Sam hadn't even been aware of until Gordon touched it.

"Ouch. Quit it."

"Uh-oh," someone muttered. "He'll probably sue."

Sam almost laughed until someone else said, "He won't sue. He's practically family."

"Don't be stupid," Ida Jane said, pushing her way past a cluster of onlookers. "He *is* family, you dolt."

The *dolt* in question—Linda McCloskey puffed up indignantly. "He's an in-law. I meant *real* family."

A twinge in Sam's belly, totally unrelated to the fall, made him flinch. Ida Jane looked him straight in the eye and said, "He's the twins' daddy. Does that make him family enough for you?"

Oh, Miss Ida, what have you done?

A hush fell over the crowd for several heartbeats. Sam was still looking at the old lady. He saw something that looked an awful lot like satisfaction in her eyes. He didn't understand it, but he knew without turning his head that her great-niece wasn't going to feel the same.

"Ida, you're mistaken," Diane said loudly. "Josh is Tucker and Lara's father. Sam's their uncle."

"Don't tell me what I know," Ida Jane said angrily. "Sam's the daddy."

Sam looked at Jenny. Stricken. Mortified.

A murmur of questions and speculation was building. Snippets like, "They had an affair when Josh was dying? How could they!" came through loud and clear.

Andi jumped atop an inverted bucket and whistled. "Good grief, people," she shouted. "What planet do you come from? Haven't you heard of science?"

She swept the crowd with her indignant glance then pointed at Sam. "Yes, Sam is the twins' biological father. He helped his brother and Jenny conceive because Josh was sick. Remember? Dying. Remember?"

The group looked uncomfortable. One or two people gave Sam conciliatory smiles. He grabbed the railing and pulled himself to his feet. Unfortunately, he stood up too fast, and black spots flashed before his eyes. He swayed unsteadily.

Gordon grabbed one arm, Jenny the other.

"We're going to the hospital and get a couple of X rays," Gordon said.

"Andi, please call the ranch and tell them we might be late," Jenny ordered.

Kristin suddenly appeared; Donnie followed a few steps behind. "What happened? Donnie just caught me. How can I help?"

"Take Ida Jane home for me?" Jenny asked.

"Of course."

Sam tried to navigate under his own power, but neither Gordon nor Jenny would let go. Donnie parted the crowd with a single command.

Sam kept his head down and focused on not stepping on Jenny's toes, but something made him look up. His gaze met his mother's. Her eyes were filled with accusations.

He swallowed a sigh. *Oh, the joy of Christmas.*

"ARE YOU Mrs. O'Neal?" the desk clerk asked Jenny.

Sam had already disappeared down the hallway, Gordon at his side.

"Yes," Jenny said without hesitation.

"I need you to fill this out," the young woman said. "Insurance forms. Medical history."

Jenny absently reached for the paperwork. She was a pro at filling out forms—she'd done a million for Josh.

Sam had been understandably subdued on the trip to the hospital. No doubt his injury was only part of it; they also had to deal with the gossip that would be flying around. Diane would want answers.

Gordon hadn't said a word about Ida's revelation, but Jenny knew she wouldn't be that lucky where her mother-in-law was concerned.

She tried to focus on the lines of the form. *Heart*

disease? No. High blood pressure? No. Kidney prob-lems? She scanned the list and suddenly felt swamped by fear. So many things could go wrong. There were so many ways she could lose him. Just like she'd lost Josh.

The antiseptic smells and the bright overhead lights of the hospital brought back memories of Josh on his downward slide. The fear and desperation. The unspoken prayer that a miracle was in the making, when deep in her heart she knew there was no hope.

Where's Sam? What if they found something wrong?

She jumped to her feet and started toward the door that said Authorized Personnel Only.

"Wait," the admittance clerk said.

"I can't. I have to make sure he's okay."

The girl—who couldn't be older than eighteen or nineteen—gave her an odd look. "You're Mrs. O'Neal," she said. "The teacher."

Jenny paused, torn between good manners and her need to see Sam. The girl walked toward her. "I'm Mandy Sogerson. You taught my little brother, Robbie. I was sorry to hear about your husband."

Jenny was still trying to pull an image of Robbie to mind, when she saw a light go on in Mandy's face. If Jenny's husband was dead, then Jenny wasn't the *right* Mrs. O'Neal.

"Thank you, Mandy. Your brother was quite a char-acter! Tell him I said hello. Now, I have to see Sam."

"Um…but…you're not…I can't…"

Jenny sympathized with the young woman's dilemma but she was beyond caring what anyone thought.

"Listen, Mandy, I'm the person who lives in Sam's house, fixes his food, raises his children. If you want to see a marriage license, you'll have to get in line. I need to be with him."

The stalemate ended a second later when the door opened and Sam walked out, followed by Gordon. He looked at Jenny. "Are you ready to go home?"

Jenny's knees felt weak, but she managed to clear the distance between them. "Are you okay?"

He hugged her tight, as if to convince her that he was healthy and whole.

"He's going to be just fine," Gordon said, patting her shoulder. "It helps to have a hard head."

"I prefer to think it was my years as a stuntman that saved me," Sam said, his tone thick with humor. He pushed back a lock of hair that had come loose from Jenny's elaborate hairdo. "No concussion. Hairline fracture of one rib, but I still think that's an old break."

He and Gordon exchanged a look. "Don't tell your mother, but I'm going to sneak a cigar before you take me back," Gordon said. He picked up his coat from the pile Jenny had been watching and walked through the pneumatic doors.

"He's a good man," Sam said, then he put his arm around Jenny's shoulders. "Let's sit down and talk a minute."

Jenny wasn't sure she could. Her emotions were all over the place: relief, residual panic, dismay at being the center of all the gossip once word hit the grapevine, and shock from the unnerving memory of Josh's image blocking her view of Sam. Maybe she was losing her mind. Her maternal grandmother had gone crazy. Maybe mental instability was an inherited trait.

"Can we go home instead?"

He steered her to an uncomfortable-looking chair in the far corner of the waiting room. "Soon." He sat beside her, then leaned close enough to take both of her hands in his.

"Jenny, Gordon and I were talking. We can do some damage control. If you move back to town—"

She blinked. "What?"

"I was wrong. I should have known this would come out and that people would think the worst. They always do."

"You don't care what people think."

"No, but you do."

Jenny looked at the admittance desk. Just the top of Mandy's head was visible behind a magazine. "I read somewhere that most people's attention span is just slightly longer than the life span of a mayfly. I'm through living my life worrying about keeping the rest of the world—even the people of Gold Creek—happy." She stood. "Can we go home now?"

FACEDOWN ON KRISTIN'S massage table the next morning, Sam blinked the last vestiges of sleep from his eyes. By the time they'd dropped Gordon off, replayed the whole fiasco for Greta and checked on the twins, it was after midnight. Lack of sleep—plus the jet lag from his East Coast trip—left him feeling slightly hungover.

"You know, Jenny thinks she saw Josh's ghost, Sam," Kristin said as she dug her fingers into the tender muscles of his upper shoulder.

He gritted his teeth when she touched a particularly tender spot. "I beg your pardon?" he asked, his voice echoing from beneath the table.

Kristin had spent the night in Jenny's room at the ranch and had offered to give him a massage before she headed home to Oregon. Despite their little talk at the hospital, Sam and Jenny hadn't really discussed what happened the night before. He'd been wiped out on the ride home, so much so he let Jenny drive.

"I believe the human spirit never dies. And I'm sure Josh is still a part of our lives, but I don't think his ghost suddenly appeared on the stairway, blocking her view of you," Kris said.

Sam lifted his head. "Ghost?"

"Whatever she saw was probably a result of a combination of stress and grief," she went on as if he hadn't spoken. "Her first Christmas without Josh...all suddenly got to her. Unfortunately, now she thinks she's lost it."

"Lost what?"

"Her mind. Like Grandma Suzy."

Sam pushed his face into the cutout and cussed.

"There's been too damn much talk about ghosts," he muttered.

Kristin plied his lower back with her thumbs. "I agree, but I *did* feel a chill right before I left. Maybe the place *is* haunted."

Sam kept his groan to himself. He lifted himself up on one elbow. "Does it really matter? My fall was an accident. I'm fine. Jenny's fine. Isn't she?"

Kristin nodded. "She and Ida are feeding the twins breakfast. They're getting so big. I can't believe they're nearly four months old. Where does the time go?"

Sam plopped back down on his belly. Time wasn't on his side. He'd locked Jenny into a five-year plan that might be the worst thing for her. She was under great stress and now the gossip in Gold Creek was going to make it worse.

Kristin added more oil to her hands then attacked his upper back, probing the tense muscles in his shoulders. After a minute, she said, "You love her, don't you?"

Sam kept his head buried. "Where'd that come from?"

"I can tell. Andi said you did, but I wasn't sure before now."

Sam wasn't thrilled to know he was so transparent. He changed the subject. "My right calf still hurts. Can you work on it?"

She applied her strong hands to his leg muscles, and Sam let out a soft groan. Neither spoke for several minutes, then Kristin said, "Maybe Josh appeared because he knows Jenny loves you, too."

Sam rolled to his side and sat up, making sure the flannel sheet was tucked securely around his waist. "You know, Kris, I appreciate the massage, but this kind of talk isn't relaxing."

Her look of chagrin made him give her a light punch on the shoulder. "It's okay. I feel great, and you have a long drive ahead of you. Thanks. I mean it."

She smiled apologetically and started to leave the room but stopped by the door. "Maybe Josh came to say goodbye. He was your brother, Sam. He'd want you to be happy. He loved Jenny and he'd want her to be happy, too. If the two of you can make each other happy, then why wouldn't he be cool with that?"

Sam didn't answer. He didn't believe in ghosts. Josh was gone, and Sam had a big mess on his hands. Not the least of which was Diane, who would no doubt show up any minute with a slew of questions. Questions Sam didn't want to answer.

"SO, HOW BAD is the gossip?" Jenny asked.

Andi had arrived twenty minutes earlier toting a six-foot spruce that she said Sam had asked her to pick up.

"Not too bad," her sister answered. "I'd say only about sixty percent of the town has heard."

A naughty grin played across her lips. "Of course, the

other forty percent is away on vacation, but most people aren't checking their e-mail, so you're safe.''

Ida Jane snickered. Jenny wasn't sure Ida fully understood the ramifications of her disclosure last night. She'd tried bringing up the subject, but with Greta popping in and out of the kitchen to work on the preparations for tonight's feast, Jenny hadn't had much private time with her aunt.

She stuck her tongue out at her sister.

Andi laughed and gave Ida Jane a kiss on the top of her head. "Lighten up, sis. Ida Jane and I did you a huge favor. Now, you and Sam can do the right thing and get married and everybody will understand why.''

"Married?'' Jenny croaked.

"Who's getting married? Jenny and Sam? When?'' Ida Jane asked, nearly dropping Tucker's bottle.

"The sooner the better in my book,'' Andi said, adding her helping hand to Ida's. "But you'll have to ask them.''

Jenny's head throbbed so badly it felt as if she'd fallen down the stairs. She hadn't slept well. Kristin talked in her sleep. She kept saying the name Zach over and over.

When Jenny questioned her about it this morning, she'd huffily snapped, "That's my business. Keep your nose out of it.''

Jenny had been too wiped out to fight. She still was. She could barely muster the energy to contemplate decorating a Christmas tree—something Josh always made a big production of. Eggnog, decorated cookies, carols on the stereo. One year he rented an electric fireplace to give their home that "holiday ambience,'' he'd said.

"Can we not talk about this, Andi?'' Jenny said with a sigh. "Poor Sam is probably—''

She didn't get her sentence out because the kitchen

door opened and Sam walked in, looking as fit as she'd ever seen him. "Good morning, everyone. Miss Ida, you look lovely. Nice sweater. Very festive." He smiled at the older woman before nodding at Andi. "Hi, Andi, thanks for picking up the tree. How much do I owe you?"

Andi made a swishing motion with her hand. "I figure we're even. Word got out about your fall and before the night was over, half the town had stopped by for a cup of coffee and to pick my brain."

Sam didn't look alarmed. "Did you get a sense of what people are thinking?"

Andi took Tucker from Ida Jane and kissed his plump belly. "Of course. Nobody is shy about speaking their mind in Gold Creek."

Sam poured himself a cup of coffee then casually leaned back against the counter. "Tell us."

"I tried telling Jenny but she got huffy."

Sam turned his gaze her way. Jenny's heart did a somersault. With the bright sunlight pouring in through the window behind him, he looked vital and alive. Suddenly she yearned for something she didn't dare acknowledge. Josh had only been dead four months. Jenny owed him more loyalty than that.

"We have a tree to decorate," she said. "And food to prepare for the employees' party. We don't have time for chitchat. If the people of Gold Creek want to think badly of us, then let them."

Chin high, she set Lara's bottle on the table and rose. "I'll be in the living room setting out the Christmas decorations."

She knew it was childish. She couldn't run from this, but she wasn't about to talk about the future until she'd had a chance to talk to Sam. Alone.

JENNY LOOKED AROUND the large spacious room. She'd set up her easel in one corner. The soft morning light and panoramic view inspired her in a way she'd never dreamed possible. Some mornings she flew out of bed charged with a sense of discovery and wonder. In many ways, she'd never been happier.

She wasn't going to let gossip or public opinion, or even Josh, run her out of this haven that felt so homelike.

Nor was she going to let anyone else dictate her morality. She knew what was going on between her and Sam. The attraction was undeniable, but they were adults. Friends. Parents. They could handle it. There wasn't going to be a hasty wedding just because the people who'd once changed her diaper thought there should be.

"Where do you want the tree?" Sam asked, waltzing the ungainly tree through the doorway.

"Where do you usually put it?"

He looked at her blankly.

"You've never had a tree here before?"

He shrugged. "Why bother? I was always invited to your holiday get-togethers at Ida Jane's. It never seemed worth the effort."

He scowled at her. "Stop looking at me like I'm some kind of Grinch. I put up lights outside. Most years. And I always take my crew to dinner at the Golden Corral. You're the one who suggested having the party here."

"I know. I didn't say you were cheap."

He manhandled the tree past the furniture, propping it up against the wall in the far corner of the room. "Where's the stand?"

She kicked the cardboard box labeled Xmas Tree Stand in Josh's neat script.

Sam went on in his own defense. "I give the guys

who live around here a big fat turkey to go with their bonuses. The bunkhouse brigade get bottles of Jack Daniel's and movie passes.''

"I know. Josh always said there were guys lined up to work at the Rocking M over the holidays. It's just that I can't imagine celebrating without a tree. Josh used to spend hours selecting the perfect one. Not too tall, not too fat, not too skimpy.''

"Just pick one,'' she'd cry in exasperation when her toes were ready to fall off from the cold.

Sam opened the box and extricated the stand, which could revolve, play music and make the lights flash. Josh had ordered it from a catalog the first year they were married.

Sam carried it to the center of the windows where the glass formed a triangle. "Here or in the corner?''

Jenny's throat closed. "There.''

She laid Lara, who was almost asleep on her shoulder, down in the fabric-sided playpen. Andi and Tucker were nowhere to be found. Probably in Ida Jane's room, plotting her and Sam's next public fiasco.

"Where are the ornaments?'' Sam said, rising to his feet after securing the tree in the stand.

Jenny looked at him. "Are you serious?''

His eyes went wide in question. "What? You don't have any ornaments?''

"Of course I have ornaments. Your brother was an ornament nut. He couldn't pass by a Christmas shop without buying something. I meant, we put the lights on first, then the ornaments. Isn't that how you do it?''

His face flushed, and he walked toward the kitchen. "I'll get some water. It takes water. Right?''

His snippy tone made her flinch. What kind of teacher

made a student feel badly about not knowing an answer? she asked herself.

Feeling crummy, she eyed the six boxes sitting beside the leather couch. She picked the one that said Lights and Decor. She peeled back the tape and looked inside. Nice and neat. Josh not only put up the tree to exacting standards, he took it down just as precisely.

Jenny yanked out the carefully wrapped strands and pitched them toward the tree. The thick carpet would keep them from breaking. When the last had made its flight and was lying on the floor like a deflated balloon, she pulled out a box labeled Angel.

"Angel?" she questioned, examining the box. She lifted the lid and looked inside.

Her hands started to shake and she nearly dropped the box before she managed to sit down. She let it rest on her thighs as she stared at the finely crafted angel made of lace and beads with a porcelain head. She remembered all too clearly the first time she'd seen it.

Last year. The Sunday before the Christmas break. Jenny had been exhausted from her pregnancy and from rehearsing the play her fourth-grade class was performing. Josh had insisted on dragging her out of their nice warm house to attend the Gold Creek Garden Club's holiday gift bazaar.

"You don't feel well enough to bake, Jen, and we can't decorate the tree without Christmas cookies and eggnog," he'd said. She'd gone along even though the smell of baked goods had made her stomach heave.

It had taken him an hour to pick out his selection of goodies—mostly because he had to talk to everyone he met. Then, just as Jenny was ready to drop, he spotted the angel.

"Jenny, I found her," he'd exclaimed so loudly everyone in the Methodist Hall turned to look.

At seventy-five dollars, the angel decoration didn't impress Jenny. "It's pretty, Josh, but what's wrong with the star we always use?"

He'd wheedled, cajoled, argued and begged, and like always, Jenny had been tempted to let him have his way, but maybe because she was tired and cranky, for once she'd put her foot down.

"No, Josh. We have a baby on the way. We can't afford it." They hadn't learned about the twins yet.

Unwilling to listen to any more of his arguments, she'd walked home. Josh had shown up fifteen minutes later full of apologies and sweet talk. He'd stashed his grocery bag full of goodies in the kitchen and put on Mannheim Steamroller—his favorite album—while they decorated the tree.

He'd hung the star without a word.

But, secretly, he'd bought the angel. Then packed it up until next year. No doubt hoping that Jenny would be too busy with their child to care about his extravagance.

Sam entered the room with a watering can. He stared at the haphazard display of lights scattered across the floor then looked at Jenny. "I take it we use all of them?" he asked with aplomb.

A funny little tickle wiggled through her chest. Sam didn't play games. He didn't plot and plan then disappear. He would never buy a seventy-five-dollar angel then hide it in a box for a year.

"Sam?" Jenny said, watching him dig through the tree's thick branches to fill the reservoir.

"Uh-huh?"

"Sam," she repeated.

He set the watering can aside and looked up from his kneeling position. "What?"

"I love you."

CHAPTER THIRTEEN

SAM REGISTERED the words, but before he could think of a reply, Kristin appeared, carrying her massage table in its zippered canvas tote.

"I'm leaving," she announced.

Sam jumped to his feet and jogged across the room. He relieved her of the strap of the weighty bag and hefted it to his shoulder. "Let me carry that for you. It's the least I can do after a free massage. Where are your keys?"

She fished them from the pocket of her jeans. "Thanks. That'll give me time to tell Ida Jane and Andi goodbye."

As he walked toward the door, he saw the two sisters embrace then head for Ida Jane's room.

Kristin's Subaru wagon was parked to the right of the flagstone walk; Ida Jane's massive pink Caddie, sat cockeyed off to the left. Sam took his time loading the table then drove the wagon across the compound to the gas pump where he filled up her tank. He also checked her oil and cleaned her windshield.

The mundane tasks helped keep his mind—and his heart—from overreacting to Jenny's unexpected announcement. Love? What kind of love? Her comment was too out of the blue to be anything but gratitude. Or holiday turmoil. Right?

He parked Kris's car where he'd found it but left the

engine on and the heater running. The early-morning sunshine had given way to valley fog that had pushed its way up the hillsides. He shivered, wishing he'd grabbed a jacket.

As he started toward the house, the sound of hooves in a hurry stopped him. Hank, atop his old favorite, Jughead, pulled to an abrupt halt in front of the gate. The bay's huffing breath appeared dragonlike in the cold air.

"What's going on?" Sam asked, sensing the urgency in his usually unruffled foreman's manner.

"Blue's down."

The health of any animal in his care was always a concern, but the loss of Blue would prove a significant setback to his breeding program. The bull was one of the Rocking M's most important longhorns, and one of Sam's favorites. "Can we reach him by truck?"

Hank nodded. "He's not far off the road. Be faster if we cut the fence."

"Load up what you need, I'll call Rich." Richard Rumbolt had been the ranch veterinarian for years; he was both a dedicated professional and a friend.

Sam dashed to the house. The three sisters were just coming out, with Ida Jane between them. "Hi, ladies. Kris, your car is gassed up and ready to go. Jen, I'm sorry, but you'll have to start the decorating without me. We have an emergency in the field."

Jenny reached out to touch his arm. "Can I help?"

Her concern made him want to take her in his arms and kiss her, but, of course, he couldn't. There was still too much between them to take anything for granted. "I appreciate the offer, but we won't know how bad it is until Rich gets here."

He handed Kris her keys and gave her a friendly hug. "Have a happy holiday."

As he hurried past, he looked at Andi and said, "You're sure we can't talk you into joining us tonight. Got a few lonesome cowboys who'd think Christmas had come early if you so much as smiled at them."

Her cheeks took on a rosy hue; she gave him a pointed look. "Thanks, but I'll be pumping caffeine into the veins of Gold Creek's finest until eight o'clock, then I'm going to crash. I still have two more days of retail, but I'll be here Monday night. Your mother and Gordon offered to pick me up."

Christmas Eve. Sam's stomach made an unhappy sound.

"You missed breakfast this morning, boy," Ida Jane said, giving him a wink. "Better grab a handful of cookies before you run off to work. Greta and I decorated them."

He gave her a quick kiss on the forehead then hurried inside. He'd been looking forward to a relaxed "family" day, but it couldn't be helped. Besides, what did he know about tree trimming? Josh had been the Christmas guru, not Sam.

"HAVE YOURSELF a merry little Christmas..."

Vince Gill's CD provided the background music as Jenny stepped away to scrutinize her creation. She'd never had this much autonomy in tree trimming before. Josh had been a control freak when it came to "his" tree.

"What do you think?" she asked Ida Jane, who'd given up an hour earlier and was now supervising from the recliner.

"The tree's absolutely lovely," Ida Jane said.

Something in her voice made Jenny drop the strand

of gold beads in her hand back into the box. "Is something wrong, Auntie? You sound a little sad."

"I was thinking about my sister. Suzy loved pretty things. Looks were important to her. Some said that's why she married Bill—for all the things he could give her."

Jenny sat across from her on the sofa. "You mean she married Grandfather for his money? She didn't love him?"

Ida shrugged slightly. "She had her reasons for marrying Bill. He was a good man. Kind…and lonely. I think they cared for each other—even if he was older."

"How many years?"

Ida smiled, as if hearing something Jenny hadn't meant to impart. "Far more than you and Sam."

Jenny realized it was no use trying to hide her feelings for Sam from Ida Jane. "Ida, I think I'm in love with Sam. I know I shouldn't be. It's too soon. It's not fair to Josh—"

Before she could finish, Ida made a rude sound. "Life wasn't fair to Josh, but you can't make up for that, Jenny. You've got no say in who lives and who dies, and you don't have a lot of control over who you love. I know, honey, believe me."

Jenny found her aunt's words reassuring, but she sensed Ida was not talking about her niece and Sam.

"Are you referring to a man in your life, Auntie? Someone you loved?"

Ida nodded. She turned her head to stare at the fire. Her profile looked impossibly young. "Yes, dear. There was a man, but, like Josh, he was gone too soon."

"He died?"

"Killed in the war."

Jenny reached across the distance and took Ida's hand. "I'm sorry."

It broke her heart to think that Ida had loved this man so much that she'd never married or had children of her own. "How come you never told us about him? Does it still hurt to talk about him?"

Ida squeezed her hand. "No, dear, death is a part of life and, if you're brave—like you are—you accept that and move on. Sometimes in my dreams I still see him. He was a charmer. So handsome. But we would never have had a life together."

"Why?"

"Because he loved my sister."

Jenny took in a quick breath. "Oh no."

"Yes. It wasn't her fault. Or his. She was so very lovely—a butterfly men yearned to hold. At the time, I wasn't terribly gracious about what I considered my sister's defection, but Suzy was just being Suzy."

Jenny sighed. She'd seen firsthand what could happen to sisters when a man came between them. Andi and Kristin had tussled over Tyler Harrison, and the episode had triggered years of hard feelings. "At least you and Grandma Suzy made up before she died," Jenny said. "And you helped her when she came back to Gold Creek to live."

Ida looked at her strangely. "She came home, but only after she'd been on the lam for ten years."

Jenny blinked in confusion. "I beg your pardon?"

Ida sighed and closed her eyes. "Suzy blamed herself for what happened with Bill. Later on, after the money was gone and she'd lost her looks, her mind went, too. Guilt will do that to you."

A shiver passed through Jenny, and she inched closer to the fire. A gray mist had moved in, giving the sky an ominous feeling. "Auntie, did our grandmother kill our grandfather?"

Ida's eyes snapped open. She blinked twice as if coming out of a trance. "No. Of course not. What gave you that idea?"

"You said she felt guilty."

Ida pushed the knitted throw off her lap and started to stand up. "There are all kinds of guilt, Jenny girl. Sometimes we feel guilty about things that aren't even our fault—like the way you feel about Sam."

Jenny helped the elderly woman to her feet and handed her the cane. "I'm going to lie down a little while so I'll be fresh for the party tonight. I want to look my best for those studly young cowboys."

Ida's use of the word *studly* made Jenny laugh. "I'll come down later and help do your hair," she offered.

Ida Jane gave her a scornful look. "You just worry about impressing Sam. I can take care of myself."

"I don't know if I'm ready," Jenny confessed. "It feels too soon to be talking about this."

Ida gave her a hug. "Life moves on, Jenny love. Whether you're ready or not. Just take what comes and try not to hurt too many people in the process."

The last sentence seemed oddly introspective, but Jenny couldn't imagine what Ida Jane had to regret. She'd been a caregiver her whole life. She'd given up a career to help when her mother was dying of cancer and her father started to fail; she'd taken in her sister and niece when Suzy's mental health crumbled, then later raised her niece's three orphaned babies.

"Ida Jane, I don't tell you this often enough, but I love you. And I'm so glad you're here with me. I don't think I could have survived Josh's death and the birth of the twins without you."

Her aunt smiled and patted her cheek. "Of course you could have, dear. You have Sam."

After Ida was gone, Jenny finished picking up the boxes and bits of paper strewn on the floor. She set the four ornaments she'd selected for Sam to hang on the end table. She didn't know why it mattered, but she wanted him to be a part of this ritual.

Although he'd celebrated every holiday for the past twelve years with Jenny and her family, this was different. The dynamics had changed, and Sam was now a part of her life in a way that meant they could never return to the old patterns. It was up to her to create new patterns. Even if it hurt.

She still had one ornament to put in place. The tree-topper. She'd left it till last because she couldn't decide whether to use the angel or the star. Swallowing against the knot in her throat, she gazed at the tree, hoping for an answer.

"Use the angel, Jenny penny. I bought it for you."

She heard Josh's voice as clearly as if he were standing beside her. "No," she said aloud. "You bought it for yourself. Because you wanted it. Because you always got everything you wanted."

"Not everything."

His dry wit—so perfectly Josh—hit her like an avalanche. Tears filled her eyes; mucus closed off her breathing passages. A harsh cry clambered up her throat and escaped like the desperate wail of a drowning woman. She sank to her knees as if in prayer.

"Oh, Josh, I'm so sorry," she whispered, clasping her arms around her ribs trying to keep her sobs inside. "I'm so very, very sorry."

She wasn't certain what she regretted most—loving Sam or not missing Josh enough. Despite all that she and Josh had shared—the laughter and tears, the squabbles and disagreements—Jenny was finding it harder and harder to hold on to the past. Maybe the time had come to move on.

IT WAS DARK by the time Sam got back to the house. The day had stayed cold and dreary. The wet chill was the kind that worked its way into the bones, and he planned to detour to the living room to stand in front of the fire before dashing upstairs to shower.

His guests would be arriving in less than an hour, but he knew that everything was ready. Hank had talked to Greta several times, updating her on Blue's condition. After Rich's initial diagnosis—a respiratory infection—they'd transported the massive animal to the barn and pumped him full of antibiotics. There was little Sam or Hank could do, but they'd stayed close by on a kind of deathwatch that seemed all too familiar to Sam.

Then just fifteen minutes ago, the bull seemed to perk up, getting to his feet to take some water and feed. Sam had been so relieved he'd had to leave so no one would see how much he'd been affected.

Sam left his manure-covered boots on the deck and walked inside. Several scents hit him—candles burning in a yule log, cinnamon and pumpkin, prime rib and pine. The whole place seemed alive with color and warmth. He hung up his coat in the closet then walked to the great room.

At the far end, in front of the windows, the Christmas tree twinkled with tiny lights of every color. Awash with ornaments too plentiful and diverse to appreciate from a distance, Sam stood with his back to the fire and smiled.

"She did a good job, wouldn't you say?"

Sam turned to find Ida Jane standing in the doorway.

She looked elegant in a silver and black pantsuit. A sprig of holly adorned one lapel. Sam walked to her and kissed her cheek. "Hello, Miss Ida. You look lovely. And my house has never looked better. You and Jenny did a great job of decorating."

He turned and looked again. Crystal snowflakes were suspended in the windows by what he assumed was fishing line. The artful arrangement actually made them look like falling snow. Colorfully wrapped gifts of all sizes clustered around the base of the tree, which made a slow revolution to the music-box-sounding rendition of "We Three Kings."

Squinting, he noticed several ornaments lying on the end table closest to the couch. "She missed a couple," he said to Ida Jane.

"She left those for you to hang."

He glanced at her. "Why?"

"So you'd feel a part of the festivities. I put up my couple, and the twins did their part," she said with a grin. "Those are yours."

Sam's heart swelled at the thoughtful gesture. He walked over and picked up one. It was a metal cast of a San Francisco streetcar. For some reason it triggered a memory.

Jenny, Josh and Sam had been in the city two years ago to see a Giants game. They'd taken B.A.R.T. in early and were wandering around SoMa, the artsy area South of Market, when Josh spotted a little shop selling Christmas things. Sam and Jenny had groaned in unison, knowing what that meant to their agenda. But he'd emerged just minutes later. "Perfect," he'd declared. "Now, whenever we hang this, we'll remember the great day we had together."

Sam took a deep breath. Instead of the pain he expected to feel, there was a warm sense of nostalgia.

"Where should I put it?" he asked.

"Wherever it belongs," a different voice said.

He spun around. Jenny.

His mouth dropped open. She was dressed in red. Her skirt was snug around the hips and stopped well above her knees. The sparkly sweater—also red—had a scoop neck that made the simple gold chain she wore look dazzling against her pale skin.

By sheer willpower he managed to say, "How do you know where that is?"

She walked toward him. "You'll know. Trust me."

He glanced at Ida, who appeared to be watching them with interest. He set the little cable car back down and shoved his hands in his pockets. "Later. I've got to grab a shower and sign the cards for my crew. I thought I'd have time this afternoon… If you ladies will excuse me, I'll be back shortly."

He sidled past Jenny, being careful not to breathe in her fragrance. He'd already stood in a chilly rain most of the afternoon, he didn't want to do anything that would require another cold shower. He paused before leaving the room, though, and said, "You both look wonderful, by the way. Really beautiful."

Then he turned and took the stairs two at a time. His shower was quick. He didn't want to give himself time to think, to wonder, to read anything into Jenny's dress and the gesture of the ornaments. And he still hadn't figured out what she'd meant when she'd said she loved him. Brotherly love? Fatherly love? Husbandly love?

"Coward," he muttered as he dressed. He opened his closet to find a tie—the least he could do was dress properly since she looked so elegant, and his gaze was drawn to a hatbox on the shelf overhead. He knew without looking what it contained: Josh's green cowboy hat.

His fist closed around a Jerry Garcia tie—a gift from Jenny and Josh. He tied it quickly and left the room. Keeping his mind on business, he took the back passage to his office, opened the door and went straight to his safe, which was located in a cabinet under a lighted drawing table.

Greta had purchased a box of western greeting cards and left it on his desk. All Sam had to do was count out each employee's bonus then sign the card and label it. He withdrew an envelope of cash that he'd put aside for this purpose and walked to his desk. It didn't take long. He'd already decided on the dollar amounts weeks before. When the last one was finished, he was surprised to see four, hundred-dollar bills remaining.

Tim and Rory. He'd forgotten about the two men who'd gotten into a fight and been fired. Rory was living at home with his widowed mother. Tim was still in jail awaiting trial. He'd have to remember to send Rory a check next week. He was a good kid—just full of piss and vinegar. Much like Sam had been at that age.

He returned to the safe and knelt on one knee to work the combination. When he heard the click, he opened the door and placed the bills on top of some envelopes. He was about to close it, when something made him look a second time. *That's Josh's handwriting.*

He took out a slightly yellowed envelope and looked at the postmark: 1992. He opened it and found a greeting card with a cheesy image of two men in a fishing boat. The caption read, For My Brother on Father's Day.

Sam couldn't remember receiving it, but that had been a long time ago. When Josh and Jenny were in college, and Sam had been feeling more alone than he thought possible. He'd tried dating for a while but couldn't find the right person. Finally, he'd given up and devoted his time to his business.

He opened the card, expecting to see Josh's sloppy but effusive signature. Instead, there was a fairly neatly written message on the inside flap.

Sam,
Just a little note to say thanks. Jenny told me I don't do that enough. She's right. But it's not because I don't appreciate everything you've done for me. I do. I just get busy and forget to say the words.

Without getting too sappy—and because Jen's standing here waiting to mail this—thanks for giving me this way-cool life. College is a kick and we both know I wouldn't be here without you footing the bills. I love you, brother, and I promise someday I'll find a way to give back a little of what you've given me.

Your loving bro,
Josh

Sam's hand trembled. Was this a sign? He didn't believe in signs.

It's okay to love her, Sam. Jenny needs you, and you need her. It's the way it was meant to be. I did my part.

Sam heard the words as clearly as if Josh were talking on the baby monitor in the next room. He closed his eyes and rocked back on his heels. "Oh, great, I'm losing my mind."

"I hope not. We have fifteen people coming for dinner."

He turned to look behind him and lost his balance, landing on his butt on the oak flooring. It wasn't far to fall but he winced. His hip was still sore from the previous night's tumble.

Jenny walked across the room, her sexy high heels snapping in a sultry manner. "Are you okay? It's not your head, is it?"

Could be. "I'm fine. I just… I'm fine."

She stopped a few feet from him and took a breath. "Yeah, me, too. Fine, but about this close to tears." She held her hand up with the finger and thumb almost touching. "Right?"

Sam nodded. He knew she wouldn't think less of him if he admitted how sad he'd been the past few months. "I found a card from him. A Father's Day card. I don't remember getting it, but you know how that goes. We always assume we'll have another holiday and another."

She walked a little closer and held out her hand to help him up. "I know. Every ornament I hung today had a memory attached to it."

He took her hand and rose. "That must have been hard. I'm sorry I wasn't here to help."

She shook her head. He liked her hair down instead of swept off her neck like last night. "It was probably better that you were gone. It gave me a chance to take my time and come to grips with what was happening."

"What do you mean?"

"I was saying goodbye." She looked at him, her eyes luminous with tears. "To Josh. To the way things were."

Sam wanted to take her in his arms and comfort her, but he didn't trust himself. He'd kissed her twice and both times he'd felt his heart would burst if he didn't tell her how much he loved her. This wasn't the time nor place.

He returned the card to the safe. "In his note, he mentioned how much fun you were having in college."

She made a little sniffing sound. "It wouldn't have been quite as carefree without your help."

"I didn't do—"

She shook her head in warning. "Sam, Josh was very frank about his finances. He didn't see anything wrong with spending your money, since you offered. He said I didn't have a problem using the Gold Creek scholarship money the town had set up for me and my sisters, so why should he turn down what you offered?"

"He was right. I was glad to help. I didn't go to college until I was twenty-five, and then mostly night school. Believe me, it wasn't that much fun. Hearing about your parties and road trips was my chance to live that life vicariously."

She didn't say anything, so he started toward the desk. "Shall we go? Our guests will be arriving soon."

Jenny reached out and touched his arm. "I wanted to talk to you about what I said this morning."

Sam's empty belly growled from the sudden shot of acid that hit. "Could it wait? I know you planned to help Andi at the shop tomorrow, but we have all of Monday before Gordon and Diane show up, don't we?" He'd made it clear that tonight's party was for employees and guests only—although he would have made an exception for her sisters. The family get-togethers were scheduled for Christmas Eve and Christmas morning.

She looked slightly crestfallen, and he couldn't stop himself from going to her. He pulled her into a light hug. "Jen, I'm not fooling myself into thinking you meant anything serious. It's the holidays, emotions run high this time of year. Let's just try to get through the next couple of days without saying or doing something we'll regret later, okay?''

She looked ready to protest, but in the distance he heard the sound of the doorbell ringing. They looked at each other a moment, then she smiled. She reached between them to fiddle with his tie. ''This looks sharp. I've never seen you wear it. Josh insisted it was too flashy for you, but I told him it would bring out the green in your eyes.''

She lifted her chin and ran her tongue over her bottom lip. ''I was right.''

She's flirting with me. It took every ounce of willpower in his soul not to kiss her. He was going to make it through the holidays if it killed him—which at this rate was a distinct possibility.

CHAPTER FOURTEEN

SAM STOOD in the middle of the kitchen enjoying the rare moment of total quiet. The twins were down for their morning nap. Jenny and Ida had just left to deliver gifts to Ida Jane's friends in town and to pick up last-minute supplies for tonight's Christmas Eve gathering. Greta and Hank were on their way to her sister's in Bakersfield.

His housekeeper had outdone herself preparing the Rocking M feast that had left every one of his guests groaning in bliss. The party didn't break up until midnight, and by then Jenny and Sam were both ready to drop.

Sunday had been hectic with Jenny pitching in to help Andi at the bordello. Sam and Ida Jane had been in charge of the twins. Jenny had returned with sore feet and a raging headache, so Sam sent her to bed early. There hadn't been time to talk this morning, either, since Jenny was up at dawn to start cooking her cioppino. "I like to start the stock early so it can simmer all day, then we throw in the fish at the last minute," she explained when he stumbled downstairs following the aroma that had woken him.

The fog had disappeared and the day, while a chilly forty-five degrees with a crisp northerly wind, was sunny and clear. She'd looked so bright and full of life, he'd longed to pull her into his arms. A part of him wanted to beg her to marry him. Right here, right now. But he knew better than to spring the idea too soon. He would ask her when the time was right. And if she said yes, they could plan their wedding for autumn, waiting the respectful year.

If she says yes. He wandered to the stove and picked up the lid of the steaming cauldron. A heavenly aroma of fish stock, basil and stewing tomatoes filled the air. He closed his eyes and took a deep breath. *I could get used to this.* He hadn't realized just how lonely he'd been.

He stirred the mixture then replaced the lid and walked to the laundry room where Jenny had wrapped presents. He'd asked her to leave everything out because he had a couple of gifts to wrap. The majority of his purchases had been wrapped at the toy store, but these last two had been impulse buys.

The utility room sat just off the kitchen. Its large window faced the driveway. He left the door open so he could hear the phone, and he set the baby monitor on a shelf.

He still couldn't get over the fact that Jenny had entrusted him with baby-sitting. Alone. Her trust was the best gift of all.

The counter was littered with scissors, tape dispensers, ribbons of various widths and colors and bright rolls of wrapping paper. He eyed one with cartoon characters. "No." He considered a green metallic paper, but settled on an old-fashioned design in wine and cream.

"Perfect," he said, withdrawing a postcard-size jeweler's box from the chest pocket of his flannel shirt.

He opened the box; a heart-shaped locket on a gold chain rested on a bed of ivory satin. His work-roughened fingers looked ludicrous touching the delicate piece, but he pried open the catch and glanced inside. Tucker on the left, Lara on the right.

The photos were ones that he'd taken with his digital camera. The images captured each child's individual personality. Princess Lara, Court Jester Tucker.

Smiling, he closed the locket and started cutting the paper. Totally engrossed in his project, he jumped when he heard someone cough from the doorway behind him.

With a muffled curse he spun around to find his mother in the doorway. "Damn. You scared the..." He dropped the epithet. "Hello, Mother, you're a little early. Jenny and Ida Jane are in town. Dinner's not—"

"I know when dinner is, Sam. Gordon and I are picking up Andrea at six—right after she closes the shop. We'll be here at six-thirty as planned."

He hastily finished wrapping the package then pushed it aside. The second gift—which he wasn't even sure he was brave enough to give—would have to wait. The last thing he wanted was to show it to his mother. He knew what she'd say about his plans.

"So, why are you here?"

She gave him a droll look. "Why do you think? To talk to you."

Sam should have known he couldn't avoid this confrontation forever. "Okay. Let's take a cup of coffee into the living room. It's warmer by the fire."

As he grabbed the monitor, he spotted his mother's car parked in the driveway. How had he missed her arrival? Why hadn't the dogs barked? Or was he that oblivious? Shaking his head, he led the way to the kitchen.

"It smells good in here," Diane said.

Sam poured two cups of coffee and handed one to his mother. "Cioppino is Jenny's specialty. She makes it every Christmas Eve.'' As he followed Diane into the living room, he said, "One year, she couldn't find any fresh crab locally, so Josh and I drove to the fish market in San Mateo to buy some. Two hours one way! God, we laughed about that, but it was the best we ever tasted.''

Diane paused at the entrance of the room to look around. She walked slowly to the tree. Sam still hadn't hung the ornaments Jenny had set aside for him. He'd been planning to do that this morning. Alone.

"It's lovely. The room looks so...lived in," she said, her surprise obvious.

"The place needed a family, and now it has one."

"Your brother's family."

Sam looked her in the eye and said, "*My* family, Mother."

She turned to gaze out the window. "Ah, yes, the test tubes. Andi explained it to me after you and Jenny left for the hospital, but that doesn't entitle you to take over your brother's life, Sam."

Sam set down his cup then walked to her side. He waited until she looked at him. "Josh is dead, Mother. I would do anything in my power to change that, but I can't."

"You're dishonoring his memory," she snapped, her eyes flashing with pain.

"How? By providing a home for the children he went to such great lengths to conceive? By loving the woman he loved? Josh would be the first to tell you that he had great taste. He'd expect nothing less. Jenny is a wonderful woman, and those babies upstairs are a part of the three of us—Jenny, Josh and me. By being a family, we honor Josh's memory. It's what he would have wanted."

Her lips curled in a sneer, but the tremor in her voice was one of pain not anger. "How can you be sure?"

"I can't," Sam confessed. "Maybe I'm wrong. Maybe I'm looking for the answer I want to hear because my life was an empty shell before this." He made a gesture that encompassed the room, with its homey decorations, toys and baby swing, candles and snowflakes.

"Maybe you're right, Mother. I didn't have a life of my own so I've taken what Josh left behind," he said, the ache in his chest almost paralyzing.

To his surprise, his mother set down her cup and dropped her purse to the floor then closed the distance between them. "If Josh were here, he'd say that your life made it possible for him to live his life so well."

Her words echoed what Josh had written on that card Sam had found. She placed her hand on his upper arm. "Sam, there are things I've never told you about my life, about Josh's childhood."

Sam didn't want to hear it. She'd try to talk him out of loving Jenny, from asking her to marry him. "The past is over, Mother. Can't we just forget it?"

"Not when it has bearing on the future. Sam, please. Listen to what I have to say. Let that be your Christmas gift to me."

Her pleading tone made him give in. He nodded toward the grouping of chairs by the fireplace. "Let's sit."

She picked up her purse and led the way. Once seated, she opened her large leather satchel and withdrew a videotape. "I also came out here to give you this. Josh sent it to me a month or so before he died. His letter asked that I give this to you and Jenny when the time was right. I called him and asked how I'd know when that was and he said, 'You'll know, Mama.'"

Her eyes filled with tears. "He had such faith in people. I never understood why. I used to disappoint him all the time. I'd say we were going someplace then something would come up and I'd cancel, but he never lost his optimistic outlook on life. And he never stopped trusting the people he loved.''

Sam's chest tightened. "I know. I once called him a cockeyed optimist, and he said, 'Beats the hell out of being a myopic pessimist.' I figured that was me.''

His mother's lips flickered in a near smile. "Or me.''

A second later she handed him the tape.

"What's on it?''

"I have no idea. It's yours, not mine.''

That surprised him, and he studied her face to see if she was lying. She'd had this tape for over six months and hadn't peeked?

"I couldn't bear to view it, Sam. I loved that boy with all my heart and, frankly, I was hurt that he sent *you* a tape. I didn't want to know what he could say to you that he couldn't say to me.''

Sam understood. "But now that you know about the twins' paternity, you figured whatever is on this video has to do with that.''

She didn't deny the charge. Instead, she asked, "Why didn't you use Josh's sperm to make the babies? I went on the Internet and read about the advances they're making in fertilization. It doesn't take much sperm to work.''

Sam sighed. He honestly didn't want to discuss this, but perhaps it would be best to clear the air. "In most cases of testicular cancer, once the diseased testicle is removed, the person still has some sperm available, but young boys who are treated with radiation and chemotherapy before puberty may be left sterile. That's what happened to Josh.''

The color drained from Diane's face. "That was my

fault, too, wasn't it? He got cancer the first time because I didn't get his immunization shots when we were in Mexico. Then he got mumps, and that left him more vulnerable to cancer.''

Sam interrupted. ''Mother, nobody knows why some people get cancer and others don't. Josh never blamed you, and neither do I. It's just the way things worked out.''

He sighed. ''I think Josh set this particular ball in motion just to cover the worst-case scenario. I've talked to a lot of cancer survivors, and they told me there's always a niggling fear the cancer will return.''

She didn't say anything for a moment. ''Andi mentioned that Jenny wanted to use an anonymous donor's sperm, but Josh twisted her arm to use yours.''

Sam nodded. ''He was a master of elaborate plans. I know in my heart Josh didn't plan to die. He was just covering all the bases—looking out for Jenny's welfare. You know how much he loved Jenny.''

Tears welled up in Diane's eyes. ''And you, Sam. He loved his big brother, too.''

Sam reached across the distance and squeezed her hand. ''Josh had a big heart. He loved us all.''

She took a shaky breath and said, ''Even me.''

She broke into tears and clawed in her bag for a tissue. Sam felt helpless; Josh's was the sympathetic shoulder to cry on, not Sam's. ''Of course he loved you. You're his mother.''

''But if it wasn't for me, he'd still be alive.''

''Like I said, you didn't intentionally screw up Josh's immunizations. It couldn't have been easy living in Mexico with a small child. The only thing I never understood is why you went there in the first place.'' He took a breath then asked the question that had been plaguing him for years. "Was it to get away from me? Because of the Carley thing?"

Diane shook her head. In the morning light, she looked older than he remembered. She looked vulnerable—not an adjective he could ever remember using to describe Diane O'Neal. "I knew you'd be mad at me about Carley. But the truth is, Carley was a spoiled brat who would have drained you dry then left you for someone with more money. Believe me, son, it takes one to know one."

Sam's mouth dropped open. Had he unintentionally married Carley because she reminded him of his mother? An odd shiver passed through him.

"I have friends who are still in show business, and they told me Carley's on husband number four at the moment," Diane said. "Who does that remind you of?"

"Wouldn't Freud have had a heyday with that one?" Sam asked, swallowing a chuckle.

Diane made an offhand gesture. "Probably too conventional—they say every man wants to marry his mother and every daughter her father. I'm a slow learner. Three of my husbands were exact replicas of my father, who, unfortunately, was a horse's behind."

Was my father one of the three?

"Your father and Clancy, bless his heart, were the two keepers—and Gordon, of course."

"Why'd you divorce him?" Sam asked.

"Who?"

"My father."

She looked at him blankly, then shook her head. "Oh, my heavens, I never told you about your father?"

Sam shifted uncomfortably. He wasn't sure he wanted to know. "It doesn't matter. Clancy was as good a father as anybody could want.'' Clancy had given Sam both a sense of identity and a secure future.

Diane had a sad, slightly bemused look on her face. ''Pat O'Neal was just a kid. Like me. We were stupid and in love. I got pregnant and he married me. My father didn't give him any choice,'' she said with a chuckle. ''But it was what we both wanted.''

Sam frowned. ''If you loved him, why'd you split up?''

''He was killed in a car accident, Sam. Six months after you were born.''

''I don't remember ever hearing you talk about him,'' Sam said.

Diane sighed. ''His death hit me hard. I was alone with a baby. My mother was no help. My father—like I said—was a jerk. I packed us up and headed west. I ran, Sam. That's what I do when things get hairy.''

Her honest self-appraisal earned her a nod of acknowledgment. Sam understood. After what happened with Carley, he had run, too. Straight to the rodeo circuit.

''I didn't set out to interfere with you and Carley, Sam,'' Diane said, changing the subject. ''I was trying to protect you. You didn't tell me there was a baby. You just blew in that morning and said you were eloping to Vegas. You didn't even give me a chance to wish you good luck.''

Sam suddenly realized she was right. He hadn't been living at home at the time because he'd despised Frank, Diane's then husband. ''Why'd you tell Carley's parents where we were?''

''I wanted them to stop the wedding before you said your vows. I know you, Sam. I knew if you married that twit you'd have stuck by her to the bitter end. Her dad was Mr. Bigshot. I figured he could talk you out of it. I didn't expect him to hire a bunch of thugs to beat you up.''

Sam believed her. Diane may have been distant and flighty but she wasn't purposefully mean or vindictive.

"I knew you'd be angry—you were usually mad at me for something. But I thought we'd get past it. We always had. This just happened to be bad timing.''

Sam didn't understand what she meant. "Timing?"

Her sigh seemed to carry the weight of the world. "I was married to Frank, remember? You hated him. But he was good to me and he adored Josh. Sometimes, when I was working late, he'd pick up Josh from the baby-sitter just so they could have quality time together.''

Something about the way she said the words made gooseflesh race across Sam's neck and arms.

"On the day I went to see Carley's parents, I couldn't find a sitter, and Frank offered to stay with Josh. The visit didn't take as long as I thought it would. I got back, and when I walked into the bedroom I saw something...terrible. Something sick.'' Her eyes filled with tears and she looked away.

Sam shook his head. "He abused Josh?"

She sank into the cushy depths of the chair and closed her eyes as if to block the image. "Years later, I saw a therapist. All I could do was cry for days on end. I thought I was the worst mother ever born.''

"What did he say?" Sam asked.

Diane opened her eyes. "She. My therapist was a woman. She told me that sexual predators like Frank are very clever chameleons who outwardly play one role just to get close to children. She said I might have saved myself years of self-hatred if I'd turned him in to the police and pressed charges, but, instead, I ran away.''

His mother went on. "For two days, Frank begged me not to call the police. He said he'd get help. I waited until I knew for sure he would be busy, then I cleaned out the accounts at the travel bureau and packed everything I could carry. I was just leaving when you showed up. You were so mad you didn't even ask me about our suitcases."

Sam's only memory of the incident was his own fury.

"After you left, Josh and I hopped a bus to Mexico. I spent the next five years terrified that Frank would find us, but one day I called a friend in L.A. and she told me Frank had been killed in a ten-car pileup on the 405."

Sam felt a knot the size of a T-bone steak in his gut. He would have given anything to be able to get his hands around that old sleazeball's scrawny neck. "Did Josh remember any of it?" he asked.

"I don't think so. I asked my therapist if I should bring it up, but she felt it was Josh's call. As long as his life seemed to be happy and well adjusted..." She shrugged her shoulders, then let out a small cry. "But what if it had been eating away at him. Underneath the surface all these years. What if *it* made the cancer come back?"

In the past, Sam might have let his mother blame herself, but not any longer. Life was too damn short to spend agonizing over old hurts.

"Mom, Josh loved you. And, frankly, it took a lot of guts to leave everyone and everything to try to protect your son. If anything, you saved Josh a lot of painful memories by leaving. Like you said, the timing sucked, but that isn't something any of us has control over."

Diane lowered her head and started to weep. He cleared the short distance, dropping to one knee. He couldn't remember the last time he and his mother had hugged, but it wasn't as difficult as he expected it to be.

"Oh, Sam," she cried, throwing herself into his arms. "I'm so sorry. I tried to blame you because you weren't there when I needed you to be." Sniffling against his shirt, she said, "Isn't that pathetic? I was the parent. I should have been the one to take care of things all along, but you were always my rock—even when you were a little boy."

Sam took the praise to heart, and felt the rift between them begin to heal.

Before he could say anything, a sound crackled from the plastic rectangle at his waist. A baby's cry grew in volume. "Tucker," he said, recognizing his son's voice.

Sam pulled back and touched his mother's wet cheek. "Your grandson is calling. Want to help?"

The olive branch hovered between them. "Okay. I have to get back to town to finish up some gift wrapping, but I always have time for my grand—for your children."

Sam stood then held out his hand to help her rise. "Let's go. Tucker hates a wet bottom."

Diane chuckled. "You were the same way. Josh never complained about anything, but you knew what you wanted and wouldn't settle for less."

They were halfway up the staircase when Diane said, "Sam, whatever you and Jenny decide to do is fine with me. I just hope you'll let us—Gordon and me—be a part of your lives."

He took her hand. "Does that offer include baby-sitting if Jenny and I decide to take a honeymoon?"

She squeezed his hand with barely a second's hesitation. "Of course. What's a grandmother for?"

JENNY WALKED in the door of the ranch house at four o'clock. Their guests were due at seven. Andi would close up shop at six. After Diane and Gordon picked her up, they'd swing by Beulah Jensen's to get Ida Jane, who'd decided to "stay awhile and visit" when she and Jenny had stopped by to drop off a plate of Greta's famous rum cake.

Jenny knew she should be exhausted after all the socializing she'd done in the past few days, but she felt oddly wired—like a kid waiting for Santa to show up. She checked her cioppino base, smiling at the rich, mouthwatering aroma. The shellfish, shrimp and hunks of halibut would be added once their guests arrived. A green salad and French bread made this a simple but festive meal.

She arranged a selection of homemade goodies—gifts from Ida Jane's many friends—on a crystal plate, then carried it to the living room. "Hello," she called out, expecting to see Sam and the twins.

When no one answered, she set down the plate and walked to the Christmas tree. The ornaments she'd left for Sam to hang were no longer on the end table. Kneeling, she depressed the switch that made the base revolve.

By the second rotation, she'd spotted each of Sam's choices. "Nice job, Sam," she said softly. She was about to leave, when she noticed something else. Two ceramic panda bears, adorned with wreaths of holly, dangled side by side from a branch. When she looked closely, she noticed one bore the name Lara, the other, Tucker.

"Souvenirs from the National Zoo," she said to herself. "That's something Josh would have done."

Shaking her head, she went in search of her family.

She found all three on Sam's king-size bed. Sound asleep.

The twins were snuggled in the curve of Sam's body. Petite, ladylike Lara was closest to her daddy, one hand curled beneath her chin. Tucker was sprawled on his back, mouth open like a little bird. A large, brightly colored children's book rested on the pillow nearby.

Jenny paused in the doorway to soak up the beauty of the scene. The artist in her longed to record it for posterity. She didn't have time for paints, but Sam's digital camera sat by the television on the built-in stand across from the bed. The thick carpet muffled her footsteps as she crossed the room and picked up the compact camera.

He'd demonstrated how to use it months ago, and although Jenny hadn't used it often, she managed to click a few shots without disturbing her subjects. After turning off the power, she returned the unit to its spot.

As she did, she noticed a video sitting half out of the VCR. The label bore Josh's handwriting. The title said, For Jenny and Sam.

A funny little squiggle moved into her chest. Was this something Sam had had for a long time but never shared with her? She nudged it into the machine and took the remote with her to the foot of the bed. She pressed the mute button and stared at the blue screen.

"I was waiting for you to get home before I watched it," Sam said in a soft voice.

Jenny almost dropped the remote. "Where'd you get it?"

He didn't answer. Instead, he slid off the bed, taking care not to disturb the children. A moment later, he sat beside her. Almost as if on cue, the screen filled with images of a party. Familiar faces, laughing and mugging for the camera.

"Last year's St. Patrick's Day party?" Sam asked.

They watched a moment longer. "Oh, yeah, there I am. Large with child," she said ruefully.

Sam's chuckle was like a pat on the back.

"I wondered what had happened to this tape," she said. "When I was packing, I went through our videos and couldn't find it. I was afraid it might have gotten erased."

They watched in silence. Every so often Josh would hold the camera at arm's length and give some kind of commentary. Jenny was tempted to turn up the volume, but wasn't sure she dared.

Josh made a goofy face—one she'd seen many times. "What a nut," she said, her voice tight with emotion.

Sam took the remote from her hand and pressed pause. "Jenny, we need to talk."

She turned slightly to face him; their knees touched. "Okay."

"I'm not Josh. I'll never be him." He sighed deeply. "He was a unique person who filled our lives with joy and silliness—" He nodded toward the TV. "I miss him too much to even try to take his place—not that I ever could."

Jenny responded without thinking. "Who's asking you to? I agree one hundred percent that you're not Josh. He was lightness and air. And, at times, he could be annoyingly shallow and petty. You're solid and substantial. Reliable. And I've never known you to act unjustly toward anyone."

"He made you laugh."

"And cry," she admitted. Remarkably, she felt no guilt at sharing this truth.

Sam studied her face. "Are you saying you didn't love him as much as I think you do?"

Jenny looked down. *What am I saying?* "No. Josh was everything to me, but in a way he kept me so distracted I never had time to be me. Some days I felt more like a press agent than a wife. Does that make sense?"

Jenny shivered. She'd never expressed those feelings before, even to herself.

"He was a bit like a celebrity," Sam said, an understanding smile on his face. "He'd enter a room and all the attention would turn to him."

Jenny nodded. "Exactly."

"Which worked great for me," Sam said starkly. "He got me off the hook. As long as Josh was around, I could hang out in the background."

Jenny felt a dawning of understanding. "That's how I felt, too," she exclaimed softly. "And I know why I craved that kind of anonymity. Until Josh moved to Gold Creek, my sisters and I were the town's pet project. Everybody had a say in our lives, but Josh distracted them. He was so charismatic and preposterous. Even Gloria Hughes was charmed. She never had anything bad to say about Josh in her column."

Jenny pictured the piece of paper in her pocket. One of the younger members of the Gold Creek Garden Club had printed it off an Internet community loop. It included a copy of the "Glory's World" column that would appear in Thursday's edition of the *Ledger*.

Sam distracted her by running a hand through his dark hair, so different from Josh's golden waves. "I used to think he came by it naturally," he said. "Rumor had it Josh's father was an actor. I don't know if that's true. I never asked Diane, but Josh did have a natural affinity for people, which I certainly lack."

"You're more alike than you think, Sam," she told him. "Look at the way you persuaded people to back your wildfire-awareness campaign. That was just like Josh."

Sam looked away—as if her words were a little too intense for him to handle. "You'd have thought he was Steven Spielberg the way he controlled that camera," Sam said, smiling.

He aimed the remote, adding volume to the action then handed it back to her. Josh's voice—loud enough to be heard over the crowd—made Jenny's heart speed up. A frame later the scene changed to the rocky summit where Sam had taken Jenny to talk after the twins were born. Josh was narrating a commentary about the glorious spring.

"Did you know he'd gone up there?" Jenny asked Sam.

Sam shook his head. "No. In fact, I told him flat out to stay off the four-wheeler and no horseback riding. Ridiculous as it sounds, I was afraid the jostling might spread the disease," he admitted, shaking his head. "I was pretty uptight. I'm not surprised he ducked out for a while."

Jenny sighed. She hadn't wanted the party, either, but for a more selfish reason. "I was mad at him, too. I told him I didn't want to share any of the time we had left with other people."

Josh's voice filled the silence between them. "Even if this turns out to be the last spring I ever experience, I refuse to be sad," he said. "Isn't this a glorious day? How can I be anything but thankful? None of us knows the time limits on our lives, but we put so many limits of other kinds on ourselves, we forget to enjoy what we have."

Jenny sighed. "He said that so often—even before he

got sick. But it always seemed kinda phony to me. Who doesn't worry about tomorrow?''

Sam leaned forward, resting his elbows on his knees. He was wearing a new flannel shirt. The dark heather color made his eyes look enigmatic. "When Josh started chemo, I acted like a coach whose star player was goofing off. It must have driven him crazy.''

Jenny snickered softly. "It did, but he loved you for it. Same with me. I was horribly bitchy at times. I accused him of not taking his illness seriously.'' Sam's look of empathy made her want to curl up in his arms.

She forced herself to look at the screen where Josh was interviewing Beulah Jensen's four-year-old great-granddaughter, Tory. Jenny turned up the volume. Josh's playful, singsong tone made her smile. He asked simple, innocuous questions that made the little girl giggle, then he said, "'Know what? My brother, Sam, is going to be a daddy soon.''

"Rewind that,'' Sam said sharply.

Jenny's hand shook so badly on the slim black device that Sam scooted over and took it from her fingers. The set made a whirring noise then replayed the clip. Sam cursed under his breath.

"He's going to be a terrific daddy,'' Josh continued. "I know because he practically raised me, and look how wonderful I turned out!''

The little girl giggled. "You are funny.''

The video camera nodded up and down. "That's me. Life-of-the-party Josh. But the party will go on without me. That's the way life is. I know it, but I'm afraid Sam might not.''

Sam started to say something but paused when Josh added, "That's what kids are for. They make you live whether you want to or not. They don't give you a choice. And Sam and Jenny are both going to need those babies if things don't work out for me,'' he finished in a serious tone.

The interview ended when Tory's attention span gave out. The viewfinder followed her running to where Jenny was organizing a sack race. ''Well, hello, beautiful,'' Josh said, his tone playfully lecherous. ''Look at the belly on that woman—isn't she gorgeous?''

Jenny laughed. Tears stung her eyes, but they weren't the painful tears she was used to.

''You were the most beautiful pregnant woman I've ever seen,'' Sam said softly. ''Josh used to talk about you every morning when I brought him his meds. 'Just wait, bro',' he'd say. 'She's going to be even more beautiful this morning.'''

In her peripheral vision Jenny saw that their shoulders were close but not touching. She craved human contact but didn't know how to ask. Shyness had never been a part of Josh's makeup.

''The last time we made love was a week after this was taped,'' she said. ''After he started chemo, everything pretty much came to a stop.''

Sam let out a sigh. ''He'd joke about it. You know, telling me to turn off the monitor because he was going to make mad, passionate love with his wife and he didn't want me turning into a voyeur. But I knew he was too sick. He'd wince when I'd help him roll over.''

Josh's coverage of the egg race continued, but Jenny tuned it out. ''I wasn't complaining, I just meant that it's been nine months since…you know.''

The fact that she couldn't say the words aloud brought a surge of heat to her face. What kind of wanton pervert thinks about sex when watching a video of her dead husband? She started to turn off the tape, but an image on the screen caught her eye. Sam. Standing on the balcony.

She reached across Sam and tapped the volume button. "There he is," Josh said. His tone was proud, boastful even. "The man of the hour. Not that Sam would ever think of himself in those terms, but that's what he is. My big brother. My hero."

Sam let out a short burst of air, as if he'd just been punched in the gut. Jenny spontaneously reached behind him and patted his back. "He loved you so much," she said, trying to ignore how good his heat felt against her palm.

"Sam has saved my life so many times he's lost track," Josh went on. "But I haven't. That's why I asked him to be a surrogate father—in case anything happened to me. Because as far as I'm concerned, he was the best father any kid could have."

Sam sighed again and cocked his head to rest against Jenny's. He brought up his left hand and put it on her knee. Josh continued to exude praise for Sam until, apparently, something caught his eye off screen. The camera panned sideways.

"'But, hark, what light on yonder balcony shines. 'Tis Jennifer, a rose by any name at all.'"

Jenny and Sam both chuckled at Josh's butchering of Shakespeare's prose.

In a softer voice, Josh added, "If you two are ever watching this, and I'm not around, I want you to know one thing. Love never dies. You both love me. I love both of you. And the greatest gift you could ever give me would be to love each other."

Suddenly, the screen went black. Jenny and Sam froze.

Sam muttered an expletive then jerked his hand from her knee and tucked it under his armpit.

"That was..." Jenny said. "Eerie."

Sam rose, turned off the TV. He took a deep breath

and slowly let it out. He felt as gut-twisted nervous as he did the first time he rode a bull.

Glancing toward his bed, he looked at Jenny. She seemed nervous, too, and he knew instinctively that they were sitting on the same fence. He returned to her side, sat down and looped his arm across her back. He squeezed her gently and nuzzled his face against the crown of her head.

"A part of me wants to throttle him. He never saw anything wrong with manipulating a situation if the outcome was the one he was looking for," Sam said, picturing his brother grinning like a well-fed cat. "But just because he wanted this doesn't mean—" He closed his eyes for a moment. "What we have to decide is whether or not we care enough for each other—"

"No," Jenny interrupted. "We need to decide if we *love* each other, Sam."

That word again.

Jenny lifted her chin and opened her mouth, but Sam kissed her before she could say anything. He engulfed her in his arms, crushing her to his chest as tightly as he dared. Her soft moan seemed more encouragement than distress. He deepened the kiss.

If it weren't for their children asleep behind them and Jenny's great-aunt puttering around downstairs, he would have pulled her into his bed and demonstrated just how much he loved her. And desired her. Instead, he pulled back.

She let out a soft groan. "You're not changing your mind, are you?"

He snickered softly. "Just the opposite." He looked around. This wasn't the most romantic setting... *Just say it, dufus,* he could almost hear his brother shout.

He scooted off the bed and sank to one knee in front of her. "Jenny, you're the mother of my children *and*" he stressed, "the woman of my dreams. I love you more than one word could possibly convey. Will you marry me?"

He fished his second gift—one that he'd spotted in a jeweler's case in a trendy little shop near his hotel in D.C.—out of his pocket. He hadn't planned on giving it to her this soon, but his talk with Diane had changed things.

He blew a speck of lint off the fat little box before presenting it to her. "It's an antique ruby. I thought it might look nice with a simple band."

Jenny's mouth was open but no words were forthcoming. "Sam," she finally cried, tears shimmering in her eyes. "I...we...oh, my. Yes." She took the ring from the box and slipped it onto her finger.

Sam hadn't realized he was holding his breath until he heard the word. He kissed her hard—losing his head in the rush of emotions that surged between them. The possibilities. The future.

"Can we...should we tell people?" she asked.

"That's up to you. You know this town better than I do."

For some reason, his answer made her laugh. She removed a folded piece of paper from her hip pocket. "Read this," she said.

Sam rocked back on his haunches. From the format and the long list of names in the header, he recognized it as an e-mail post. After a few sentences he realized it was an advance copy of Gloria Hughes's column for the upcoming edition of the *Ledger*.

In related news, it turns out Sullivan triplet Jenny isn't so "perfect" after all. Word has it she gave birth to her brother-in-law's twins last summer—

just hours before her husband passed away. Did she actually believe she could keep something like that a secret?

Blood racing with fury, he crumpled the offending missive. "That small-minded bitch," he growled. "We'll sue that cowardly excuse for a newspaper into oblivion."

Jenny's delighted laughter caught him off guard.

She cupped his jaw, which he'd clamped together in rage. "Don't you get it, Sam? The reason I tried so hard to *be* perfect is that I always felt like I owed it to the town of Gold Creek because its citizens did so much for me and my sisters when we were growing up."

Sam wasn't sure he understood her logic, but his anger disappeared at her touch.

"And later on, when Josh and I got together, he was adamant about staying here. He loved this town, and he wanted so badly to belong that I tried to be perfect for his sake."

Sam's gut twisted at the sadness he heard in her tone.

But suddenly she brightened. "However, you read what Gloria wrote. It's there in black and white, so it must true. I'm *not* perfect."

Sam pulled her into his arms. "You are to me."

She snickered softly. "Don't tell anybody, okay?"

Sam kissed the corners of her lips. "So, should we announce our engagement in the ridiculous *Gold Creek Ledger*?"

She hesitated. "I don't care about the town's opinion, but what will your mother say?"

Sam smiled. "Who do you think gave me the video?"

She pulled back in astonishment. "Really?"

"Josh sent it to her with instructions to give it to *us* when the time was right."

She thought a moment, her teeth worrying her bottom lip. "What made her decide today was the day?"

Sam shook his head. "I don't know. You can ask her when you see her."

Jenny looked momentarily blank then glanced at her watch. "Oh my God," she exclaimed. "We've got to get ready. It's Christmas Eve. We have company coming."

The twins, disturbed by their mother's outburst, moved restlessly. He caught her hand before she could go to them.

"Jenny love, just one thing. I know this is going to sound hopelessly old-fashioned, but I'd like to be able to tell our children that, as improbable as it seems, we waited until we were married before we had sex."

She did a double take. "I beg your pardon?"

He pulled her back into his arms and kissed her. "I don't think Josh would expect us to wait a full year from the date of his death. In fact, after watching this video, it occurred to me that St. Patrick's Day might make a fine day for a wedding. We can wait till then, right?"

She relaxed in the circle of his arms. "Well, I'll have to change my plan to seduce you tonight." She grinned at him. "I think Josh would love it. What better day to become Jenny O'Neal O'Neal?"

Their mutual chuckles were muffled by their kisses.

A minute later, she tilted her head, as if silently doing the math. "I guess I can wait that long. If you can."

There was something challenging about her smile; Sam silently groaned. She wasn't going to make the next few months easy for him, but he had a feeling he was going to enjoy every sweet minute.

CHAPTER FIFTEEN

THE CIOPPINO HAD BEEN a great success, but everyone had been too full to do justice to the four pies his mother had brought, so Sam decided to deliver one to the bunkhouse, where his employees without family in the area were spending a quiet Christmas Eve.

The night had turned cold, but after the steamy warmth of the kitchen, Sam relished the brisk night air. He'd grabbed his lined denim jacket and the hat hanging on the peg beside the door then made his escape.

With one hand carrying the pie and the other a plastic container of whipped cream, he had to use the toe of his boot to make his presence known at the bunkhouse door.

The door opened and a head popped out. Harley. The mysterious stranger who'd been dropped off by Sam's miner pal, Lars. "Care package," Sam said.

"Great," the man said. He seemed an easygoing sort, eager to learn, though often baffled by the simplest of tasks. The disparity between Harley's obvious intelligence and his functional skills frustrated Hank, but Sam liked the guy. In some ways, Harley reminded him of Josh. Just as good-natured and affable but far less self-confident.

Sam passed the dishes through the gap in the door but didn't go inside. He had a lot on his mind and needed a few minutes alone before returning to the family gathering. "Merry Christmas," he called as he left.

"You, too. And tell the missus—I mean, Jenny, we said thanks," Harley returned.

Sam touched the brim of his hat in acknowledgment. Harley's mistake would be rectified in March. Jenny had made the announcement over dinner. She'd called Kristin with the news while Sam greeted their guests and served eggnog and mulled wine.

Sam had suggested that they hold off on the announcement until after the holidays, but Jenny said she couldn't wait to share the good news.

After Gordon's eloquent prayer, Jenny had risen and held out her glass in a toast. "This is a very special holiday for us all. We have so much to celebrate—" She'd smiled at the twins who were sitting in their bouncy chairs, having already been fed. "And yet, we can't help but miss Josh." She lifted her glass. "To Josh. Forever in our hearts."

After the ceremonial clinking, she'd reached to take Sam's hand. The table had grown instantly quiet, as if each guest knew what was coming. "Sam and I are getting married," she'd said without preamble.

To Sam's surprise, the reaction was unanimously positive. Andi had chortled with delight when she heard the proposed date for the nuptials. "Too cool. That means Kristin owes me twenty bucks. She said you wouldn't tie the knot until after that whole year-of-mourning thing. I told her she was full of…garlic bread. More bread, anyone?"

While consuming heaping bowls of fish stew, Ida Jane, Diane and Gordon had discussed the pros and cons of a St. Patrick's Day wedding. His mother volunteered to hire someone to play the bagpipes, but Jenny politely declined the offer. "We want to keep it simple but festive, don't we?" she'd asked Sam.

He'd nodded as if he had a clue, but in truth Sam felt overwhelmed. Life had changed—and was still changing—at Mach speed. *But is this the right trajectory?* he asked himself. After shoving his cold hands into the side pockets of his jacket, Sam walked blindly toward the corral instead of returning to the house.

Building this corral had been Josh's first job after they moved the travel trailer onto the property while the log house was being built. With the typical cockiness of a seventeen-year-old, Josh had promised to complete it in one day if Sam would purchase tickets to some rock concert Josh wanted to take his new girlfriend to see.

"You've only been in town two days and you already have a girlfriend?" Sam had exclaimed.

Josh had removed his glove to puff on his nails and polish them against his grimy shirt. "That's me. Josh, the Stud Muffin. Too bad you're only into cows, man. I could give you lessons on the art of love."

Sam chuckled at the memory. A sudden gust of wind lifted his hat—which he just then realized didn't feel quite right on his head—and sent it tumbling across the hard-packed ground. He chased it a few steps. When he picked it up, it dawned on him that the felt was too stiff to be his hat. Holding it up to the light of the half moon, he saw the color—green, not black.

"Damn," he cursed.

After dinner, Jenny had passed out copies of her poem/story. With Sam's permission, she'd retrieved Josh's green cowboy hat from his closet and had set it on the table while Andi read the story aloud.

Everyone had loved the piece. His mother had cried, of course. Ida Jane had insisted the story needed to be published, though Jenny was reluctant to submit even a query letter until the illustrations were complete.

"I plan to work on the drawings once the holidays are over," she'd explained. "From everything I've read, getting something published is no easy task, but I promised Sam I'd look into it."

Sam hung the hat on a nearby post. It tilted at a jaunty angle just the way Josh liked to wear it. A shiver—entirely unrelated to the freezing temperature—passed through his body. "Weird," he muttered under his breath.

Another rogue breeze made the hat rattle as if in answer.

Sam sighed. Just what he didn't need was for people to see him talking to a hat.

Since when do you care what people think?

Sam looked behind him, almost positive he'd heard the words spoken aloud. When he turned back, he saw the green hat sitting atop his brother's head. Josh was perched on the fence. As healthy and vibrant as Sam could remember.

Sam's automatic expletive made Josh laugh.

I'm here to say goodbye and that's the best I get?

The pressure on Sam's chest made it almost impossible to breathe. "No," he choked out. "Wait."

Josh gave the hat a nudge so it tilted back on his head. The starlight made Josh's form shimmer like magic. *I can't, Sam. This is my path. Yours is here. With Jenny. Make me proud, Sam. Live it well.*

He grinned, then disappeared.

Sam dropped to his knees the same instant the hat clattered to the hard ground. Deep, racking sobs echoed in the stillness.

"Sam?" Jenny called, rushing out of the darkness. "What's wrong? Are you okay?"

He struggled to his feet, wiping his cheeks with the sleeve of his jacket. His throat was too tight to speak.

Jenny flew to his side, wrapping her arms around him as if to protect him from whatever demons were attacking him.

"Josh," he managed to say through his hollow sobs.

She nodded, kissing his wet face. "I know, honey. It's hard to say goodbye. I went through this months ago, but you've kept it bottled up inside."

He wasn't sure how to make sense of what he'd seen—or didn't see. Maybe it was an illusion brought on by all that had happened—his and Jenny's decision to marry, viewing Josh's video, the talk with his mother.

"It isn't fair," he managed to croak. "I should have been the one to go. This is Josh's life, not mine."

Jenny grabbed him by both arms and gave him a stern shake. "Don't ever say that again, Sam O'Neal. We don't *own* our time on this planet. It's a gift. Josh's life was way too short, but it was beautiful. And he left us so much. Two babies. Each other. Our families, united and whole—except for Kristin, but I'm working on getting her to move home."

His pain began to subside. Her words were a balm to his soul.

"Sam, your mother and I were just talking. I told her that in my opinion the best way for us to honor Josh's memory is to live with passionate optimism." Her beautiful smile quelled his anguish. "Doesn't that sound like something Josh would say?"

Sam took a deep breath. The frigid air was healing and invigorating. He felt more alive than he had in months.

He gave her a quick but meaningful kiss. "You're

right, Jenny. Life goes on, and we're going live it with gusto—just the way Josh would have wanted.''

He grabbed her hand and pulled her toward the house, pausing only to pick up the hat. ''Your sister was whining about not getting to open a gift, so I think we should resurrect an O'Neal family tradition. We each open one gift on Christmas Eve, then the rest on Christmas morning.''

''I thought you didn't remember anything positive about your childhood?''

''We had our moments. Especially after Josh was born. He loved Christmas. I used to lift him to my shoulders so he could put the angel on the top of the tree.''

Jenny suddenly grabbed the railing that had been installed along with the ramp to accommodate Ida Jane's wheelchair.

''What's wrong?'' he asked.

''The angel,'' she said. ''I thought it was just Josh spending money.''

Sam shook his head. ''What are you talking about?''

''Come with me,'' she said. ''I have to fix something and I need your help.''

Jenny shed her coat in the entry without bothering to hang it up. She kicked off her shoes and was about to walk to the living room, when Ida Jane suddenly appeared. The older woman managed to get around quite well, but she insisted on using her cane—as if afraid to be without it.

She still had moments when she seemed depressed or lost in the past, but those had been noticeably fewer since moving to the ranch. Jenny credited Greta and the twins for the improvement.

''Oh, there you are, dear,'' Ida said cheerfully. ''I want to talk to you a minute.''

Jenny was in a hurry to fix her oversight. She knew what she needed to do. "Can it wait, Auntie? I have to—"

Ida interrupted. "I just wanted to tell you that I'll be leaving soon."

Jenny halted so suddenly Sam bumped into her. "W-what did you say?" she sputtered.

Ida gave them both a knowing look. "A young couple doesn't need an old lady around to cramp their style."

Sam walked to Ida Jane's side and put his arm around her shoulders, much the way Josh would have done. "Miss Ida, you can't leave. You're our chaperon. The town gossips—Gloria Hughes, in particular—would have a field day. She'll butcher us in her column then I'll have to sue. We'll spend a fortune in court and won't have anything to show for it. So, please say you'll stay."

Ida Jane looked unconvinced until Jenny added, "Please, Auntie. I have so much to do between now and March. I'll need your help more than ever."

Those words seemed to be what Ida needed to hear. Jenny reminded herself how important it was to hold the ones you love close to your heart and never forget to tell them how much they mean to you. Josh's death had taught her that.

"Well…okay," Ida Jane said. She started to return to her room, but Jenny took her hand. "Come with us, Auntie. We're starting a new tradition. One I think you'll like."

Five minutes later, Sam gave Jenny a questioning look.

She nodded, after winking at her sister who was sitting on the couch with Ida Jane. Diane and Gordon—each holding a twin—stood nearby.

Sam bent down and picked her up, his strong arms

wrapped around her thighs. His face was level with her belly. Jenny remembered another time when he'd held her like this. Then, she'd been flustered, this time she felt she could stay in his arms forever.

With her left hand, she removed the crystal star and replaced it with Josh's angel.

Once she took away her hand, Sam stepped back and eased her down. But he didn't let go.

"Can we open our presents now?" Andi asked as petulantly as she had when the triplets were children.

Sam's lips—his wonderful lips—turned up in a smile. Some gifts were worth the wait. And Jenny knew that in two and a half months they'd share the best gift of all—a love that was meant to be.

*   *   *   *   *

*Please turn the page for
an excerpt from Andi's story—*
WITHOUT A PAST.
*You won't want to miss this second title in
Debra Salonen's compelling trilogy,*
THOSE SULLIVAN SISTERS.

Watch for it next month.

ANDI SULLIVAN STOWED the last of the boxes in the basement storage room then brushed off her hands and looked around. She'd forgotten about the spacious and surprisingly snug area. As children, the Sullivan triplets had avoided the cellar because of the threat of spiders, but now Andi evaluated it through the eyes of a businesswoman.

"If we make that window into an egress…" She peered out the cloudy glass. By investing a few bucks, she could probably rent out the space and pull down six or seven hundred dollars a month. Maybe more.

A few bucks. Finding that money could prove to be a hurdle taller than the surrounding mountain peaks, she thought grimly. She'd invested nearly all the cash she'd saved while in the military, but no amount of venture capital seemed enough to stem the steady drain on their resources. Sooner or later, she'd have to admit that the old bordello was a losing proposition.

So why am I fighting so hard to save it? She didn't know the answer.

She was about to head back upstairs, when the phone at her waist rang. *Jenny again, no doubt.*

"What now?"

"Andi? Why are you always so grumpy?"

Wrong sister. This was Kristin. "I thought you were

Jenny. Again. I'm busy getting ready for Ida Jane. A week ahead of schedule.''

Instead of walking up the open wooden steps, Andi sat down, plopping her elbows on her knees. She wanted to complain to somebody. Why not Kristin?

"I just heard," Kris said. "Can you believe Jenny sent our eighty-two-year-old aunt off with a stranger?"

Andi smiled to herself. Kristin's take on any given subject was usually a hundred and eighty degrees opposite of Andi's. Always had been.

"Harley Forester isn't exactly a stranger. He's been working at the Rocking M for three months."

"Am I supposed to find comfort in that?" Kristin asked facetiously. "The man is an amnesiac. What if he suddenly remembers he's a serial killer?"

Andi chuckled. She couldn't help herself. She was no great judge of men, as evidenced by some of her boyfriends over the years, but she'd bet the deed to the old bordello that Harley Forester was a decent human being with a past no more nefarious than Andi's or either of her sister's.

"Hey, this wasn't my idea, but it's a done deal. They'll be here any minute." Unable to resist teasing her sister, Andi added, "Unless he's dissecting Ida's body as we speak."

Kristin hissed with outrage. "You're impossible. I only called because Jenny told me to tell you that we need to be especially gentle with Ida. Apparently she's been restless and unhappy all week. Jen said she found her crying a couple of times."

Andi closed her eyes and frowned. Sweet and gentle was Kris's thing. Kind and understanding was Jenny's thing. Andi was pretty sure none of her *things*—whatever they were—would prove beneficial to Ida Jane's emotional well-being.

"Could be she's homesick," Kristin suggested.

Andi wished it were that simple, but she'd witnessed a steady decline in her aunt's mental acuity over the past year. Neither of her sisters believed it was serious, but Andi feared otherwise.

"I'd better go," Andi told Kristin. "If Ida's feeling depressed, she'll really flip out when she sees the For Rent signs. We'd planned to talk to her about that when you got here, remember?"

Kristin, who was due back in town Friday for Jenny's wedding, said, "You're right. I wish I could talk to her right now, but I'm just leaving the house. I have to go to a… I'll call later. As soon as I get back."

Typical, Andi thought sourly. Kris always seemed to be gone when there was an emotional confrontation of any kind. She'd been running since high school and hadn't stopped. "Don't worry. I'll handle it, provided Harley gets her home in one piece."

"You like him, don't you?"

Andi jumped to her feet. "No."

"Yes, you do. I could always tell when you liked a boy."

Andi made a rude sound and started up the stairs. "Nu-uh," she returned, purposely trying to sound like one of the teenage girls who frequented the coffee parlor at the old bordello. Double mocha freezes were all the rage at the moment.

Kristin snickered. "You're attracted to him. But who wouldn't be? He looks like that actor from *Ever After* with Drew Barrymore. Do you know who I mean?"

Just as she reached the basement door, Andi heard the

sound of a truck engine turn into the parking lot. Her heart rate went up a notch.

"Never saw it," she lied. She'd rented it twice—for that very reason. And it irritated her to no end that her sister—her beautiful sister—saw Harley as an attractive, sexy man.

"You should. He's a cutie. Wish I could remember his name. Oh, well. Gotta go. Good luck with Ida Jane. Tell her I love her, and I'll call later."

Andi quickly entered the kitchen, closing the door securely behind her. She tried to shake off the sense of anticipation at the thought of seeing Harley Forester, as he called himself. A man who—while probably not a serial killer—was definitely no cowboy.

He was an enigmatic stranger playing at being a ranch hand, when anyone could tell he knew nothing about the business. Andi's attraction to him was just a silly diversion—probably the result of too much worry and not enough of a social life.

"I need to get out more," she muttered as she dashed to the porch. She didn't want to miss her chance to watch Harley getting out of the truck. He might not *be* a cowboy, but, damn, he looked good in Wranglers.

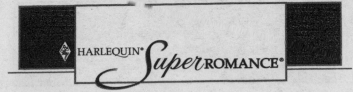

HARLEQUIN *Super*ROMANCE®

The Healer
by Jean Brashear

Diego Montalvo's life changed forever after the
Special Forces mission that nearly killed him.
Now a *curandero*—healer—whose healing tradition
calls into question everything that cardiac surgeon
Caroline Malone believes, he may be her key to
regaining the career that's her life. Except,
success in healing means losing each other.
Because he can't leave his home in West Texas…
and she can't stay.

**Look for more
Deep in the Heart
Superromance titles
in the months to come!**

**Heartwarming stories with
a sense of humor,
genuine charm and emotion
and lots of family!**

**On sale starting
January 2003 from
Harlequin Superromance.**

**Available wherever
Harlequin books are sold.**

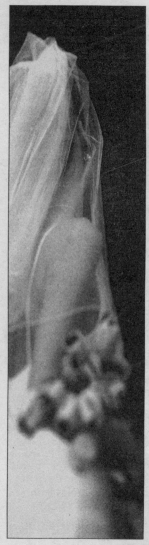

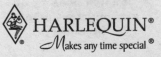

Michael's Father
by Melinda Curtis

Who is four-year-old *Michael's father*? That's a secret Cori's grandfather, patriarch of Messina Vineyards, wants to know—especially now that Cori's returned home. But she can't ever tell him because her grandfather has vowed to destroy Michael's father. And Cori could never do that to Blake, the man she still loves....

For the same reason, she can't tell Blake he has a son he doesn't know about!

Available wherever Harlequin books are sold.

Watch for *Michael's Father*— the first book by an exciting new author— in January.